THE SAINT GOES WEST

FOREWORD BY WILLIAM J. MACDONALD

THE ADVENTURES OF THE SAINT

THE SAINT
GOES WEST

LESLIE CHARTERIS

SERIES EDITOR: IAN DICKERSON

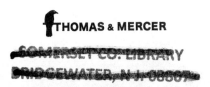

THOMAS & MERCER

Text copyright © 2014 Interfund (London) Ltd.
Foreword © 2014 William J. MacDonald
Introduction to "Palm Springs" from *The Second Saint Omnibus* (1951)
Introduction to "Hollywood" from *The Saint's Choice of Hollywood Crime* (1946)
Publication History and Author Biography © 2014 Ian Dickerson
All rights reserved.

Published by Thomas & Mercer, Seattle

www.apub.com

ISBN-13: 9781477842829
ISBN-10: 1477842829

Cover design by David Drummond, www.salamanderhill.com

Printed in the United States of America.

To Mary and Denis Green
to whose always welcome interruptions
this opus owes so much of its distinctive dizziness

PUBLISHER'S NOTE

FOREWORD TO THE NEW EDITION

The Saint . . . well what can be said about our legendary swashbuckling avenging-angel-cum-Robin-Hood that hasn't already been said by so many sage acolytes?

My journey with the Happy Highwayman began in the early '90s rather unexpectedly. I was attending a car auction in London when a beautiful 1966 Volvo P1800 rolled onto the docket with the notorious ST 1 license plate. This jogged memories of my youth in San Francisco where many of my classmates had enjoyed the ITC series starring Sir Roger Moore. I made inquiries about the literary rights and ultimately secured the rights at Paramount and we made the feature that was eventually released in 1997.

Several years passed after the film's release, and in 2006, by sheer coincidence, I inquired about the television rights and met Sir Roger's son, Geoffrey, who was very keen on developing a series. Along with Roger, we formed a partnership, and my odyssey with Simon Templar began anew. This parsec on our trek has involved years of effort to bring the legend to audiences in the twenty-first century. Aside from creating a truly familial bond with the Moores and Ian Dickerson, the boy genius from Hampshire who has brought this first re-release of Leslie Charteris's timeless hero to the digital world in this work, we learned much about how, evidently, the world had grown so cynical relative to its prior incarnations, that chivalry and a gallant esprit de corps was, on the surface, a bit too "aged." This merry band has persevered nonetheless proving the fact that his world is timeless and that these new generations need a hero who is more brains over brawn, more clever rather than brutish, more insouciant rather than just wantonly rebellious . . . in a word, the Saint.

As of this writing, our team has successfully developed and produced a pilot for the new series starring Adam Rayner and Eliza Dushku, a terrific teaming, a truly fantastic modernization of the characters of Templar and his cohort in his unique brand of larceny, retribution, and justice, Patricia Holm.

I and our team invite the readers to immerse themselves anew in one of fiction's most endearing, if irreverent characters . . . Simon Templar, aka the Saint, and enjoy him as we do.

—*William J. MacDonald*

THE SAINT GOES
WEST

ARIZONA

1

Simon Templar checked the fit of the specially built silencer on his .357 Magnum for the last time, and settled more snugly into the screen of tumbled rocks from which he was watching the road below. The crisp Arizona sun baked down on him out of a sky of such brilliant blue that it would have seemed artificial if it had not been so certain that no artifice on earth could have copied it, and his blue eyes that matched the sky as closely as anything could match it were narrowed slightly against the glare that came up from the open desert. A grey lizard lay and watched him from a little distance with one cold flat eye, its soft stomach pulsing quickly with breaths, but otherwise as motionless and as much a part of the landscape as he had become since he had seen the lazy billow of dust creeping along the twisted ribbon of dirt trail that wound past the foot of the knoll where he was lying.

There were many men in the world who would have been surprised to see him there, much as they had learned to accept Simon Templar's sudden and disturbing appearances in all kinds of unlikely places: men in the variegated police uniforms of a dozen European and South American countries, as well as a staidly bowler-hatted Chief Inspector of Scotland

Yard, and a certain gruff grey-haired detective in New York City, men who could have met at any time and talked lengthily on one common ground apart from their professional interest in the enforcement of the Law—namely, their separate and individual reminiscences of the impudent outlawries which had blazed Simon Templar's trail around the earth. There were also an even larger number of public enemies from just as many places, who could have joined in the chorus with no less indignation, who would have been equally surprised to find him in a setting so different from the urbane backgrounds against which he was usually tracing his debonair and dangerous saga of adventure. But these surprises would have been purely geographical: there would have been no surprise that he lay there on the threshold of more trouble, for trouble was a thing that clung like an aura to the presence of Simon Templar, whom some imaginative newspaperman had christened the Robin Hood of modern crime, but who was much better known to police files and the unwritten records of the underworld as the Saint.

The dust-cloud lengthened sluggishly towards him, churned up by the wheels of a well-worn car whose labouring engine sent a faint grumble of protest to his ears through the great stillness, and the Saint waited for it with the ·infinite patience of any Indian who might have lain in the same ambush more than a hundred years before, watching a covered wagon crawl through the scrub-sprinkled valley below his eyes. You might have seen something of the same Indian, too in the intent lines of his tanned reckless face, but that would have been an easy illusion. The same lines would have fitted as naturally into the picture of a conquistador scanning the shore of a new world, or of d'Artagnan mocking the courts of France: they were only the heraldry of a character that would have been the same in any age or place, the timeless brand of the born buccaneer. Perhaps that was another reason also why he seemed as much at home there as he would have been against the shining sophistication of a city boulevard—because it was inevitably right that he should fit in wherever adventure offered, because he himself was the living embodiment of adventure . . . But the Saint himself would never have thought about it so romantically as that, being strictly concerned at the moment with the mechanical job that he was there to do.

The car rattled around another curve, with the driver nursing it gingerly over ruts and washboard, and then it was as close to where he was hiding as it would ever be. At that, he estimated the range at a little more than a hundred yards, and rested his brown right hand on a rock in front of him as coolly as if he had been trying a trick shot for his own amusement. Judgment of distance, speed, and elevation merged into one imperceptible coordination as he squeezed the trigger. The Magnum jarred in his grip with a discreet *flup!* but he still held the aim until he saw the car swerve on one flattened front tyre, bump a little way off the road, and come to a grinding stop. It had never had enough speed to be in any danger of overturning, and he had had no such fate in mind for it anyway.

Satisfied that he had done no more and no less than he meant to do, he slid away down the other side of the hillock, straightened up as soon as he was safely below the skyline, and walked quickly to the big Buick parked in the sandy arroyo below the sheltering slope, unscrewing the cumbersome silencer as he went; a few minutes later the long sedan jounced out of the wash on to the dirt road half a mile south, turned back, and battered its way north again over the tracks left by the car which he had just brought to an effective standstill.

Simon braked as he came up with it, and a white-haired man in a neat but incongruous business suit eased his back from a pained and unprofitable scrutiny of the deflated tyre. Simon leaned out and grinned amiably at him.

"Anything wrong?" he inquired.

The white-haired man gazed back at him through silver rimmed spectacles with the peculiarly sadistic tolerance reserved by all right-minded voyagers for those persons who ask futile questions in unspeakable situations.

"We had a blow-out," he said, with admirable restraint.

"Maybe I can help," said the Saint cheerfully.

He swung out of his car and inspected the evidence of his marksmanship with concealed satisfaction. His single bullet had done its job as neatly as he could have desired, ripping through tube and casing without leaving any evidence of its transit except for an expert. But the Saint only said, "Do you have a spare?"

"You could help me to get it out," said the girl.

She backed her head out of the trunk to say it, and Simon placed a cigarette between his lips as he turned to look at her with a casualness that was only another concealment. For this was a part of the encounter which he had irrelevantly looked forward to all day—in fact, since he had first caught a passing glimpse of her the evening before.

She was only a minor character in the business that his mind was on, and yet he had been hoping that the impression he had been saving wouldn't be destroyed. Now he saw that he need not have worried. Even with her brown hair a little scattered, her face a little flushed, she had the same quality that had caught in his memory. It was not the standard prettiness of blue eyes, of a smiling generous mouth, of a small nose that was still a cameo of classic modelling, but something much more, much rarer, and yet so simple that the only words for it seemed inadequate. You could only say that in one glance at her you knew that without being naive or stupid she was utterly without guile or coquetry or deceit, that her mind was as clean-cut and untrammelled as her sapling figure in its plain white shirt and blue slacks, and that whatever she did would be as real and honest as the friendly hills. But to the Saint, who had known so many other fascinations, this was one of the most arresting certainties that he had ever known.

"I'd love to," he said.

He struck a match and put it to his cigarette as he strolled over, but he didn't throw the burnt stem away. As he wrestled the spare wheel out, and carried it around the car, he kept working the match-stem into the valve, letting the air escape whenever there were other noises to mask the hiss of it, so that a few minutes later he could press the tyre flat with his hand and say, "It's too bad, but this seems to be another dead one."

"Now, that's perfectly swell," said the girl.

Simon let the wheel drop, and philosophically revived his cigarette.

"The nearest garage is back at Lion Rock," he remarked. "I'll leave word there later if you like. Or could I take you anywhere?"

The man said, "We were heading for the Circle Y—it's three miles further on, off this road."

"Visiting?"

"No. I . . . er . . . I happen to own it."

"When were you going to be back at Lion Rock?" asked the girl. "We don't want to take you out of your way, but it's getting late. I mean . . ."

The Saint smiled down at her, rumpling his dark hair with apparent thoughtfulness. It was indeed getting late, as he had hoped it would be: bright as it still was, the sun was already dipping towards the high range to westward, and under the slanting light the barren battlements that ringed three of their horizons were putting on soft chiffons of rose and purple against the promise of an early twilight.

He said, "It might be quite a while before I see Lion Rock again. Perhaps I'd better take you to the Circle Y and you can send in to the garage tomorrow."

"We hate to trouble you," said the white-haired man half-heartedly.

"Don't give it another thought," said the Saint. "Have you got any parcels or things you want to take along?"

Five minutes later the Buick was rocking and rolling north again with two extra passengers, and the older man was making conversation from the other end of the front seat.

"I suppose we ought to introduce ourselves. My name is Don Morland, and this is my daughter Jean."

"I'm Simon Templar," said the Saint.

The name meant nothing immediately to them, and was not meant to. But he had known who they were before he lay down to wait for them not long after breakfast, behind the pulpit of erupted boulders which had already merged into the violet-shaded diorama behind.

"I'm sure glad you happened along," Morland went on. "I wouldn't have enjoyed trying to find my way home from there if we'd been caught after dark."

"That doesn't sound like a rancher talking," Simon remarked lightly.

"I'm not really a rancher—of course you could tell that. I just happen to own a ranch. As a matter of fact, we've only been here a couple of days. It's all quite an accident."

Simon grinned.

"You won the Circle Y in a raffle?"

"It belonged to my brother. He died just recently, and I inherited it. I was a dentist in Richmond, Virginia. I'd been thinking I was about ready to retire, and Jean always wanted to see the West. So we thought we'd give it a trial."

"Too bad it had to happen that way," said the Saint. "I mean through your brother."

Morland began filling a stubby pipe.

"Yes. It was very sudden. His horse threw him and kicked him—fractured his skull. He only bought the place himself about eighteen months ago . . . Well, if he could turn himself into a rancher I expect I can."

"You think you'll keep the place."

"Probably. Our next-door neighbour from the J-Bar-B made me a rather attractive offer as soon as we got here, but I don't think I'll sell. I think I might get to like it here. Jean is going to buy me a big hat and some high-heeled boots and try to make me look like the real thing."

The Saint's strong hands worked on the wheel with imperturbable skill, his calm eyes picking the smoothest path over the derelict track as nonchalantly as though his role had actually been as fortuitous and disinterested as it was meant to seem. But into his mind went just a little more information than he had had before, and with it a repetition and revival of one grim question that he had already asked himself a great many times. Yet no one could have guessed that there were such things as murder in his thoughts.

Jean Morland was studying him with straightforward interest, taking in his quietly checkered blue shirt, his well-worn Levis, and coming back again to his lean tanned face with its hint of mockeries and mischief that must have known even wider fields than those traditionally great open spaces.

"I don't think you've lived around here all your life, either," she said.

He smiled at her.

"That isn't really very hard to guess. As a matter of fact, I haven't really been around here for about ten years. But I can still give a working imitation of the genuine article. I was riding herd in the Panhandle when you weren't any further than the fourth grade. You need a good hand on the Circle Y?"

"You've got a nice car to look for work in," she said.

"That's part of the build-up. All of us cowboys ain't bums. We seen ourselves in the pitchers, an' we know better. Next time I'm going to be a straw boss, at least."

She laughed.

"Seriously, what are you doing now?"

"You might call it vacationing. Wandering here and there, and seeing what may turn up. I haven't a plan from one day to the next. But I love this country."

"So do I," she said. Then: "What do you think of doing right here?"

The Saint lighted a cigarette, taking his time.

Presently he said, "I thought I might do some hunting."

It seemed to him that this might be a truthful way to put it, even though she would never guess what a deadly kind of quarry he was thinking of. Even though she might never know that the spoor he was following had been started months before when a certain Dr Ludwig Julius paddled out of his office on the Wilhelmstrasse and set off on an odyssey that had already taken him more than half-way around the world, by way of the Trans-Siberian railroad to Vladivostok, from Vladivostok to Yokohama, from Yokohama to San Francisco, and from San Francisco, after a pause at the Nazi consulate there, to the peaceful Arizona county where Simon Templar was on the trail of bigger game than his state hunting licence had ever been intended to include.

2

They sat on the porch of the ranch house after dinner, listening to the far-off yipping of coyotes and the nearer croaking of frogs down at the spring.

Simon had stayed, of course. He had always meant to stay, although he had put on a proper show of diffidence. In fact, he had taken quite a little trouble to make sure of becoming a welcome friend at the Circle Y. And with the insidious intimacy of dinner added to his acquaintance with Jean Morland, he was even more sure that it would be no hardship to spend the time that he expected to spend there.

"How much stock do you have here?" Simon asked.

It was one of those desultory conversations full of long pauses and random twists, but rich with warmth and contentment.

Morland said, "About five thousand head. Not very much, but not enough to be too big a headache."

"Pretty good range?"

"Not so bad as you'd think. Eh, Hank?"

"We go back quite a ways into the hills," said Hank Reefe. "They do pretty good back there. It's handy havin' the stream. They don't ever need to go short of water."

Reefe was the foreman. He sat in the fourth chair, on the other side of Jean, rocking himself gently, his long thin legs stretched out. He was probably not much more than thirty, but his weathered face was deeply carved with the lines that a man gets from staring into hot shimmering distances. He had good level eyes and the kind of long sinewy features that are an unmistakable inheritance from the stock that first fought its way through that untamed country.

"There's no mining in these parts, is there?" Simon asked casually.

"Not right around here. Sometimes the prospectors'll come through. But they'll go anywhere."

He had a slow, rather musical drawl, which to a sensitive ear was the same as a lapel badge would have been to the eye.

"You wouldn't be a Texan, I suppose," said the Saint.

"Yes, sir." Reefe poured Bull Durham into a gutter of thin paper and spread it with his forefingers. "I heard Miss Jean say you worked in the Panhandle yourself."

"A long time ago."

The foreman's deft fingers shaped and rolled. He sealed the cigarette with a flick of his tongue, and said, "Smoke?"

The sack of Bull Durham landed in Simon's lap. Lazily Simon slid a paper out of the folder, curved it with thumb and fingers of one hand, poured tobacco, and rolled the cigarette while his other hand pulled the string of the sack against his teeth and tossed it back. His eyes met Reefe's tranquilly over the match that the foreman leaned across with.

Neither of the Morlands would have realised that two men had measured each other, with challenge and answer, like two proud animals. And yet Jean Morland was very clearly a part of that watchful speculation, for Simon had seen something more in Hank Reefe's manner towards her than the strictly dutiful respect to which her position as the boss's daughter entitled her.

Reefe dragged on his own cigarette with an expressionless face, and said idly, "I was raised right around Hereford. Worked around two or three ranches up there 'fore I came west." Smoke curled in the lamplight as he let it out through his nostrils. "There sure used to be some interestin' characters around there."

"Quite a few," said the Saint.

"Was one feller I remember hearin' about, came from England or somewhere. Everybody thought he was a dude. So when he asks for a job, first off, they put him on an outlaw horse for a laugh. Well, he was the guy who did most of the laughin', because it turned out he could fork a bronc better 'n 'most any cowboy in that country, an' he rode the horse out an' kept him. After that they found out he could throw knives like somebody in a circus, an' shoot the pips out of a six of spades just as fast as he could pull a trigger . . . I guess he couldn't find anything wild enough for him around there, because later on he went south of the border an' fought in one of those revolutions, an' got to be a general or something. At least, so I heard. He was quite a young feller then, an' I was only a kid myself, but I never forgot him because he had such a funny name for a chap like that. They called him the Saint."

Simon Templar tilted his head back and blew leisured rings at the lamp.

"He must have been quite a guy."

"Yeah . . . I've often wondered if he turned out to be the same Saint I've read about in the papers since. But I never met him myself, so I wouldn't know."

"I wonder what a man like that would be doing these days?" Morland said. "Fighting with the RAF or something like that, I suppose."

"No," said the girl. "That would be too conventional for him." She hugged her knees and gazed out in to the dark. "He'd be rescuing prisoners from the Gestapo, or catching spies in London, or something of that sort."

Simon looked at her thoughtfully.

"You mean, you really believe those stories about him?" he said teasingly, and again he had to encounter the disconcerting calm clearness of her eyes.

"I want to believe in a few things like that," she said simply.

They went on looking at each other for a while, with the same quiet steadiness, and then Reefe's chair creaked abruptly as he sat forward.

"Seems as though we have some late visitors," he said.

The lights of a car were creeping up from the desert, two yellow eyes that quivered under the punishment of the road. They all watched them coming closer, twisting jerkily up the hillside, until the station wagon that carried them jolted to a stop in front of the porch.

The headlights went out and under the porch light Simon could read the words "J — B Ranch" on the door of the station wagon as it opened.

"Our neighbour," Morland said.

The man who came clumping up the steps with the spurs jingling on his high-heeled boots was big and broad, and everything about him had a heavy swagger that was as aggressive as a clenched fist. Under the brim of his black hat he had thick black brows and a square dark jaw that looked as useful to hit as a chunk of granite. He was dressed with the curious contradictions of a man who liked his western fopperies and was still ready to do a day's work with any of them. There were rubies and gold flowers in the buckle of his hat-band, ruby eyes in the longhorn steer's head knotted in his scarf, jewels and gold inlay in the big silver buckle of his belt, but all of them had been smoothed and scarred with service, like the fancy leather trim on his dusty gaberdines. He showed a perfect set of white teeth and said, "Hullo ev'rybody."

Unexpectedly, his voice was a soft tenor, not quite light enough to be effeminate, and yet light enough to strike a note that set the Saint's delicate sense of menaces on edge.

Morland said pleasantly, "Hullo Max." He made the only necessary introduction. "This is Mr . . . er . . . Templar. Mr Valmon."

"Glad to know you, Mr Templar."

Max Valmon's grip was as hard as his voice was soft. Simon was expecting that. He smiled gently, and used some of the strength of his own right hand. It gave the encounter an air of rather excessive cordiality, and made Valmon's eyes harden a little under his heavy brows.

"Glad to know you, Max," said the Saint affably.

Valmon's glance held another moment of suspicious calculation, and then he turned away and tossed his hat in to a chair. He sat on the arm of the chair and said, "Well, Don—got any news for me?"

Morland knocked out his pipe and began to refill it.

"I don't think so. We haven't done very much. Went into town this morning and got stuck with a blow-out coming home. Luckily Mr Templar came along, and—"

"I don't mean that sort of news."

"Well, really, there isn't—"

"I mean, haven't you made up your mind to accept my offer for the Circle Y?"

Morland blinked.

"Why no, Max. I told you the other day I wasn't planning to sell. Jean and I like it here."

"But I told you I was planning to buy." Valmon's voice was still soft and friendly. "I'm obstinate. And I was here first. Why don't you face it? You don't know much about this country, Don. It won't feed both of us."

The older man frowned in a sort of innocent puzzlement, his thumb poised over the bowl of his pipe. Reefe's chair became still, as if chilled into suddenly watchful waiting, but Morland didn't seem to be ready with a lead. It was as though he had just begun to sense something in Valmon's undertones that was so foreign to his experience that he was afraid of being mistaken about it.

It was the Saint who hooked a leg over the arm of his chair and said diffidently, "Not that it's particularly my business, but you make it sound like peculiar country. What makes it that way?"

Valmon turned with his flashing smile.

"Water," he said. "I've got a spring on my side of the hills, but it goes dry every summer."

"We do all right," Reefe said quietly.

"I know." Valmon's smile was untouched. "But your stream rises on my land. Only it doesn't stay there long enough to do me much good, especially when it runs low. To do any good, I'd have to blast a new channel—turn it around that shoulder up there, and let it run down my way to where I could build a dam. Of course, that's the same as starving you out."

"The law won't let you do that," Reefe said.

Valmon shrugged.

"I don't know. The water comes from my property. The law couldn't say much after I'd done it, and it wouldn't take much doing. Just a few sticks of dynamite in the right places, and you'd be dry. Then I suppose you could go to court and try to get an order to make me blast it the other way again. But before you could do that, and make me do it, you wouldn't have any stock. So where does it get you?"

He had divided his words between Reefe and Morland, and he was looking at Morland when he finished, but then his eyes went back to the Saint, as if somehow Simon was the only one that he was in doubt about. And curiously, the others seemed to wait for the Saint too, as though without any assertion he had become felt as the man who was the most natural match for Valmon.

And yet the Saint hadn't moved. He only seemed to become longer and lazier in his chair as he lighted another cigarette with his eyes narrowed but still casual against the smoke.

"You make it all sound so much like the plot of any western picture," he remarked, "that I can only think of what the answer would be in any western. If I were Don, I guess I'd just cut down your fence and drive my cattle right through to your beautiful new dam."

"And you know what happens in westerns when somebody does that," Valmon said in the same tone.

"I don't want any fighting," Morland said, with the slightest jerkiness in his voice. "If you're really in trouble, and you come to me properly, we'll see if we can work something out. Perhaps I could let you water your cattle over here. I just don't like you pretending to threaten me."

"It's the ham in him," murmured the Saint, so lightly that for a second he didn't seem to have said anything, and then calmly, astonishingly, so unpredictably that somehow it was not instantly believable, he began to sing something to himself to the tune of "Home on the Range":

> *"Oh give me a ham*
> *With a lovely new dam*
> *Where the skunks and the coyotes can play—"*

Valmon snapped to his feet, and his smile was gone.

"All right," he said. "I've made you a fair offer. I'll give you just twenty-four hours to take it. You can come and tell me tomorrow night. If you think I'm pretending, don't come. You'll find out when I start blasting the next morning."

Morland stood up also, more slowly, his face a little paler.

"I think you'd better go, Valmon," he said tightly.

Valmon picked up his hat and clapped it on at an insolent slant.

"Thanks," he said. "I'll go—while there are three of you telling me. But I'll be back here after you've gone. And then we'll see who makes the funniest cracks."

His voice was still soft and well-modulated, but instead of taking the sting out of his words, that incongruous dulcetness gave them the malignance of a snake's hiss. It whipped a dull flush into Morland's face, but his lip quivered with the uncertainty of a man unused to violence. Hank Reefe started forward with a low growl, but Simon caught his arm and stepped ahead of him. Very courteously the Saint bowed Valmon towards the steps.

"Good night, Maxie dear," he cooed, and Valmon gave him a long stare.

"I'll know more about you before that," he said.

"Maybe."

Simon leaned on the porch rail and concluded his improvisation while Valmon strode across to his car and slammed the door.

> "*Where nothing is heard*
> *But the Razz and the Bird,*
> *And the boss can make faces all day . . .*"

The line ended in a vicious rasp of angrily meshed gears, and the station wagon's engine roared as Valmon jarred in the clutch and pulled away.

Simon watched the lights bumping down the trail, and turned back with a little of the humorous mischief fading from his eyes.

"So," he said slowly. "That seems to have done it."

Jean Morland was hugging her father's arm.

"Did you see?" she said wonderingly. "He looked really—wicked. Did you see, Daddy?"

"I'm afraid it's my fault," said the Saint. "I knew just how to get under his skin, and I couldn't resist it. I've got an evil gift for that sort of thing. You're right, Jean—he's bad. But I suppose it still wasn't my business. Now I've blown everything up for you. I'm sorry."

"Perhaps it's just as well," Morland said quietly. "At least we've seen him in his true colours . . . I'll go in to town tomorrow and see the sheriff, or whoever you have to see."

The Saint shook his head slightly.

"You're going to have trouble," he said. "Maybe you'll need some extra help. I kind of brought this to a head, so my offer still goes."

Morland fumbled with his matches, trying to get his pipe going again. His hands were just a trifle clumsy, not quite so steady as they would otherwise have been.

"It's very nice of you, but—we haven't any right to bother you. I'm not going to worry."

"But we can't turn Mr Templar out at this hour of the night," Jean said quickly. "At least we can find a bed for him."

"We . . . we don't have any room to offer him dear."

Simon smiled at the girl.

"I can put up with the bunkhouse," he said, "if you can put up with me. I'd like to stay."

"There's a spare bed in my room," Reefe said detachedly. "He's welcome to that."

Half an hour later Simon Templar sat on the spare bed in Hank Reefe's room, pulling off his boots and watching the foreman silently roll another cigarette. With the smoke going, Reefe dug under his bed and pulled out a well-worn suitcase. Out of it he extracted an almost as well-worn cartridge belt, from which the holster hung heavy with a Colt .45. He took the revolver out, sprung out the cylinder and spun it, checking the load.

"At least you didn't think I was kidding," said the Saint.

Reefe looked at him with his lean poker face.

"I've seen trouble build up before," he said. "My father saw a lot more of it, when he wore this belt all the time. Things don't change very much, out here."

Simon Templar peeled off his socks and sat rubbing one instep, developing his own estimates.

3

They were drinking coffee after breakfast at the long communal table outside the kitchen with the four cowboys, Jim and Smoky and Nails and Elmer, and Don Morland said, "How far can Valmon really go?"

Jim drained his cup and got up, hitching his belt, and as if he was the spokesman for the others he said, "Well, you can go as far as you like, an' if he wants to fight we'll be right there with you."

The others nodded and grinned in the slow slight way of their kind, as they also got to their feet, and Nails said, "You bet."

"Let's git goin'," said Jim, with the speechmaking finished.

Hank Reefe watched them go, dawdling to roll a cigarette.

"They're good boys," he said.

"But what can Valmon do?" Morland protested.

"He can do enough."

"But there's still some law and order here, isn't there?" The older man seemed to be arguing with himself. "There must be something about water rights in the title to this property. Valmon can't do just what he likes and get away with it."

"You heard what he said last night," Reefe persisted woodenly. "He can do what he likes on his own land. If that damages you, you can sue him. Dunno if that does you much good, after the damage is done. An' if we go in on his land to interfere with him, that's trespassin', an' maybe he can sue you. Guess that wouldn't help him so much either, if we had him stopped."

"So he wouldn't let us stop him," said Jean. "He'd fight."

"Sure," Reefe agreed. "But he's not the only one who can do that."

"It's ridiculous," Morland said. "Things like that just don't go on any more. I'm going to town and talk to the sheriff."

Reefe nodded.

"You can try that," he said expressionlessly, and shaped the brim of his hat as he straightened up. "I'll get on with my job."

They watched him walking away down towards the corral, the well-worn cartridge belt drooping under his right hip and the holstered Colt purposefully tied down to his thigh. He could so easily have looked melodramatic, and yet the stoical naturalness of him made that word impossible.

Morland turned to the Saint with a little bewildered gesture, as if all these things were too much for him.

"What does he mean? Does he think the Sheriff would be on Valmon's side?"

"You can never tell," said the Saint philosophically. "Such things have happened."

Morland's lips tightened.

"Well, I'm going to find out!" He stuck his pipe in his mouth at a stubborn angle which to Simon had the ironic pathos of unconscious futility. "If . . . if I could borrow your car, I could pick up my wheels on the way in and have them fixed, and then someone could fetch the station wagon in this evening."

"Help yourself," said the Saint cordially, and held out his keys.

Jean Morland came slowly back to the porch after she had seen her father start. She turned again beside the Saint, who was smoking a cigarette there with one hip hitched on the rail, and looked down the canyon where Morland's dust was creeping down towards the desert.

One of her hands curled into a small fist, but it was much longer than that before her eyes moved. And then suddenly she turned on him, almost savagely, and said, "Why are you all so cruel to him?"

"Nobody's been cruel, Jean," he said steadily. "The boys are ready to fight for him. Hank Reefe is toting the old family six-shooter for him. They just don't talk a lot."

She brushed back her hair helplessly.

"Oh, I know. I'm sorry. I shouldn't ever have said that. But it seems cruel. As if you were all laughing up your sleeves at everything he says."

"We could be, in a sort of way. If he had some of these boys back on his home ground in Richmond, Virginia, he could probably make them look pretty naive. Well, out here he looks pretty naive to them. But it isn't unkind. He seems to have a lot of ideas of his own, so they figure the best thing is to leave him to it and let him find out for himself. Then he'll get it out of his system. You see, they know."

"And you think you know, too."

"I don't know much. I've only just arrived. But if I have to take somebody for an authority, I'll take Hank and the boys. After all, they've been here for a while . . . I only want to do the best I can for you."

He smiled, and the Saint's smile could be as quietly irresistible as it could be quietly deadly. Quite naturally he touched her arm.

"Why don't you show me around this morning," he said, "and let me get my bearings on the battlefield?"

"Of course," she said, and she went on looking at him with that open-eyed straightforwardness that was more baffling than any coquetry. "Yes, I'd like that." And there was nothing but the sincere direct statement of fact in her voice. But it was as if she was realising, with a little surprise and puzzlement, that they were not new acquaintances any more. Or had they ever been strangers? . . . "You could go on ahead and saddle the horses, and I'll be ready as soon as I've cleared up some of these dishes. Mine is a pinto—the only one in the corral. You can choose your own."

"Okay," he said.

After he had saddled the pinto his own choice was immediate—a beautiful golden palomino with lines that would have stood out in any company. He was just tightening the cinch when he heard the girl's step behind him, and turned to find her standing with her eyes fixed on the horse in an uncertain kind of stillness.

"I should have known you'd pick Sunlight," she said slowly.

Simon unhooked the stirrup from the horn and returned her gaze innocently.

"What's wrong with him?"

"He's the horse that killed my uncle. Nobody else has ridden him since then."

The Saint paused to light a cigarette, and then he deliberately put his foot in the near stirrup and swung lightly into the saddle. The palomino didn't stir. Simon stroked its sleek neck.

"It seems like an awful waste of a good horse," he murmured.

"Let's follow the brook up to Valmon's boundary and see what the scenery's like around there."

The stream crossed the boundary line near the north-west corner of the Morland ranch. For a full mile around that corner the country was a cluster of tall rolling hills, but it seemed to Simon from where they halted to survey it, with Jean Morland pointing out the landmarks, that all the higher crests were on the Circle Y. She confirmed this.

"But the spring starts lower down," she explained. "It rises on Valmon's side. Then it does a horseshoe turn back on to our land."

"Which I suppose makes it easier for Max to turn it back again," said the Saint.

He gazed thoughtfully at the painted grandeur of the landscape, wishing that he had nothing else to look for than the beauty which Nature had squandered there in a riot of heroic sculpture. He had a passing notion that with water established in that sort of formation it should have been possible to tunnel or drill on Morland's side of the hills and bring a new stream gushing from the same buried reservoir, but he was not much of a geologist, and anyway the point was not instantly constructive or even closely related to his original quest. He wished too that he had been free to share the spell of the scene, with no other consideration on his mind, with the girl who had so simply and so unaccountably, in less than a day's span, become one of his oldest friends, but that also was just an unprofitable dream, so long as Dr Ludwig Julius was in Arizona. His face was a tanned mask studying the terrain, and his right hand rested unconsciously on the butt of the Magnum that he had belted on that morning as automatically as Reefe had put on his Colt.

"Let's ride on some more," he suggested.

He turned the palomino into a trail that looked as if it might find a way to the top of one of the higher slopes from which there should be a fair panorama of Valmon's property. As they climbed, the wild brush-pocked hills opened and spread below them, pushing back the rugged horizon to let broad tablelands press up to the north-west. The trail, if it had ever really been a trail, petered out unobtrusively, until the Saint was breaking new ground all the time and his eyes were kept busy in search of ways to circumvent steeper slopes and increasing obstacles of tumbled rock. Presently he was on a spoon-shaped ledge from which at first sight all progress seemed to be blocked by a precipitous mass of broken boulders.

He reined his horse there and turned cross-saddle to estimate the view, as Jean Morland urged the pinto's nose up to his knee. Below and to the left, near the foot of the hills which they were climbing, he could now see some of the scattered buildings of the J-Bar-B, looking like toy models at the distance of two miles or more. There was one section of shallow canyon behind him where he could see a stretch of water sparkling in the sun, but he couldn't locate the rest of its course.

Then something said *BOOM!* in a thick throaty cough like the bursting of a giant drum, and the sound went echoing and rippling through the hills in a thinner diminuendo of repetitions. The horses started and moved nervously, their ears rigidly cocked, and Simon's face hardened.

"Max isn't wasting any time," he said.

But Jean Morland was frowning at the settling cloud of dust that had mushroomed from behind one of the rock castles some way to the north.

"The stream doesn't go there," she said.

"Maybe that's where Max is planning for it to go," said the Saint. "He'd get his new channel ready in advance, but he won't set off the last blast that would turn the stream until his ultimatum has run out."

The girl turned to him with her lips and eyes divided between fight and pleading.

"But why do we have to let him do it—get everything so that he only has to press one button to ruin us?"

"It won't hurt him or his men to put in an honest day's hard work," said the Saint calmly. "They haven't pressed that last button yet, and what makes you think that we're going to let them?" He reached for her hand, and took her fingers lightly into his. "Let's go on a bit and see if we can't see some more."

"There might be a way over there—"

She urged her horse on to squeeze past him, and forced it out on to a narrow shelf that looked as if it might sneak around the barrier. It was foolhardy riding, for if the shelf had proved to be a blind alley there would have been no chance to turn round and come back, and he wondered whether she did it in ignorance or recklessness. But he followed her because it was too late to argue, and was relieved to find that in a few yards the sheer drop that fell away from the ledge eased into a less perpendicular slope of rubble—still dangerous enough to navigate, but not offering the same prospects of instant and irrevocable disaster. He kept close behind her, skirting a pile of smaller boulders; she seemed quite unperturbed, and she kept looking off the trail towards the point where the blast had been, as if there was much more on her mind than any casual risk of the route.

Perhaps that was why she never saw the rattlesnake curled sleepily on a rock that rose waist-high from the slope as she rode past it. The Saint saw it, and his hand went like lightning to his gun, but from the start of that movement everything seemed to happen at once. He saw the rattler's tail dissolve into a quivering blur of warning, but before the sound even reached his ears the pinto had heard it and lurched sideways, losing its foothold on the treacherous scree. Simon thought that he fired at the same moment as the snake struck, but he had no chance to meditate about it just then. He had had no time to wonder whether the horses were gun-broke, and it would probably have made very little difference if he had. It turned out that they weren't. His palomino reared up on its hind legs like a tidal wave, twisted wildly as its rear hoofs skidded and took a half-sideways leap into space that landed it twenty feet down the slope. Through some incredible agility it remained upright, but there were seconds of frantic scrambling and sliding after that before the Saint had a chance to realise that he was still definitely in the saddle. It was a feat of horsemanship that an audience of bronc riders and mountain cavalry could have stood together and cheered, but he was less concerned with that than with the slim figure clinging to the slope above him.

"Jean—are you all right?"

It sounded to him like particularly stupid dialogue, but it was the only thing to shout as he drove the trembling palomino back up a ladder of precarious zigzags. Then as he reached her he saw that she was shaking half with laughter.

"I can't help it, Simon! You floated gracefully through the air on a flying horse, while I was landing on my behind . . . Oh God, the romance of the great open spaces!"

He lowered himself from the saddle beside her, and helped her to sit up.

"You're sure you aren't hurt?"

"Only some undignified bruises."

But she looked at the rattlesnake writhing and lashing a few feet away, its back almost cut through by the Saint's bullet. He edged over and crushed its head with a stone, and looked at her more closely when he came back.

"'I'm hoping it didn't touch you," he said.

The tone of his voice made her raise her right arm slowly to see where his eyes were fixed. There was a tear in her shirt—two tears, actually, close together and parallel, near the firm swell of her breast. Simon knelt beside her and opened one of the rents with steady impersonal fingers. He saw golden skin, softly rounded, unmarked.

"Another half-inch would probably have done it," he said. "You're going to make me believe you haven't got any nerves."

She met his eyes with sober directness.

"I just didn't want to be sloppy about saying thank you."

That was when it seemed so natural to kiss her.

He stood up abruptly.

"Hold on a minute and I'll get your horse," he said.

He led the palomino up the slope first, to a more level stretch of firmer ground. Then he went back for the pinto which by some other miracle seemed to have also avoided rolling over or breaking a leg. He stroked the animal's nose and talked to it until he had calmed it down enough to struggle back up the incline with the reins in his hand.

Beside Jean Morland again, he gave her his other hand and got her to her feet. She stumbled at once, almost into his arms, as another patch of loose surface slid from under her, but as he steadied her, somehow, he was not looking at her but over her shoulder at the ground behind her, where the weathered surface was freshly scarred and churned up by the varied scuffles of feet and hoofs. Then, quietly, he bent and picked up a broken chunk of red rock and squeezed it into his pocket before he gave her his hand again and helped her up on to where the palomino was waiting.

Even after he had turned the pinto loose there, it still seemed spontaneously inevitable for their hands to stay linked together until they sat side by side on a bench of rock and he had to light cigarettes for both of them. There was nothing to say about it. All their lives it had been certain that this would happen if they ever met.

With the smoke from his mouth curling and vanishing in the lazy air, Simon Templar took out the piece of rock he had picked up and turned it in his hands, while the girl glanced at it curiously.

"What is it?" she asked. "A souvenir? Or are you going to find gold in these hyar hills?"

He shook his head.

"No, darling. Not gold. That would have been rather corny, somehow. But some people would give a lot of gold for it. It's more useful, in certain ways . . . I think I'm beginning to get somewhere."

He turned the rock this way and that. It was heavier than one would have expected for its size. One face was caked with brown limestone, that matched many of the surrounding formations. But the rest of it was a hard greenish-grey, quartz-like stone, faintly dappled with darker shadows. And in this quartz ran veins and beads of bright magenta.

The Saint, as had been admitted, was no great geologist, but there were a useful few ores which he could recognise at a glance, and he knew now why Dr Julius must be greatly interested in Max Valmon's feud with the Circle Y.

4

"They've rounded up some cattle for branding in a canyon a couple of miles over that way," Jean Morland said. "I think I can find it, and we can have lunch with them."

They had found another way down through the hills without any more accidents.

"Just one thing," said the Saint. "Don't say anything about my mineral studies yet. I'd like to get a few more ideas and do some figuring first."

Her eyes were clear and level.

"Okay."

Hank Reefe straightened up from untying a calf and held her horse while she dismounted. Away from the branding fire, there was another fire where three pots stood steaming, and Nails was stirring one of them experimentally with a large ladle. Reefe's tanned face was lighted with a quiet smile of pleasure when he saw her, and just as quietly the smile went away when he saw the rent in her shirt which she had roughly pinned together. His glance shifted evenly to the Saint.

"A rattlesnake did that," Jean explained, and told the story.

The foreman's steady gaze only left her again when she had finished. Then it went back to the Saint and he smiled again, but differently.

"That was nice shootin', Simon," he said. It was as if he had shaken hands. The Saint grinned and said, "We're starving."

"We were just goin' to have a bite."

When they were sitting on a rock with fragrant bowls of stew balanced on their knees, Reefe said, "I thought I heard a shot once, but they've been blastin' too, so I wasn't sure."

"They've been blasting, all right," said the Saint. "We saw one charge go off. But they haven't touched the stream yet, and until they do that we'll have to be careful how we interfere. Max Valmon can blast holes all over his property if he wants to, and we haven't any right to stop him until he does us some harm. In fact, if he's got the sheriff in his pocket it'd only make things worse for us. We might give them an excuse to lock us up legally and keep us out of the way until the damage was all done. Valmon might even be playing for that."

"All the same," said Reefe, "that feller I was talkin' about last night—the Saint—he wouldn't 've sat around doin' nothing."

"Too bad we can't send for him," said the Saint. "He might be handy to have around."

He went on eating without saying any more about it, and Reefe seemed to draw back into himself in a disappointed way, as if Simon had let him down. Presently he began to talk to Jean in a rather strained manner, making stiff and trivial conversation. The girl answered him more easily, but every now and again her eyes turned back to the Saint in silent puzzlement.

Simon was too preoccupied with his own speculations to do much about it. They finished eating, and one of the cowboys brought mugs over and poured them coffee. The conversation of Reefe and Jean dried up again, and again they seemed to be waiting for the Saint's lead. Simon lighted a cigarette and stared frowning at the tinted hills.

At last Reefe got to his feet.

"You want to try your hand at helpin' us rope some of these calves?" he asked stolidly.

Simon shook his head. He finished his coffee and stood up.

"I think I'll ride back to the house. Mr Morland should be back with my car before long, and I want to drive into town."

Hank Reefe considered him lengthily. Then he spoke with deliberation, as if he had finally made up his mind and was satisfied to go through with his decision.

"You ain't figurin' on doin' anything about Valmon at all?"

Simon looked him in the eyes, with the faintest glimmer of a smile.

"Hell no," he said. "It wouldn't be legal. In fact, I might even think of taking some dynamite over and helping him a bit . . . Of course, I couldn't do that now, though—not in broad daylight. I think that Max has a proud and sensitive nature, and he wouldn't be happy if he knew about it. But if you and I rode over very quietly after dinner, we might be able to do a couple of little things for him . . . Of course, that'd just be a little secret between us."

Reefe's face relaxed so slowly that there was not a movement of a muscle which could have been identified, and yet the change was so profound that he no longer looked like the same man.

"Why, sure," he agreed. "It's nice ridin' around here after the moon's up."

"I'll go back with you and show you the way," said the girl.

Simon knew how Reefe looked at her without watching. He said, "You don't really need to. It won't be any trick to find."

"It's time I was getting back, anyhow. I want to know how Daddy made out."

The Saint shrugged.

On the way back he said, "Hank is good people."

She said, "Yes."

It was all there. He didn't have to say, "You know he's in love with you, of course. But how do you feel?" And she didn't have to answer, "I don't know now, since you came here. So what about you?" And that saved him from having to say, "We should be afraid of this. It's got to be something we're both imagining. It musn't be anything else." But those words were all there, intuitively, unspoken, so that it was as though he knew she was reading it all out of his mind just as her mind couldn't deceive his, and he knew it and couldn't stop it, and didn't want to, only it was not so cold that way as it would have been in words. And so they talked idly about everything else, and this was all they said all the time.

It was soon after two when they rode down to the ranch house. There was an unfamiliar car parked outside, a green coupe, and an unfamiliar man rose from a chair on the porch as they stepped up, and bowed with insinuating politeness.

"Good afternoon," he said.

He wore a greenish speckled tweed suit, conventionally cut on city lines and complete right down to the waistcoat with a gold watch-chain strung across the stomach, and he carried a green felt hat with a feather in it, so that he looked rather as if he had been outfitted to correspond with a Bronx tailor's specifications for a country gentleman's costume. He was of medium height and soft in the middle. His face was round and pink and a little shiny, and his smooth brow extended back over the top of his head, like a polished atoll surrounded by a surf of sandy grey hair. His eyes were pale gunmetal, and looked like small marbles behind the thick lenses of his gold-rimmed spectacles. They anatomised the girl rather completely, and turned back to Simon.

"Are you Mr Don Morland?"

"Mr Morland isn't here," said the Saint coolly. "But I'm his manager. Can I help you?" The other pursed his small red lips.

"Of course. Of course. Mr Morland would be an older man." He spoke English perfectly, yet he could have been neither American nor English. His accent was faultless, but his voice was pitched in the wrong part of his mouth. "So you're his manager. Yes. You mean you are in absolute charge of all his affairs?"

"Just that," said the Saint pleasantly.

It is only a matter of history that he never even paused to wonder whether Jean Morland would fail to back him up, but without looking at her he could sense that she hadn't betrayed him by the flick of an eyelid.

"I see." The tone was much too ingratiating to be sceptical, but the cautious advance was there just the same. "So that any business proposition he received would have to be referred to you?"

There were ethereal emphases and question marks in just the right places.

"Exactly."

"Even quite a private matter? . . . Such as . . . if I were interested in buying this ranch?"

"Even that," said the Saint cheerfully. "But as a matter of fact, the ranch isn't on the market."

"Of course not. No. But I could be permitted to wonder whether a sufficiently attractive price—let us say, perhaps, double Mr Valmon's offer . . ."

Simon looked at him unhelpfully.

The visitor sat on the arm of a chair and dabbed his pink forehead with a large silk handkerchief.

"Perhaps I should make a fuller explanation. I've always wanted to own a place of this kind. It so happens that I'm a temporary guest of Mr Valmon's—he used to have business connections with a cousin of mine, who sent me to him with an introduction. I had never met him before. Naturally, I heard about what happened last night. I hate to say it, but I feel that Mr Valmon's behaviour must have been very bad. And yet of course I have no control over him. But I do feel that his attitude absolves me from some of my ordinary obligations as a guest."

"So that you're free to go behind his back and bid for a place that he's interested in?" Simon suggested politely.

"Indeed, no. I don't see it that way. I feel rather that I'm trying to make some amends, by proxy, for his bad manners."

"Did he tell you what he was threatening to do—about the stream?"

"He did say something about trying to cut it off."

"Which would make this place practically worthless."

"That would be a great pity. But it might not happen."

"You must think quite a lot of your drag with Valmon."

The pink-faced man fluttered a plump deprecating hand. His smile was so unshakably sweet that a baby would have been ashamed not to give him its favourite rattle.

"Perhaps I should have a slight advantage—through my cousin's business connection. Perhaps I'm just too proud of myself as a psychologist. But I'm quite willing to take my risk. Even if I lost, I should be satisfied to think that you hadn't suffered."

"Now I come to think of it," said the Saint, "my mother did tell me about Santa Claus."

The pale grey eyes gleamed limpidly.

"Will you give Mr Morland my message?"

The Saint lighted a cigarette, and in doing it confirmed an impression that he had caught out of the corner of his eye. His Buick had just then turned the corner in from the desert, but he did not want to help the other to notice it.

"Sure," he said. "I'll talk it over with him, and he'll do what I advise."

"Mr Morland must have great confidence in you."

The probing dubiety was still there, but the man's saccharine accents made the words sound like a compliment.

"This is Mr Morland's daughter," said the Saint easily. "She'll tell you."

Without looking at him, the girl said, "My father always does what Mr Templar tells him."

There was a stillness in which the whole earth took part. It seemed as if no living thing could be moving or breathing anywhere. And yet all of that hush was mental, without any change of expression anywhere to which it could be attached. Jean Morland must even have been unaware that it had taken place at all. The visitor went on looking at Simon with his deferential smile and appealing spaniel eyes, his fingers pulling on his soft lower lip.

He said, almost apologetically, "Then . . . surely . . . Mr Templar could tell me now—whether I have any hope—"

"Give me a day or two to think it over," Simon said.

"But this wild threat of Mr Valmon's. He said he had given you some sort of ultimatum. It's absurd, of course, but he's the type of man who might be capable of carrying it out. Then this property would be spoiled. Then, of course, I shouldn't have had even a sporting chance to make good with it. So then it wouldn't be fair to ask me to repeat my offer. I don't want to rush you, but you must see why my proposition can only be good for tonight."

Simon Templar gazed at him levelly. The stillness had left him bubbling away before a spring of deep inward laughter that didn't stir a muscle of his chest. The same laughter seeped into the depths of his eyes, like the shift of something stirring far down in a blue mountain lake, without changing a facet of the surface.

He felt quite unreasonably happy. But to the Saint there was always a reckless delight like no other mirth in the world when the wolves split the first stitch of the first tiny seam of their well-tailored sheepskins, and he knew that the cards were coming on to the table and the fight was going to be on. All the sparring and exploring and the rubber stilettos were great fun in their time, but they were only shadows until those moments of reality touched them like magic wands putting life into a picture . . .

"I'll see you tonight, then," he said.

"With something definite?"

"With something definite."

The other's hopeful eyes searched his face, as though they were seeking an innuendo that could have been confirmed there, and yet that hadn't been hinted by the minutest inflection of a single syllable.

"I hope we shall both be pleased about it," said the visitor at last, wistfully, .and stood up. He bowed obsequiously to the girl. "It's been a pleasure, Miss Morland." He put out his hand towards her. There was only the faintest hesitation before she responded, and then his head dipped again infinitesimally over her fingers. He turned at once. "Until tonight, then, Mr Templar."

His soft white hand hovered persuasively in front of the Saint.

Simon enclosed it in brown steel fingers, in a grip like the caress of a hydraulic press set to crack eggshells. He smiled with incomparable hospitality.

"I'll be looking forward to it," he murmured cordially, "Dr Julius."

The other's eyes misted at him through thick distorting lenses for an infinite instant, and the pink tonsure bobbed at him with impeccable punctilio before it turned away.

Simon Templar put his cigarette back in his mouth and drew long and deep as he eased his hip carefully on to the porch rail, before he turned to meet the inevitable unwavering challenge of Jean Morland's calm clear eyes.

5

The green coupe had started away before she spoke. And then her voice had the same inquiring detachment as her gaze.

"He never mentioned his name," she said. "But you knew it."

The Saint nodded.

"How did he know mine?" he asked.

"I told him."

Quite clearly she had no idea of the meaning that he might have placed on the word "know." She went on, as though she was methodically determined to work through to something: "Why did you tell him you could speak for Daddy?"

"Why did you back me up?"

"I thought you must have something in mind, and I didn't want to spoil it."

"You must have great confidence in me," he said, in smiling mimicry of Dr Julius's saponaceous lisp.

"But now it isn't fair to keep me guessing."

The Saint took one of her hands.

"Did I forget to tell you that you were perfect, darling? You were. No old campaigner could have done better without a rehearsal. You only made one mistake, and that simply wasn't your fault."

"What was it?"

"It doesn't really matter. Ludwig would probably have found out anyway, in next to no time, and it was fun to see him do his frozen-fish take . . . But as for the rest of it, I just didn't have any deep-laid motives. I became your father's manager to find out what went on. If it was a legitimate visitor I could always back down. If it was the Ungodly, I might be able to draw the fire. In case you still feel there are loose ends, it was the Ungodly."

"Then Valmon was only bluffing?"

"Oh, no. Valmon would always be effective in an emergency. You heard the subtle way the threat and the ultimatum were repeated? But Ludwig Julius is smarter than Valmon. He'll go a long way to avoid trouble, because when there's trouble you never know what may blow off. He'll even go so far as to double the ante, which is a long way for a guy like that to go. I give you my word, if he were sure of getting away with it, Comrade Julius could play so much rougher than Valmon that he'd make Max look like a squeamish school-teacher."

Her eyes still held him.

"You still haven't told me how you know so much about him."

Simon's glance switched off the verandah again. His car was just pulling up in front of the house.

"There isn't time now," he said. "I'll tell you presently. Just for now, it'd be so much better if your father didn't know anything about it. He's a swell guy and everything else, but he just doesn't know these games. You've backed me so far. Will you back me some more?"

She took a long quiet breath. She was aloof in a dispassionate appraisal that few other women he had ever known could have simulated, let alone made sincere. Yet it all died in the helpless quirk of her shoulders and the surrendering downward turn of her lips.

"I'm nuts," she whispered. "But I'd back you to hell and back."

"One way is enough," he said. "There are no bets on the return journey."

But his eyes said everything else that there was no time to speak.

And then he was rising to greet Don Morland as he came up the porch steps, as though nothing at all had happened since they had parted.

The old man's step was quick and nervous, and he asked the obvious question in the most obviously conventional way.

"Who was that fellow I passed on the road?"

"He was working his way through correspondence college," Simon replied gravely, "with a line of hogwash and fertiliser. I told him we didn't keep hogs and we weren't farming, and he went away."

Morland nodded as if he had scarcely heard. His face looked lined and fretful with worry.

The girl took his arm.

"We want to know how you got on," she said.

"I didn't get on at all," Morland said flatly, and her shoulders drooped.

"Then—"

"The sheriff wasn't there. The sheriff wasn't in town. The sheriff was away. Nobody knew where he was. The sheriff was busy on some case. Nobody knew anything about the case or how to get in touch with him. Nobody knew when he'd be back."

"But didn't he have any deputies?"

"Oh, yes, there was a deputy in the office. He'd be glad to do anything he could for me. But this was a bit too much. He didn't rightly know what the law was in a case like this. He reckoned this was too much responsibility for him to take on his own. He'd have to talk to the sheriff about it. But he didn't know exactly how to get hold of the sheriff. Of course, he'd be back. Maybe tomorrow. Or the next day. Certainly before the end of the week . . . And that was all I could do."

The pounding of clipped bitter sentences died away with the last one into a dull hopelessness. Morland gave his daughter's hand a little squeeze and turned towards a chair. She looked at the Saint, and he gave a faint tight-lipped shrug.

He said, "What is technically known as the good old runaround. It might be a coincidence, but it's a hundred to one the sheriff has been got at. Only he couldn't come out in the open and refuse to do anything—that'd be as good as putting a rope round his neck. So he just can't be found. When he can be found it's too late, and then it's just too goddam bad. You can go on from there."

Morland sat with his hands clasped and his forearms on his knees; not fuming or fidgeting, and Simon realised that he was not really weak and foolish. He was just stumbling in a new language.

Then he looked up suddenly, and his eyes were hard and bright.

"Now I know what you all meant this morning," he said. "You must have thought I was very stupid. I was. But I won't be any more. If I've got to fight to keep this place, I'll fight. I don't care what happens. I'll get a gun and fight for it with every one of you who'll stand by me."

A slow smile came to the Saint's lips.

"That's the kind of talk the boys are waiting to hear, Don," he said, and took himself off the porch rail. "Tell 'em 'bout it when they come in. They'll cheer you." He flipped the end of his cigarette away on to the drive. "Now I'm going into town and attend to a couple of little things myself."

Jean Morland said slowly, as if she was asking for a new hope to be kindled, "Perhaps you could find the sheriff—"

The Saint shook his head.

"I'm not even going to try. This is something much more important. I'll be back in time for supper, and I may be able to tell you about it then."

Morland stood up.

"That wheel is still in your car—I had to buy a new tyre," he said. "If you're going out again you might as well drop me by the station wagon and I can bring it back. I'd rather have something to do than sit here waiting."

"Good enough."

The three of them went back to the Buick together. The girl took her father's arm again, but she took the Saint's arm as well. He tightened his arm against his side in answer to the pressure of her fingers . . .

Besides some important research in the county records, he had a couple of purchases to make in Lion Rock, and the dusk was deepening as he drove back towards the Circle Y. It had been a profitable trip, and he was humming idly to himself as he nursed the big Buick over the unsuccessful imitation of a road. He felt it as one of those happy intermissions of adventure, the twilight between the cold daylight and exciting darkness, the empty stage between the acts, the gathering pause that was platitudinously called the calm before the storm. But to him it was only in those moments that the full flavour of an episode could be savoured in anticipation, like the bouquet of a rare wine before tasting, before it had changed for ever into retrospect. This one had been a little slow to grow upon the senses, but now he knew that all the analyses had been worked out and the vintage would prove to belong with the most distinguished aristocracies of such brews. Even his wordless understanding with Jean Morland belonged with it—but he didn't want to think about that too much yet, when thinking only brought back too many questions that would have to be answered before the end Just then he only wanted to be glad that they had met and talked a little, without saying anything. It would have been enough to leave it like that, perhaps; and yet he was aware of a moment's absurd contentment as he drove up in front of the ranch house and switched out his lights, and saw her coming to the head of the porch steps, with the lamplight behind her limning the eager cleanness of her silhouette.

He ran up the steps and took her hand.

"I told you I'd be back for supper," he said, "and I'm starving."

"You'll get pork and beans," she smiled.

But her smile was something that came quickly, just for the moment of greeting him, and then lost its spontaneity as quickly as it had found it. Her eyes left his face, and seemed to search the background behind him.

"I'll bring it out," she said, and turned back towards the kitchen.

Simon Templar strolled over to the table that was already set up on the verandah, and tossed his hat over a pair of stag horns nailed to one of the rafters. He pulled out a chair and sat down and tilted the chair back, opening a new pack of cigarettes and tapping one out on the stretched denim over his left knee. As definitely as if a bell had rung, he realised that the interlude was already over.

A little way along the porch, Hank Reefe gazed at him steadily from the rocking chair where he sat with his gun belt across his knees, and said, "You come back alone?"

"Yes. I dropped Papa off where the station wagon was ditched yesterday. He was going to change the wheel and bring it in."

"You didn't see him after that?"

Little electric needles stitched a ghostly seam up the Saint's spine.

"No. The station wagon wasn't there when I came by just now. I thought he'd be back here."

"He hasn't been back."

Jean Morland came through the kitchen door and set bowls on the table.

"We'd better go ahead and eat," she said. "Hank must be starving too."

The foreman came over silently and sat down on the other side of her. He sat looking at Jean, and the Saint looked at her too. Her eyes went to one of them after the other, and she smiled again, rather quickly and nervously. Reefe stretched out his big hand and took hold of her arm gently.

He said, "You might be worrying about nothing, Jean. He could've remembered something he forgot to buy, and gone back into town for it. Or maybe he thought he'd have another try at getting hold of the sheriff or somebody."

"I know," she said mechanically.

"Let's face it," said the Saint evenly. "The question is whether anything could have happened to him."

His bluntness hit her with a kind of chilling shock that only lasted for a fraction of a second. And then it was as if a light had been turned on in a haunted room. Whatever had to be faced could be seen and estimated, and no matter how it looked it could never be worse than the creation of imagination feeding upon fear. She had had many thoughts about the Saint already, but never before had she sensed the quality of power that gave life to every other impression that could be caught from him. All at once, with a curiously calm relaxation, she had a ridiculous feeling that he was a man who could never fail, because he would never know when to be afraid of failure.

He smiled at her as he crushed out his cigarette.

"I'm going to eat, anyway," he said. "It won't do your father any good for us to starve ourselves, and we won't be able to do nearly as much to help him with our stomachs sticking to our spines like punctured balloons."

He ate thoughtfully for a while, without talking, as if nothing could disturb his appetite or his enjoyment of the food, but his face was intent, and his brain was coldly sorting one speculation after another, as dispassionately as though they were moves in a casual chess game. Yet he avoided looking at Jean Morland while he was thinking, because he was not certain whether the fine edge of his detachment would stand up to that.

Presently he said, "We can start working from this: Don Morland hasn't been killed, and won't be—barring accidents. But for that matter he could always fall down in a bath tub and break his neck. The Ungodly certainly wouldn't encourage that."

Jean said, "But they're trying to get the ranch—"

"How would that get it for them? They aren't his nearest relatives. The odds are that if anything drastic happened to him, you'd inherit it. If they used . . . various persuasions to force him to sign a new will before he had an accident, you'd probably contest it and the estate would be tied up for years before they got anything, if they ever did. And there'd also be a lot more publicity than they want."

"They might think Jean'd be easier to deal with than the old man," said Reefe.

"Then it would've been much more practical to kidnap her. Look, this way, the old man first has to die, and then either they've made him sign a new will leaving the ranch to them, which could be fought through every court in the country, or Jean inherits it and they have to start all over again working on her. Either way, the deal would be held up till there were whiskers on it that you could weave into blankets. They don't want that. They want quick results. See their ultimatum. Any plot of that kind is much too complicated—it takes too long to work out, and it could spring leaks in too many places. Therefore they certainly wouldn't kill Don Morland."

The girl bit her lip.

"But if they just . . . tortured him and tried to make him sell—"

"Why go to all that trouble when there's an easier way? Maybe they could break him—almost anybody can be broken if he doesn't die on you first—but they'd have to kill him afterwards so he couldn't tell about it. And that still wouldn't keep the rest of us quiet. These people aren't amateurs. If they'd wanted to work that angle they'd have tried to take Jean; then they could have had anything they wanted from her father, and the rest of us wouldn't have dared to say a word."

Reefe studied the Saint unexpressively over his spoon.

"You kept on saying 'they,'" he observed. "You figure there's somebody else in on this with Valmon?"

"I'm sure of it."

"I figured you were," the Texan said placidly, "from the way you talk. You seem to know quite a bit about them. You know they aren't amateurs. You know they're pretty clever. You knew this man Julius who was here this afternoon, Jean told me. An' he seemed to know something about you. If we knew some of these things ourselves maybe we could've done quite a bit of figurin' ourselves."

His tone was reserved and sensible, exactly the same as he might have used to call a hand of poker. There was no belligerence or animosity in it. He was inquisitive and he could be wrong, but he had a right to find out what was sitting across the table, in a polite and impersonal way.

Simon Templar gazed back at him appreciatively, but still with flakes of steel resting in his eyes to match the challenge that was almost imperceptible in the foreman's courteous simplicity.

"Yes, I know quite a bit about them," he said. "I know that they don't want any more commotion than they've got to have—which is why Valmon's performance last night, when I made him mad enough to be stupid, must have been worrying Comrade Julius no little. I know why Comrade Julius must be even more worried since he was here this afternoon, I know that they may be able to make a small county sheriff play ball, but that there are other departments that they couldn't even begin to talk to—which is why they'd much rather not get involved with kidnappings and killings."

"All right," said Reefe. "Then wouldn't it help if we all knew?"

Simon pushed away his plate and took out a cigarette.

"Maybe it would," he said at last. "I wouldn't have told you any sooner because it's kind of dangerous to know. But by this time they're liable to think I've told you anyhow. So just for fun you could start worrying about this—"

He got no further, because at that moment they were all aware of quickened footsteps scuffling up the hill from the lower mesa where the other ranch buildings were.

The girl stiffened and checked her breath. Hank Reefe, with a different instinctive reaction, turned and began to stretch out a long arm towards the chair where he had shed his gun belt. The Saint crossed his legs and dragged quietly and deeply on his cigarette; Don Morland's footsteps couldn't have had that weight, and the Ungodly would have been much stealthier.

The dark shape of a man loomed into the aura of lamplight beyond the porch, and his upturned face showed as a suddenly lighter patch picked out of the night.

"What is it, Elmer?"

Jean Morland said it. She was already at the porch rail as Simon got to his feet.

The cowboy came to a stop, catching his voice after the haste of his climb.

"It's Smoky, miss," he said. "He stayed out to watch the cows tonight so we wouldn't have to round 'em up again in the mornin'. His horse just come home alone—an' there's blood on the saddle!"

6

It seemed like a crazy thing to attempt—to set out to look for a man's body at night, in wild broken country, with several square miles of it to cover. But they did it.

They belted on guns and picked up flashlights and rode out in a reckless cavalcade. But it was possible only because the moon was bright and clear, brilliant enough to throw hard black shadows against the ground that it washed with luminous grey, so bright that for any ordinary observation the flashlights were less than unnecessary. It was one of those amazing subtropical desert moonlights which are unknown to any other parts of the earth, which seem to have been designed expressly and solely for soft music and romance, and the Saint rode beside Jean Morland and reflected that this sort of thing always seemed to be happening to a lot of good moments in his life. Perhaps it was part of the price you paid for living that way: the same trail of adventure that led towards romance just as inevitably had to lead on and lead away again . . .

They headed for the canyon where they had had lunch, and found Smoky's camp fire still burning; his bed-roll was opened beside it, but hadn't been slept in. There was no sign of any disturbance. Apparently he had just mounted his horse and gone on a late patrol, or gone to investigate something that had aroused his attention or his suspicion.

They broke up and spread out from there; after arranging their signals Simon took the spoke of the fan that pointed most directly towards the hill from which he had reconnoitred Valmon's territory that morning, and it was he who found Smoky, with surprising quickness, lying out on an open slope only a few yards from the boundary. He looked at the crumpled figure very briefly, and then fired one shot in the air and swung his flashlight round and round in a vertical circle for a while until he had received five answering twinkles from different directions.

Jean and Hank reached him first, and they looked at the sprawled heap that had been Smoky while Jim and Nails and Elmer rode up one by one and clumped stiffly into the circle.

Nails said it first.

"The same way as Frank Morland. His haws musta throwed him an' then trod on him."

It looked just like that; there was the clear print of a horseshoe on the side of Smoky's pulped face, and others, just as clear, in the bloody mess where his chest had been crushed in.

The Saint lighted a cigarette.

"I just don't know very much," he remarked diffidently. "I've seen a few trick horses in my time, but Smoky's must be something to tell Ripley about. Maybe you could sell him to a circus."

Hank Reefe stared at him levelly, but it was Jim who growled, "What for?"

"There was blood on the saddle, wasn't there?" said the Saint. "It must be a pretty acrobatic horse if it could have done this to him while he was still on top."

"I've knowed a hawss to r'ar up an' fall back on a man so's he got the horn in his chest," Nails said slowly. "I've seen hawss an' man fall together an' the hawss roll over on him."

"The blood wasn't on the horn," answered the Saint, "and the saddle hadn't been rolled on. It was quite a new saddle, and there wasn't a scar on it."

It was a strangely dramatic scene, all of them standing silently there around Smoky's body with the silver moonlight carving out shadows as sharp and flat as a woodcut and drawing a kindly vagueness over the ugly details of death. So the moon would never mean soft music and romance to Smoky anymore, and its light on his broken body was only the same light that it had shed on hundreds and thousands of other broken bodies in European cities where soft music was also only the memory of a dream. But it seemed to Simon Templar that even in the timeless hush of those Arizona hills he could hear the grinding mutter of the mad machinery of destruction that had reached half-way around the world to lay a simple cowboy on the same altar with the peasants of Poland and the villagers of Greece.

Hank Reefe was nodding quietly.

"Sounds right enough," he said. "So it could've been the same way with Frank Morland."

"It's been done before. Makes it look like a good accident. But they muffed Smoky a bit, or the saddle wouldn't have given it away. He must have been shot or stabbed first, before they went to work with the big mallet with horseshoes nailed to it."

"But why?" demanded the girl.

Simon shrugged grimly.

"Probably he saw something he shouldn't have seen. Probably your Uncle Frank did the same. They won't tell us."

The foreman hooked his thumbs in his belt.

"Well, what now?"

It was purely an invitation, but it was curious how inevitable it sounded. Now that a leader was plainly called for, there was not a moment's question about who it was to be. The leadership was offered and accepted with such unconscious naturalness that perhaps nobody even realised at the time that it had happened at all.

"Somebody'd better take Smoky back to the house," said the Saint. "Nails, you do it. Jim and Elmer—you stick around here. You might see some more of what Smoky saw, and if it means trouble you can help to look after each other. Jean, you go back with Nails. Hank, you can go with her. Take a car and drive over to Valmon's. Raise hell. Talk a lot. Demand to see the foreman and the boss and everyone else. Tell 'em about Smoky. Say that you're sure there's dirty work going on, and you're going to know more about it, or else you're going to shoot up the place or roust out the sheriff or anything else you can think of. I'll leave the dialogue to you. The one thing is to cause plenty of commotion and make it last as long as possible and keep as many of them occupied as you can."

"While you're havin' a look round?"

"Exactly. The more you can distract their attention, the more I may be able to do. So try and keep 'em bothered without actually letting it go into a free-for-all. But when the time comes—and it'll probably be my time too—come out shooting."

"I'll do that."

Simon turned and handed his reins to Nails.

"You can put Smoky on my horse—I'll be walking from here on."

Then, as he must have expected, Jean Morland was the only one who had to be answered. She came and took his arm while the men were picking Smoky up and mounting him for his last meaningless ride, and the Saint was finishing his cigarette and staring over the shadowy terrain of the J-Bar-B.

"You've got quite a way of taking charge, haven't you, cowboy?"

"Everybody knows what has to be done," he tried to tell her. "Somebody just has to say it."

"I suppose that usually turns out to be you."

"I'm sorry," he said. "You're really the boss, when your father's away. But you haven't been here so long, and—well, you could have too much on your mind."

"That's just it," she said, and this was not what he had expected at all. "I have got too much on my mind. And I wouldn't be any good. And I know I ought to be left out. I don't want to be the stupid wench in the story who gets heroic and keeps dashing in where she doesn't belong and messing everything up. I know you wouldn't have any use for that. I just wish I knew why I was so sure that you know so much."

He put his hands on her shoulders and faced her.

"I think Hank will tell you about that one day."

"Couldn't I want you to tell me?"

"There isn't time now."

"But something."

He drew a breath and held it for the slightest pause.

"Do you happen to remember that there's a war on, Jean?" he asked quietly. "Well, this is part of it. Even here. Just a little frontier skirmish that the history books will never write about. But one day thousands of men will be killed and cities will be blasted with what there is on this ranch. I'm trying to make sure that they're the right men and the right cities."

She was standing quite still, and the moonlight glossed out all the subtleties of expression so that he couldn't be sure how much she understood or whether she understood anything.

She said in that clear steady voice of hers, "Just be careful, Simon. So you can tell me the rest."

She took a step closer, and for an instant he felt her lips cool and tremorless against his. Then she turned away, and he turned back with her to the others and saw that Smoky's body was already wrapped in a blanket and tied over his saddle. Jim and Elmer stepped back, and Nails led the palomino over to his own horse and bridged his stirrups. Jean Morland mounted without another word, and Hank Reefe turned to the Saint with his reins in his hand.

"Good luck."

"You too."

They gripped. Then, as the foreman set the brim of his hat and put one hand to the saddle horn, he said, "One day I'm goin' to know why you remind me of that feller I was talkin' about—the Saint."

That was all. He swung a long leg over the cantle, and the Saint turned away, grinning, and was starting down the slope without waiting to see them get away.

He figured that he might have a little time to spare, and he was interested to see not only what preparations Max Valmon might have made to carry out his threat to blast the stream out of its course but also what other engineering arrangements might have been initiated in the vicinity.

He also knew that from there on he was taking risks not only with his own life but also with the entire outcome of that frontier skirmish which were entirely unauthorised by any of the published books of rules. One telephone call to the right number, when he was in Lion Rock, would have taken the whole thing out of his hands and delivered it into the lap of a highly organised team of genial gentlemen with elegant badges and all the resources of the Law at their disposal. But to the Saint there was personal pride in certainty as against wild suspicion, and a delight in danger for its own sake that eliminated all such prosaic solutions. From the beginning this had been his adventure, and if he could drop it now he could have dropped it from the beginning, and there was no clear dividing line. And there would have been nothing to remember. It was all very reprehensible, no doubt, and respectable officials in Washington would get ulcers about it; but if the Saint hadn't been doing reprehensible things all his life there would never have been a Saint Saga, and this chronicler would have had to devoted his genius to writing a syndicated column of advice and good cheer to lovely hearts.

It was easy for Simon to find the stream, and he followed it over the boundary line as it traced a wide rising quadrant. Then it turned sharply and came tumbling down over steeply rising boulders in a series of chattering cascades. The Saint climbed beside it, and presently found himself on a high grassy flat across which the brook rustled through a broad ribbon of wild alfalfa. This, then, must have been the place where it could easily have been diverted, for the mesa fell away to his left through a rim of jagged rocks beyond which there must have been plenty of natural channels to lead it clear out to the open acres of the J-Bar-B. In fact, one path had already been cut in that direction, but it was not an aqueduct. It was a wide, nicely graded, soundly surfaced road.

Simon stood and gazed at it with profound interest. He had studied maps of the district enough to know that there should be no public highway there. And ranchers did not normally build private roads of that quality so that they could drive out to odd corners of their estates and admire the view. This road had been constructed for the efficient movement of heavy loads, and it was still new enough not to have been much scarred by the traffic.

Turning, the Saint thought that he could look across from there back to the slope where he had found Smoky, and while he looked he saw the red mote of a cigarette-end dance and brighten like a tiny firefly in a patch of shadow, and his lips hardened grimly. The road itself would not have been visible from where Smoky had been, since it lay safely below the raised rim of the plateau, but Smoky might have seen something on it that he should not have seen, and might have betrayed his presence with a carelessly handled cigarette exactly as Jim or Elmer was doing then . . .

Simon followed the road up, and the road followed the brook. They turned north together, into the rocky hills on the other side of the mesa where the ground went on climbing in ragged steps towards the general level of the place where the Saint had killed his snake that day and found crystals like blood in a broken stone . . . He realised that in fact the place where he had picked up the stone could not have been much more than half a mile from where he was going, and must have been part of the same geological outcropping . . . Then he was at the end of both the brook and the road.

They separated about a hundred yards before that, towards the foot of a sheer rock cliff where the meadow ended. He followed the stream first. It climbed precipitously up a funnel of steep falls, and abruptly he was at its source where it sprang clean and sparkling out of a natural cleft in the rock. Above there was nothing but the soaring battlements of age-eroded stone.

The Saint worked westwards along the foot of the escarpment towards the road, and now he practically knew what he would find there. Without any feeling of surprise he saw the angular spidery shapes of machinery that certainly had nothing to do with agriculture, the gaunt utilitarian forms of buildings that were not barns or granaries.

The entrance of the mine was a square patch of blackness in the side of the bluff. Simon picked his way over to it, and reached for the flashlight in the hip pocket of his Levis. He was still a few steps from the opening when a voice that was not at all western spoke out of the darkness.

It said, "Reach for some stars, buddy, and keep coming."

7

The Saint raised his hands slowly, and walked the last four paces to the mouth of the mine.

The voice said, "Drop the flashlight."

Simon dropped it.

He stood in front of the pitch-black gap, trying uselessly to penetrate its inky opacity.

"Take out your rod," ordered the voice. "Put it on the ground. Then turn around and go back six steps."

The Saint obeyed. There was nothing else for it. Out there in the open, bathed in the moonlight, he was a perfect target while the Voice was only cold words out of utter emptiness. He could have been dropped where he stood before he even knew what to shoot at.

He stood where he had been told to stop, feeling cold ripples inching up his spine, not knowing when the tearing smash of a bullet would blast through his chest and hurl him forward into eternal nothingness. Behind him he heard crunching steps—it sounded like two men. They paused momentarily, picking up the Magnum, and came on. Something hard and blunt prodded his back.

"Walk to that first building on your right."

Simon walked, with the hard bluntness in his back all the time. He was steered to a door, and told to open it and go in. When he had taken three or four steps into blackness, a switch clicked behind him and a dim bare bulb lit up over his head. He saw that he was in a corner of some sort of ore mill, but he didn't know enough about it to identify any of the machines that loomed away beyond the limits of the little patch of light where he stood.

The gun muzzle ceased pressing against him for the first time

"Okay, buddy," said the voice. "You can turn around now."

Simon turned.

He saw two men, both in dirty blue overalls. One, who was unmistakably the owner of the Voice, was big and square, very broad-shouldered and a little paunchy. He carried a submachine gun. He had a close-cropped sandy head and small crinkly eyes and a heavy stubbly chin. The other, who held the Saint's Magnum, was smaller and thinner. He had brown hair and big black eyes with a moist flat look to them, and a very pale narrow face gashed with a pink slit of a mouth.

The big man studied Simon's face with satisfaction.

"It's him," he announced to his companion. "I thought so."

"Well, I'm surprised," said the Saint reprovingly. "If you were expecting me I should think you'd have hung out flags and ordered a brass band."

The big man ignored this.

"Better call Valmon," he said over his shoulder.

The thin man nodded, and went over to a corner where there was an old-fashioned wall telephone. He took off the receiver and cranked it.

Presently he said, "This is Eberhardt. The Saint is here. He came to the mine, and Neumann and I caught him."

His voice was as thin as he was, with a strongly accented whine. He listened for a while and said "Ja." Then he said "Okay," and hung up the receiver and came back.

"They'll be right up," he said.

Simon gazed at the two men pleasantly.

"It's rather an unusual way to announce a visitor," he remarked, "but I suppose you have the real welcoming spirit underneath it all. By the way, will you offer me a cigarette or shall I smoke my own?"

"You can smoke," Neumann said stolidly. "But don't try any funny business."

The Saint took out a pack of cigarettes, and took a cigarette from the pack. He flicked a match with his thumb-nail and lighted it.

"Incidentally," he went on, in the same easy conversational tone, "how is the good old Bund making out these days? You must feel sort of lost with your Gauleiter in the sneezer and so many new laws everywhere about your marching around and heiling Hitler."

"Can it," said Neumann coldly. "Or I won't wait till Valmon gets here."

"Maybe you could fool them by saying 'Heil Schickelgruber,'" Simon suggested helpfully.

The other glowered at him without movement, and Simon smiled faintly and turned to pick himself a seat on a packing case against the wall. He leaned back and enjoyed his cigarette, while Neumann and Eberhardt watched him like wooden sentries. They were certainly not the most convivial company he had ever been with, but he could console himself with the expectation that Max Valmon would soon introduce a brighter note.

The whole picture was complete now, so simply and comprehensively that the only surprise was in the amount of insolent audacity that had laid out its composition. If he had only known just how the disappearance of Don Morland fitted in, he wouldn't have had one question left to ask. And it wasn't likely to be much longer before he had that final answer.

The only real problem was, what good his knowledge was going to do him. He hadn't expected to be caught so suddenly, if at all. And Hank Reefe wouldn't have had time to ride back with Smoky and drive over to Valmon's estancia yet. It was a situation that would have been more than slightly discouraging to most men, but to the Saint it was a tightening of nerve and sinew, the firing spark to an unquenchable fighting recklessness that had never yet admitted that any corner was hopeless. At that moment he had no idea what miracle he could possibly perform to equalise the reversal that had so catastrophically placed him where he was, but until that last and perhaps inevitable exception when The End would be written unarguably and for ever, he would always have his ridiculous and magnificent faith that if the tables could be turned once they could be turned again . . .

There was the sound of a car purring up outside and stopping. Then footsteps. Then the door opened, and Valmon came in.

After him, almost apologetically, came Dr Ludwig Julius.

Simon stood up in his own easy-going time. He gave them a smile so casual and carefree that it was hard to believe that he was not himself the host of the interview, instead of a prisoner at the mercy of four men, a Tommy gun, and a few other items of assorted ordnance.

"Hullo, Maxie dear," he drawled. "I know you asked me to drop in tonight, but I didn't think it was going to be such a formal affair. Comrades Neumann and Eberhardt have been frightfully zealous about turning themselves into a guard of honour—in fact, if I wasn't so well up in these military traditions I might have been afraid I was being kidnapped."

Valmon stood looking at him with that dark heavy swagger, his thumbs hooked in his carved and jewelled belt, his black brows drawn down unsmilingly.

"You should have come to the house," he said. "I was waiting for you."

"I thought I'd take a stroll around first," said the Saint. "It was such a lovely night, and I knew there'd be lots of interesting things to see."

"What made you so sure of that?"

"It sort of dawned on me gradually. But I suppose I was really quite sure when I picked up a chunk of cinnabar this morning, about half a mile from here, on the Circle Y."

Neumann and Eberhardt had drawn back unobtrusively towards the shadows. They were still on watch there, but they had left Simon with Valmon and Julius grouped under the dim spotlight like the principals in a theatrical stage setting.

Valmon and Julius looked at each other, and Julius moved in a little from his self-effacing place a little behind Valmon.

Simon beamed at him encouragingly.

"Of course," he admitted, "I'd started to get a few ideas before that. I suppose I really got the first one when I happened to find out that Dr Ludwig Julius, the great mining expert and one of dear Adolf's Deputy Kommissars of Supply, was taking a personal trip to Arizona for a nice healthy vacation."

"How did you know that?" Julius asked gently.

"My spies," said the Saint, "are everywhere. It sounds awfully funny, I know, but it's quite true. All kinds of people tell me things—people I've never met and probably never will meet. They just think I might be interested and do something. That's what happens when you get to be such a notorious character. You must try another purge in your Department, Ludwig—that is, if you ever have the chance."

Julius's bald head shone like smooth wet coral.

"How very interesting!" he said softly. "Do you wish to tell us anything more?"

"Anything you like . . . Of course, when I knew you were here I wanted to snoop around. So I took a little trouble to get into the next-door ranch. I didn't know at the time that they were so very closely connected. But when I heard about the previous owner's unfortunate accident, I did begin to wonder."

"And then?"

Valmon's modulated tenor was a melodic organ-note of challenge. His lips had drawn apart in a set way that bared his glistening teeth.

The Saint inhaled and blew out a leisured drift of curling smoke.

"Then, you were so anxious to buy the Circle Y. In fact, you were more than anxious—you insisted. Quite rudely. I thought your technique was rather crude at the time, and I didn't see why you had to be so corny. And there was all that yawp about damming the stream, with all the trimmings straight out of Hopalong Cassidy. There had to be something phony about that but I couldn't get it at first."

"And now you know all about it," suggested Julius.

"I think so—since I came this way tonight."

"We are waiting breathlessly."

"You've already driven an exploratory shaft. It confirms what I would have guessed from the cinnabar I found. The vein runs clear through. More—the whole mountain is probably fuller of it than a ripe Limburger is full of mould. You might want to cut acres of it away in chunks. But no matter how you work it, you're practically certain to break through the reservoir that feeds the stream. There'll be a small but exciting flood, more or less according to how big the source is, and then—no more stream."

The small pale grey eyes of Dr Julius were like melting marbles behind their thick lenses.

"You must have been a promising student of geology Mr Templar," he said milkily. "That wasn't so difficult."

"Has anything been difficult for you?"

It was dulcet sarcasm of the most treacly kind, but it was also another delicate challenge to go on.

The Saint threw away the stub of his cigarette and lighted another, without hurrying. It was all taking time—time in which Hank Reefe could catch up with his assignment. And that would give the Saint at least one ally within useful distance, and according to his irrepressible arithmetic, leave him almost nothing to cope with himself except four men, a Tommy gun, and a few other items of assorted ordnance.

And there was no reason why he shouldn't go on talking, as long as Valmon and Julius wanted to listen. He was telling them nothing that they didn't know already, except how much he knew himself— and they could have used unnecessarily unpleasant methods to try to find that out. But in the circumstances he had no objection to telling them. It was a convenient way of verifying his own deductions—and at the same time he was steadily building up the subtle moral advantage that he had assumed from the first instant, the gnawing doubt in their minds that any man in his position could talk so coolly and cheerfully without having at least one ace up his sleeve. He wanted that idea to germinate in them all by itself . . .

"It's all been a most amusing plot," he murmured. "Valmon makes this strike on his ranch, or somebody makes it for him, but anyway, he's still a good Heinie under his ten-gallon hat, so the nearest Bund heeler is the first to hear of it—unless Maxie wears that exalted title himself, which is most likely. Anyway, there's no commotion. There is a little quiet geologising and assaying, and the word goes back to Berlin that this is rich. Awful rich. And one of the things that the Fatherland needs quite badly, to kill a few more un-kultured barbarians with. So badly that the great Dr Julius comes here in person to organise it. Now unfortunately the nasty Jewish-controlled and plutocracketeering United States have passed a lot of unsympathetic embargoes against giving nice little Nazis materials to make fireworks with. But that might be gotten around. This is a pretty deserted part of the world, and a lot of machinery could be quietly brought in, and you could rake up plenty of demobilised Bundsmen with the skill to work it, and get a mine going that nobody else knew anything about—and smuggle the produce out and away to a suitable coast where it could be sneaked on to a freight-carrying submarine and carted off to dear old Deutschland. A very pretty and enterprising scheme, and well worth the trouble when you figure that a lode like this must be good for hundreds of tons of pure mercury. And if I'm not mistaken, mercury is the stuff that makes the detonators that pop off the bombs and shells that your Aryan heroes are distributing to illuminate the beauties of the New Order to the admiring women and children of the world."

He had all the confirmation he needed in Max Valmon's fixed ivorine smile, in the softly perspiring pink attentiveness of Ludwig Julius.

He went on after a moment, with the same hibernal confidence that was holding them at arm's length almost like a sword in his hand, even though he knew that his dialogue was running out and he was coming to the dizzy end of certainty like a downhill skier racing towards a precipice.

"However, there was one other snag. A little more prospecting showed that aside from the business of busting up the stream, your operations were going to be dangerously close to the Circle Y—in fact, some of the richest deposits were across their border. So the Circle Y had to be taken over. Of course it had to be done in a phony way—they mustn't know about the cinnabar, partly because you didn't want to have to pay that much more for the place, but most importantly because nobody at all must know that there's cinnabar here and a mine ready to produce. That's why you had to murder Frank Morland not long ago, and one of our cowboys tonight—because they could have seen you moving machinery and asked questions or talked about it."

"Murder is a very unpleasant word, Mr Templar," said Julius, and suddenly in his lisping way he was almost jovial. "Why not call it . . . er . . . liquidation of enemy agents to prevent vital information?"

"I prefer calling it murder," said the Saint, no less amiably. "It's such a help to clear thinking. Murder to conceal grand larceny."

The black scowl darkened over Valmon's rigid smile.

"What larceny?"

"Larceny of a large quantity of quicksilver from the people of the United States." The Saint smiled. "I made a check of your title in the County Records Office this afternoon. I found that when this ranch was first homesteaded, the Government specifically excluded certain mineral rights from the patent granted. The same on the Circle Y. Mercury was just one of the mineral rights reserved by Uncle Sam."

"I am learning to admire your thoroughness more and more every moment," said Julius ingratiatingly, but for the first time there was the faintest strain in the smooth surface of his indulgent superiority.

Simon Templar caught it without an outward sign, but his pulses moved into a sharper tempo of tentative delight. This might have been it—the break that he had been waiting for, the first hint of a crevice into which a wedge might be driven that might split the trap wide open. He pressed at it with the nerveless restraint of a master cutter attacking a priceless diamond.

"It was just routine," he said modestly. "But you certainly have stirred yourselves into a pot of soup, haven't you? You go around murdering people—and you might have gotten by with it once, but tonight was too often: I was able to prove that tonight's job wasn't an accident, and that throws doubt on Frank Morland's accident, and all the boys are going to remember it and talk about it. You're trying to start up an illegal mine, and they're going to talk about that too—"

"You told them about that?"

"Naturally," Simon lied. "Did you think I'd be dumb enough to come over here and keep it a secret, so that you'd have nobody to knock off but me?"

"But a little while ago you said that you really only understood everything after you came here tonight."

Because he was the Saint, Simon didn't even flip a muscle, though it seemed to him that his heart stopped for an instant.

"That was just on corroborative evidence—did all my guessing long ago," he said smoothly, and went on quickly: "So you'll never be safe unless you can wipe out the whole personnel of the Circle Y with no questions asked—which is going to be quite a problem, even for you . . . And then on top of all that you had to kidnap Papa Don Morland, which is a Federal rap all by itself. A bad break, Ludwig— very bad. And my poor little brain can't see what good you ever hoped it would do you. You might possibly be able to force him to sign the ranch over to dear Maxie or some other stooge of yours—"

"I beg your pardon," interrupted Dr Julius humbly.

"By all means."

"You should be more precise in your use of the conditional. Let us at least face facts, and admit that we have already persuaded Mr Morland to give us his signature."

The Saint's eyes turned colder, and Julius smiled.

"Really, we weren't very brutal," he said. "Only just enough to make him psychologically receptive. Then I told him in considerable detail about all the things that would happen to his beautiful daughter if he was obstinate, and he signed almost at once."

"You mean he believed you?"

"I can be very convincing, especially when I don't have to bluff. As a matter of fact—"

The wall telephone broke in with a tinny stutter, and for some reason everything else went quiet.

Eberhardt answered it. He put the receiver to his ear and then took it away again and looked at Julius.

"Pardon me," said Julius punctiliously, and went to the instrument.

He spent most of the time listening, with an occasional monosyllable of acknowledgment. It was not long. Then he spoke one sentence in German, which the Saint understood perfectly, and hung up the receiver and came back. He seemed even pinker and shinier and squirmily complacent than before.

"As a matter of fact," he resumed, as if there had been no interruption, "Miss Morland is with us already. Party Member Nagel has just brought her in. You knew him, I understand, as 'Nails.'"

8

Time crawled over the Saint's head—long-drawn-out intense dissected months of it, it seemed. He stood absolutely motionless, like a statue, through a crawling eternity, and this was solely because he knew that the slightest movement he made would betray him. He had to wait until his muscles and nerves linked themselves up again, as they would have to do after an unwarned smash on the head.

Actually it could only have been very few seconds, and Dr Julius was still facing him with that smug and pseudo-deferential leer.

The Saint said, "You're fairly thorough yourself, aren't you, Ludwig?"

"After all, it was a rather obvious precaution, to make sure that we had at least one friend in your camp."

"The famous fifth-column technique, in fact."

Julius almost giggled in happy agreement.

"And incidentally, Mr Templar, of course it makes one less of your men who will have to be convinced of how absurd the theories are which you have been scattering around."

"I was working that out."

"While it does make it easy for me to have a very important private talk with Miss Morland."

The Saint's gaze was a caress of ice.

"Dear Ludwig," he said, very gently, "I hope you won't be brutal with her. Because if you are, if I have to come back from the grave to do it, I swear that I'll cut a hole in your stomach and pull your guts out inch by inch and roast them over a slow fire."

Julius cocked his head on one side like a bird.

"You're quite fond of her, aren't you?"

"A mind like yours wouldn't understand it, but I am."

"Then that should be helpful . . . In fact, it gives me a most amusing idea. Let us go down to the house for a little while."

He turned and went to the door, with Valmon following him. At once Neumann and Eberhardt closed in behind the Saint and forced him after them.

There was no chance to make a break for it. Even after the dim light inside the mill, the moonlight outside was still bright enough for him to have been a certain notch on Neumann's Tommy gun before he had run half a dozen yards. Valmon and Julius were already getting into the front of the station wagon. Eberhardt opened the door to the back, and went around to the other side to cover him from there. It was all handled as efficiently as if they had had their training in the old-time gang wars of Chicago—which, Simon reflected, was perfectly probable.

Valmon drove in silence to the ranch house, and stopped. Neumann and Eberhardt got out, one on each side again. The Saint followed. They moved a little way from the car.

Julius said to Neumann, "Bring Morland here."

Eberhardt, standing a little behind the Saint, touched the small of his back with his revolver to remind him that he was still helpless.

The Saint looked around. They were standing near a corral fence. There were other cars parked a little way off, and among them he recognised his own Buick. So there was probably no doubt that Julius was telling the truth about Jean having been taken. And in another moment Simon had his final proof, when he saw her come to the window of a lighted room with Nails looming behind her. He seemed to be about to drag her back, but Julius called to him with sudden volume, for the window was some distance off: "Let her stay there."

Neumann came back from the direction of one of the other buildings with another man in overalls. They were half leading and half dragging Morland between them.

"Tie him to the fence," said Julius.

There were ropes around Morland's arms already, and the two men deftly rearranged them so that his arm were spread out along the fence and bound down by the wrists, his body bent slightly forwards to conform with the height. The headlamps of the station wagon, which had been left on, illuminated the scene. He twisted his head around and looked up at the Saint with a grey hopelessness that was incapable of even properly rendering surprise.

Simon was aware that Julius had left his side for a moment, but he was back now. He had a three-foot whip in his soft hands, running its supple length affectionately through his fingers.

"I'm not anxious to be too unkind to Miss Morland," he said syrupily. "But it is necessary for Mr Morland to receive a little extra discipline. To be exact, his sentence is ten lashes. I am going to ask you to administer them."

'What the hell," asked the Saint, involuntarily and incredulously, "do you think I am?"

Julius had so obviously been expecting such an answer that he scarcely paused for it. "There is, of course, an alternative," he admitted. "Miss Morland herself may need some . . . er . . . psychological conditioning. I was hoping that this would be sufficient. But if you object, it can be applied to her direct. She can be brought out here, and stripped. And then she can be beaten by Neumann. Neumann is quite an expert—he was a guard in Dachau for a time. She would have to receive one hundred lashes: ten for every one which you refused to give her father. The choice is entirely up to you."

Simon stared at him.

Julius held out the quirt.

"You mustn't keep us waiting too long, Mr Templar."

His voice was wheedling, succulent, with a kind of obscene eagerness in it.

Mechanically Simon took the whip. He looked at Julius, at the distant lighted window with the girl's silhouette in it, at Don Morland. He had a sense of frightful unreality contending with inescapable belief, much as an intelligent savage might have had on first listening to a radio. It was impossible, but it could not be denied. Julius was absolutely capable of making good his threat. There was no answer to it. And the gun in Eberhardt's hand prodded him in the back again.

"Let's talk this over," said the Saint stupidly.

"Afterwards, if you like. But you must do what I tell you. Otherwise I shall send for Miss Morland at once."

Don Morland spoke, his voice desperate but clear.

"Please do what he tells you. Please. Please."

Simon stepped forward like an automaton into the harsh glare of the headlights. The whip whistled as he raised it. He hit Morland once across the shoulders. There was no strength in his arm.

"One," counted Julius contentedly. "But you must try to make it look more convincing—otherwise I shall still have to let Neumann demonstrate on Miss Morland. However, we will count that as a first attempt. There are still ninety lashes that you can save Miss Morland."

It was a nightmare, a Grand Guignol horror that made the Saint feel as if black clouds were creeping into his mind. His arm rose and fell, quickly, because he knew that in a flogging the pause and waiting between blows while the curling agony of each stroke sinks into the flesh is half the torture. He put everything that he knew of control and timing into the job of seeming to throw all his weight into every blow, and pulling his arm at the last fraction of an inch to let it land as lightly as possible, always trying to land on a loose fold of Morland's shirt that would make the maximum noise while it helped to cushion the shock.

Even so, he must have hurt the old man. He couldn't tell how much. He hoped that most of Morland's writhing and groaning was in co-operation with him, to make it look good. He would a thousand times rather have been flogged himself. But that was not the alternative. He could see Jean Morland there, the red bars creeping up her white skin, and red beads swelling and trickling down to criss-cross them in a ghastly network, Neumann's powerful muscles bunching and stretching, Eberhardt's hungry black eyes and damp pink mouth . . .

". . . ten," said Julius.

Simon stepped back and threw down the whip. He felt sick. The inside of his head was numb and throbbing, as if he had taken a terrific pounding in the ring.

"A little hasty and unskilful," went on that sugary voice. "Neumann would have done much better. But it will do."

"I only hope," said the Saint, "the practice will come in handy when I have the chance to do the same to you."

Julius sniggered delightedly.

He turned to Neumann.

"Take him back."

Simon felt for his pack of cigarettes. There were only two left in it. He chose one with exaggerated care. For once in his life, his hands were unsteady.

Neumann and the other man were untying Morland and dragging him away. There was no one to be seen in the lighted window any more. Julius was speaking to Valmon.

"I shall leave you to begin explaining things to Miss Morland, while I finish with Mr Templar. Eberhardt and I can take care of him . . . You will not need to make any apologies for what Mr Templar has just done. You understand? Mr Templar is one of our best allies."

Into Valmon's dark face came a thin thread of white, the spreading gleam of his teeth.

"I get it."

He waited while Simon was steered into the back seat of the station wagon. Julius took the wheel. Eberhardt sat in the middle seat, facing around, the barrel of the Magnum resting on the back and trained on the centre of Simon's chest.

There was an idea in the Saint's head, a picture that he was trying to round out, but his brain still couldn't quite get hold of it. He sat back and tried to chase the fogs out of his mind.

When they stopped at the side door of the mill again, the disembarking was as efficient as before, even though Neumann was not there. Julius covered one side of the car, to forestall any break in that direction. Eberhardt backed out the other door and made the Saint follow him out. They entered the building in loose procession—Simon first, Eberhardt on his heels, and Julius a little behind. Once again, under the light, Simon was told to turn around. Eberhardt had stepped to one side of the door, and the Saint faced Julius. The Komissar of Supply had an automatic in his hand now, and it was clear that he knew how to use it. He stood just far enough away to be out of reach of any sudden spring.

"Now, my dear Saint," he said, and it was the first time he had used that name, "I hope you are quite satisfied with my thoroughness."

The Saint was conscious of his pulses, and they were as steady as perfectly balanced reciprocating motors again. He glanced at the dwindling cigarette between his fingers, and the smoke went up from it as cleanly cut as a vein in marble. His mind was clear and cool—as cool as a Himalayan stream.

"No," he said regretfully. "No, Ludwig, I'm afraid I'm not."

"You will tell me why?"

"You've had a nice little excursion at my expense. I admit it. And I suppose it was a great moment of triumph for your sadistic little maggoty soul. But it hasn't changed a thing since we left here."

"Please go on."

"You've made Morland sign something. All right. But there are still five people who are going to fight it, whatever it is—unless you can get away with killing us all. Which, as I said, is liable to attract some attention. You may have a conniving sheriff in your pocket, but I expect most of us have got friends and relatives here and there, and someone is going to get some publicity for it that even he can't stop. Then—"

"Let me answer your points as you make them. Frank Morland's death has already been disposed of—officially. I have seen a report of the inquest. As for this cowboy tonight—you proclaimed a theory. It was a rather nebulous one, and the men you spoke to aren't too imaginative. Remember that they still accept Nagel as one of themselves. After he talks to them some more, I think they will soon stop worrying."

"And will they forget about your secret mercury mine?"

"Yes," said Julius. "Because you never told them."

Simon looked at him steadily.

"It's your neck," he remarked. "You risk it."

"There really isn't any risk. In the first place, you contradicted yourself when we were talking—you remember? Then, I've spoken to Nagel since then. He said nothing about it. If you had divulged anything so important, he would certainly have mentioned it. I confess that you had me bothered for a moment, but now I'm completely unconcerned."

The Saint shrugged.

"If you want to draw to an inside straight, I can't stop you. But there's still Morland."

"What about him?"

"Whatever you've made him sign, he'll repudiate it as soon as you turn him loose. Therefore you can't turn him loose. But if you kill him, that'll be a third mysterious death, and even Nails is going to have a tough time talking that one off. On the other hand, you can't hold him for ever, or his daughter either. Not in this country. Sooner or later—"

Julius smiled.

"Pardon me again," he said, "but there is no question of holding Mr Morland in this country."

It seemed to Simon that a frozen cataract had exploded over his head. The chill of it went down into his bones like a distilled essence from the immemorial bleakness of the dark side of the moon . . . He wondered how he could ever have been so naive.

"Now you go on," he said.

"Mr Morland," Julius explained, enjoying it, "has been persuaded to sign an unlimited power of attorney made out to his daughter. He will now be taken, as quickly as possible, and by various special routes which I need not tell you about, to Germany. There he will be placed in a concentration camp. You have heard about our concentration camps, no doubt. And of course Miss Morland has heard about them too. Valmon at this moment is probably giving her some additional information. And with your co-operation, we have just been able to show her a small sample of the treatment which her father might receive. But that, of course, is entirely up to her. The Gestapo has great powers of discrimination. If Miss Morland is disposed to help and obey all our instructions, I'm sure that her father need not suffer any more inconvenience than if he were confined to a sanatorium."

It was all there, and the petty details could fill themselves in . . . Jim and Elmer could be sent away on some pretext, and other demobilised Bundsmen like Nails would take their place—as Julius had said, they were not very imaginative men, and they would not be hard to deal with . . . Even Hank Reefe might be got rid of, with a little more ingenuity. Jean could get rid of him . . . Jean would do whatever she was told, with that fear held over her—exactly as he himself had done a much more improbable thing that night.

"All of which," said the Saint in a very even voice, "is just as beautiful as I might have expected . . . if you leave me out of it."

"I'm afraid I was proposing to do that," said Julius unctuously. "You've been very kind to make it so easy for us. I can hardly tell you how much I appreciated the service you did for me a few minutes ago. But you can imagine it for yourself. Without that, if Miss Morland reciprocated your tender feelings, as she probably did, your disappearance might have made her harder to handle. But now that she has seen you flogging her father, with her own eyes, she will not even need convincing that you have been on our side all along. So she will feel even more alone and helpless, and she will be even more amenable."

It was the rest of the picture, the link that Simon had tried to find in the car when his brain was still out of step—the clinching knowledge that had been foreshadowed when Julius gave that significant inflection to "Mr Templar is one of our best allies."

The Saint found himself nodding.

"Did I ever happen to tell you," he inquired carefully, "that out of a lot of yellow-bellied swine that I've met, you could take a very distinguished place?"

Only for an instant Julius's face took on a deeper flush, and his pale eyes burned behind the thick glasses. And then he smiled again.

"Fortunately your opinions will soon be of no consequence," he said, and the Saint's eyes were lazy with contempt.

"You mean after I've been—what was your polite totalitarian word for it?—liquidated?"

"Precisely."

"And when does that happen?"

"Immediately."

The Saint looked again at the remains of the cigarette in his fingers, and reached for his package. He took out the last cigarette and lighted it very deliberately from the stub. A great deal seemed to depend on that simple action. But when there is so little between a man and the end of his life, not even the smallest thing can be taken lightly.

When he looked up, his eyes were almost gay.

"Do tell me," he said. "I'm sure you've got something picturesque thought out."

"You had better let Eberhardt tie your hands behind you first."

A man does these things. Even on the march to execution, he obeys. He becomes trapped into a kind of automatism, in which there is only the one hypnotising thought that death waiting at the end of a few seconds is still not yet death.

With the cigarette held between his lips, Simon put his hands together behind his back. He placed them with the edges of his wrists together and his muscles tense. Eberhardt walked around behind him, and he felt the roughness of cords tightening on his skin.

When Eberhardt stepped away again, pulling out the gun which he had temporarily thrust into one overall pocket, Julius went to the door and switched on some more lights. Deeper reaches of the long barren shed with its Martian islands of machinery sprang into sight under the crude glare of more powerful bulbs hung from the roof.

"Since this was your great discovery, I think it deserves to be your last memory," Julius said.

He crossed to a larger and much more complicated switchboard which had become visible on one of the side walls, and made another connection. The air trembled with a deep and almost musical note that soared quickly and settled into a thin but tangible whine that Simon could feel in the soles of his feet. He recognised it in a moment as the hum of a mighty generator.

"I don't know how familiar you are with the process of extracting mercury from cinnabar," Julius said conversationally.

"Not so familiar as I might be," said the Saint in the same tone. "Do you stick a glass tube in it and put it in an oven so that it climbs out like a thermometer, or do you sit over it with a microscope and pick it out with tweezers?"

"Here we use some improvements on the Almadén method," said Julius, rather like a pedantic lecturer. "But the process is fundamentally the same. First the ore is crushed with some new machinery designed by Bruechner of Essen. Then it is carried by a conveyor belt to a continuous furnace. As it passes down through the furnace, it is roasted at high temperature."

He selected a heavy lever and threw it over, and the shed suddenly trembled with a tremendous thumping clatter like a regiment of cavalry trotting over an iron drumhead. A second similar lever added a harsh groaning whirr to the din.

"The fumes, which contain the mercury, are passed through a condenser which consists first of a masonry chamber, and then pipes of earthenware, wood, and glass," Julius continued, raising his voice calmly. "The soot which is deposited in the condenser is also worked over for mercury, with an extractor designed by Colonel von Leicht . . . Let me show you some of this."

He led the way to a short flight of steps that climbed to a railed catwalk that ran around the nearest huge cylindrical engine. Prodded by Eberhardt, the Saint followed. He stood by the inside rail at the top of the stair, with Julius on one side of him and Eberhardt on the other.

He looked down into something like a huge round vat. From an elevator tower outside the building, a broad chute led down through one wall to the edge of the vat. There was a layer of coarse broken ore on it, and as Julius pulled a mechanical lever near the rail the ore began to trickle down like a slow steady avalanche. Inside the vat, operating from a central axle, a double ring of iron pile-drivers like the multiple legs of a fantastically symmetrical spider rose and fell with monotonous precision, marching round in an endless circle and pounding up and down with a tireless thundering force that shook the girdered framework. Beyond the vat, another conveyor drew crumbled ore from the bottom and raised it to an opening high in the side of a gigantic grey-white kiln.

"This is Bruechner's reducer," Julius explained, "which prepares the rock for our fine-ore furnace. It would, naturally, prepare anything else for the same treatment."

Then the Saint knew just what he meant.

So . . . this was it. Now and for ever. And there would be no retakes.

He turned the flat of his wrists together, and his upper arms stiffened and his shoulders bowed quietly as if under the load of an unutterable surrender. But he had never been farther from surrender. His lungs locked, and under his shirt, invisibly, the leathery muscles swelled and crisped and strained into corded knots. The ropes cut his flesh, but he never felt them; only one question mattered at that moment, and it sounded curiously academic: how much did Eberhardt, with all his efficiency, know about Houdini . . .

The Saint straightened up again at last, as if with a final resolution. He took a last deep pull on his cigarette, and half turned, and opened his mouth to let it fall on the platform behind him.

Then he faced Julius again.

"I'm glad you haven't disappointed me," he said. "It's a very charming idea."

"Will you step off by yourself," asked Julius, "or would you prefer to be pushed?"

He was not joking. In those words and in his face was the whole evil softness of the man. His round face gleamed with a thin film of sweat, and his small protruding slaty eyes were liquid with pleading. He licked his lips, leaving them wet.

Simon turned and looked down into the pit again, where the terrible revolving iron pistons jolted up and down. He seemed to have lost the power of speech.

"You must make up your mind," Julius insisted at length.

Simon waited as long as he could before he raised his head.

"I would much rather be pushed," he said.

Then they took hold of him, one of them on each side.

And at that moment the last cigarette which he had dropped behind him went off, for he had prepared it for just such a desperate diversion with a roll of toy caps and some photographer's flash powder which he had bought that afternoon. It was not a new trick, even for him, but it could always be counted on to create one or two precious seconds of disorganisation. And such stolen seconds often made all the difference between reminiscences and obituaries.

It went off with a sharp crack like a small-calibre pistol shot, and a brilliant burst of blue-white luminance that splashed through the shed as if a bolt of lightning had gone through it. The other two men would not have been human if they hadn't loosened their hold on him and started to turn to see what had happened. And that was as much as he needed. He slipped one hand out of the rope around his wrists, and took hold of them in his turn.

He took Julius's right wrist in his left hand, and Eberhardt's left wrist in his right hand, and with simultaneous reverse twists he wrenched each man's arm backwards and around and high up between the shoulder blades. The agonising leverage bent them forward over the rail. They struggled and kicked deliriously but there was nothing they could do against that lock clamped by fingers of steel. Eberhardt yelled out inarticulately, and the Magnum in his free hand crashed twice like a cannon, but he couldn't get it around to aim it.

The Saint didn't even notice it. His legs braced apart like a Colossus, his back straight and rigid, his arms thrust out, he pressed the two men over the rail until their weight was all hung on it. Still he forced them away, inch by inch, until their centres of gravity teetered infinitesimally over it. The sweat broke out on his forehead, and his mouth was a line of stone. And then, with one last convulsive effort, he forced them clear over and let go.

There was one shrill wailing hideous scream that reverberated hollowly through the clangour of the machinery and then nothing but the relentless rhythmic thudding and crunching of the multiple steel shafts trampling their endless circle.

9

Simon Templar stepped back, turned, and went slowly down the stairs. His face had the impassive coldness of a bronze casting. He walked to the door, and methodically turned out all the lights. He didn't try to stop any of the machinery. Let that finish what it had begun. He went out into the moonlight night.

With the door closed behind him, the deafening clatter sank to a steady rumble. Moon silver lay on the rocks and hills, and etched its sweeps and stipples of jet over the broken spaces; there were stars twinkling in the clear sky. Here, still, was peace. He got into the station wagon, switched on lights and engine, turned, and drove down the road. In a moment there was not even the grumbling of the machines any more, only the whispering hum of the engine and the cool night air slipping by.

He drove to the place near the ranch house where he had been taken before, and stopped there. The next step might have been a little ticklish, but it seemed as if his guardian angel, having at last come out of an alarmingly prolonged siesta, was determined to make amends. He had not even had time to worry over the problem when he saw a man coming towards the car. It was Neumann, carrying his sub-machine gun slackly under his arm.

Simon left the headlights on, to dazzle Neumann as much as possible, and opened the door beside him. Without getting out, he swung around on the seat so that he was clear of the steering wheel and his legs were out of the car; then he bent over as if he were fumbling for something he had dropped on the running board. He heard Neumann coming close, but he waited until he saw the man's feet and knew his distance exactly.

"Heil Schickelgruber," said the Saint, and straightened up like a spring.

His fist smashed squarely on to Neumann's fleshy nose in a co-ordinated extrusion of the same movement that had the vicious potency of a mule's hind leg. Neumann gave a weird squeaky hiccough and went reeling and back-pedalling and windmillng back for three or four paces until his heel caught and he went sprawling.

It was no time for any of the polite gestures of refined combat.

The Saint took one step, and jumped on the man's chest with both feet. It sounded as if something cracked, but Simon didn't wait to be sure. He grabbed the Tommy gun out of the man's limp grasp and pounded the butt on the man's head several times, until he was quite sure that Party Member Neumann would take no further active part in the festivities that night, if ever.

Simon went back to the station wagon and switched out the lights. The episode had not been entirely silent, but it seemed to have attracted no attention. There were no sounds of interest anywhere. The lighted window in the ranch house was still lighted, but the shades had been drawn and nobody had looked out. The Saint thought that he saw the silhouette of Max Valmon pass across it, as if pacing up and down, but he could not be sure.

He headed towards the outer buildings from which Don Morland had been brought. Chinks of light showed there from between the crevices of closed shutters. He had no way of guessing how many demobilised Bundsmen there would be inside, but he had an idea that there would be several. But he had the grips of the Tommy gun in his hands now, and the exact number was not too important.

Actually, there were nine. They looked up with the blank faces of frozen fish when he threw open the door. Three of them were lying on the cots which were ranged along both sides of the big barrack-like dormitory; the other six were apparently having some quiet fun for themselves with Don Morland, who was tied to a chair in the centre of the room.

The Saint's forefinger was feather-light on the trigger of his machine gun.

"I'm sorry to interrupt a happy cultural evening, boys," he said affectionately, "but this is round-up time. Two of you can untie Mr Morland. The rest of you will please move to the back of the room with your hands high in the air. You may try any tricks you like, but I must tell you that nothing would amuse me more than blowing large holes in your dinners."

None of them, it seemed, felt overly ambitious. They herded sullenly towards the back of the room, to be joined in another few moments by the two who had stayed behind to untie Morland.

The old man half fell out of the chair, and then pulled himself up and limped towards the Saint.

Simon waved him to one side, out of the line of fire.

"Have you been around long enough to know any good place where we can lock them up?" he asked.

"There's a sort of store-room right back there," said Morland. "It doesn't have any windows, and the door only opens from this side. That's where they kept me."

"Then they must know it's all right," said the Saint and raised his gun and his voice a little: "Into the doghouse comrades."

The men went in. It was rather a tight squeeze, but they all made it. Morland closed the door on them and slid a heavy wooden bolt into its socket.

Simon went up and inspected the fastening. It looked solid enough, but nine muscular Aryans were a slightly different proposition from one old retired dentist.

"Better give me a hand with the beds," he said.

He hauled one cot out and set it against the door, facing out lengthwise. Between them, they jammed four more cots up against it in the same direction, until the line reached to within a foot of the far wall. The remaining space they wedged full of chests and chairs and other assorted furniture until it was certain that nothing less than a tank could have broken out of the back room.

Simon surveyed the barricade with approval.

"I can't help thinking it's going to be quite uncomfortable for them," he remarked. "Rather like the Black Hole of Calcutta. But then, they'll only appreciate Leavenworth so much more when they get there."

It was then that he heard two muffled shots from a distance outside.

He snatched up the Tommy gun and ran out of the bunkhouse. Instinctively he headed towards the ranch building—there was no other place in the vicinity from which it was likely that the reports could have come. But after a few yards he paused. There was no other noise or commotion. The one lighted window in the ranch house still glowed steadily, a single blank square of yellow in the halftone dark.

Simon went towards it more slowly and cautiously. He stepped on to the verandah, and found a door near the window. Light came from under it. There was no sound at all, inside or outside.

The Saint kicked the door inwards and took two steps into the room. Across from him, unbound but unarmed, Jean Morland stared at him with wide-eyed horror and contempt. Between them, on the floor, Max Valmon and the man called Nails lay in the grotesque attitudes of sudden death.

He heard a single footfall behind him, and a gun jarred into his back. A voice that was somehow familiar, and yet distorted so that he didn't recognise it at once, said, "Drop the gun."

Simon stood still and dropped it.

The voice said, "Go on in."

Simon obeyed. It seemed as if a time machine had been turned back and he was repeating a scene that had already been played once that night.

"Now turn round."

The Saint turned, and saw Hank Reefe standing square in the doorway, frosty-eyed and expressionlessly leather-faced, with his old-fashioned Colt held level at his hip.

"I want you to see it coming, you rat," said that only half familiar voice.

The Saint looked at him steadily.

"It's good to see you, Hank," he said in a very even tone. "I'm glad you were able to get Max and Nails for yourself. I was afraid—"

"Save your breath Templar," said the Texan coldly. "Jean's told me about you already. Now stand up and take it."

Simon Templar's lips curled in a faint smile that was almost cynical. He gazed at ironic death with clear blue eyes and found it a little funny.

It was the perfect moment for Don Morland to rush in and clutch Reefe's right arm and gasp frantically: "No, no! They made him do it to save Jean from being beaten. I heard them."

***

"I left as soon as we got back to the house," Reefe explained. "I started off all right when I got here, but Nails couldn't 've been more than a few minutes behind me. I was doin' fine when there was a knock on the door an' one of the men went out. When he came back, he just said a couple of words in German to the others, an' they all jumped on me at once. Knocked me out cold. When I woke up I was tied to a chair in the kitchen. Took me some time to get loose."

"Nails fixed me a drink after Hank had gone," said the girl. "There must have been something in it, because suddenly I felt dizzy and everything started to go black. The next thing I knew, I was here."

"So," said the Saint, "I guess this winds up the interlude."

He had already told them his own story and completed the background for them.

"What do we do now?" asked Reefe.

"You'd better drive into Lion Rock and phone the FBI in Phoenix," said the Saint. "You can drop Mr Morland and Jean off at the house on your way. I'll wait here and look after the prisoners till the flying squad arrives, and give them the whole story. They'll take a few hours to get here."

"Okay," said Reefe.

He stood up and hitched his belt. There was a slight softening of amusement in his dour face.

"I guess I know now why you kept remindin' me of that feller the Saint," he said.

Simon looked him in the eyes.

"I guess you do," he admitted.

They shook hands, and Reefe and Morland started towards their car.

Jean Morland linked her arm with the Saint's as he rose and followed. "I'll wait for you," she said.

"Don't wait too long," he answered lightly. "It may be some time, and you're going to need some rest."

They took two or three steps more, quite slowly.

"It's dreadful to think that Hank might have killed you," she said, and the Saint chuckled.

"I've had a few happier moments myself. But he was quite right, according to what he knew. He's a good guy. He'll always be a good guy . . . He kind of likes you I think."

She said nothing.

Morland and Hank were already in Morland's station wagon. Just a few yards from it, Jean Morland stopped, and turned in front of him.

"Thank you so much," she said, "—Saint."

Her arms slipped around his neck, and for a long moment he felt the pressure of her lips.

Then she was gone.

He stood and watched the station wagon drive away.

After several minutes, he turned and walked over to the bunkhouse. The buttress of cots and furniture was undisturbed, and looked likely to remain that way until somebody from outside moved it. There was very little noise from the store-room where the nine Bundsmen were imprisoned. There was not likely to be much. A shortage of oxygen is highly discouraging to violent effort.

Simon went back to the ranch house and explored a bit. He found a bottle of Peter Dawson, and a bottle of Benedictine.

He decided that the occasion deserved the more expensive drink. He poured himself some Benedictine, and went back to the living room. There, after some searching, he gathered together some paper, a pen, and a package of cigarettes.

He sat down at the dining table, with his drink and a lighted cigarette, and for more than an hour he wrote steadily in his neat individualistic hand. When he had finished, the complete synopsis of the story, with all relevant facts and avenues of inquiry, was there for the forthcoming G-Men to read. He signed it with his name, and below that he carefully sketched a skeleton figure crowned with a correctly elliptical halo.

He finished his drink while he read it over and put it down again and nailed it to the table with the pen. Then he lighted one more cigarette, put the rest of the pack in his pocket, and went out to his car.

He got in and drove to the so-called main road, and there without hesitation he turned to the right and drove away westwards—which was not the way to the Circle Y. He had the greatest admiration for the FBI, but they were liable to lead into formalities that he was too busy to be annoyed with.

He drove quickly, with the softness of Jean Morland's lips on his mouth, and his heart singing.

PALM SPRINGS

INTRODUCTION

Palm Springs, if anybody doesn't know it by this time, is an oasis in the desert a little more than a hundred miles east of Los Angeles. When I first went there, the business district was about three blocks long and a block wide; there were about three hotels, much too big for the town, a reasonable number of homes, a few auto courts, and a dude ranch on the outskirts. Today the neon signs of the motels greet you miles out in the desert and escort you in unbroken procession to a main street as long as the whole village used to be when I first knew it, and the houses have spread way out where we used to ride after jackrabbits, and they have flowed all around the dude ranch on the other side, and then for about fifteen miles out on the highway beyond more villages or communities have sprung up in an almost uninterrupted chain to take advantage of the overflow that even this enlarged Palm Springs cannot swallow; I seldom go there anymore, because it is too different from the place I used to love.

But I spent six consecutive winters there in the good old days which ended at Munich, and it would have been strange if I had never set a story there.

The actual process of doing it, however, suffered some vicissitudes.

My first attempt was when RKO was making Saint movies. Thinking how pleasant it would be to work on a picture in my own favorite location, I cleverly suggested that we should make one called *The Saint in Palm Springs*. They liked the idea very much, and I went to work on the script. It turned out to be an excellent story; so naturally the producers (who always knew that they could have written much better Saint stories than I did, only they never got around to it) didn't like it much. They hired various wizards to improve it, and did such a thorough job that the final script contained absolutely nothing whatsoever of mine except the title. I have never been able to guess why they flinched from that ultimate alteration, unless it was because they feared they might obscure the genius of the inspired executive who decreed that this epic should be shot at Palmdale, which is only a hundred and fifty miles away from Palm Springs.

Then in early 1941, Dan Longwell, chairman of the Editorial Board of *Life* magazine, paid me a visit in California. I had known Dan many years before, when he was one of the editors of my New York publishers, a firm then known as Doubleday, Doran & Co. (Everything in this busy life keeps changing, as we reminiscent ancients are continually being reminded.) Dan, or somebody on his staff, had abruptly recalled that in 1841 Edgar Allen Poe had published *The Murders in the Rue Morgue*, that therefore in 1941 the world should theoretically be celebrating the centenary of the detective story, and that therefore *Life* should somehow be represented in the chorus of tribute.

Dan's idea was that *Life* should mark the occasion by publishing the first "mystery" story of the new era, and for reasons which I am far too bashful to speculate about, he wanted me to write it. It was, of course, to be done in a series of photographs with captions, rather like stills from an unmade movie.

Again I thought of Palm Springs, and what could be better than a trip there, in good company, at the expense of *Life*?

But RKO still owned (and for that matter still owns) the original Palm Springs story I had written, since they had paid me handsomely for it—even though to this day they have never used a line of it. (This is why it costs you so much to go to the movies.)

So I wrote another story, and was especially careful to include three beautiful girls in it. And since *Life* magazine, at that time anyway, had not discovered that it was as great a creative genius as the current crop of producers at RKO, they stupidly accepted it as I wrote it. We went to Palm Springs with three models and a photographer—and they not only left me to direct the shots but, God help me, made me play the part of the Saint as well.

This was my first and only appearance as a film star, even on static film, and I am not going to pretend I didn't enjoy it. A hell of a time was had by all.

The resultant million-dollar comic strip was duly published in eight pages of *Life* magazine in May 1941. And there again an immortal Palm Springs story might have been decently interred.

But I am a very persistent, or at least economical, writer. I still wanted a Palm Springs story, and even after a lapse of years I thought this was a good one. I went to work elaborating it. And the story you are about to read is what came out.

—Leslie Charteris (1951)

1

"Look," said Freddie Pellman belligerently. "Your name is Simon Templar, isn't it?"

"I think so," Simon told him.

"You are the feller they call the Saint?"

"So I'm told."

"The Robin Hood of modern crime?"

Simon was tolerant.

"That's a rather fancy way of putting it."

"Okay then," Pellman lurched slightly on his bar stool, and took hold of his highball glass more firmly for support.

"You're the man I want. I've got a job for you."

The Saint sighed.

"Thanks. But I wasn't looking for a job. I came to Palm Springs to have fun."

"You'll have plenty of fun. But you've got to take this job."

"I don't want a job," said the Saint. "What is it?"

"I need a bodyguard," said Pellman.

He had a loud harsh voice that made Simon think of a rusty frog. Undoubtedly it derived some of this attractive quality from his consumption of alcohol, which was considerable. Simon didn't need to have seen him drinking to know this. The blemishes of long indulgence had worked deeply into the mottled puffiness of his complexion, the pinkish smeariness of his eyes, and the sagging lines under them. It was even more noticeable because he was not much over thirty, and could once have been quite good-looking in a very conventional way. But things like that frequently happen to spoiled young men whose only material accomplishment in life has been the by no means negligible one of arranging to be born into a family with more millions than most people hope to see thousands.

Simon Templar knew about him, of course—as did practically every member of the newspaper-reading public of the United States, not to mention a number of other countries. In a very different way, Freddie Pellman was just as notorious a public figure as the Saint. He had probably financed the swallowing of more champagne than any other individual in the twentieth century. He had certainly been thrown out of more night clubs, and paid more bills for damage to more hotels than any other exponent of the art of uproar. And the number of complaisant show girls and models who were indebted to him for such souvenirs of a lovely friendship as mink coats, diamond bracelets, Packards, and other similar trinkets would have made the late King Solomon feel relatively sex-starved.

He travelled with a permanent entourage of three incredibly beautiful young ladies—one blonde, one brunette, and one redhead. That is, the assortment of colorings was permanent. The personnel itself changed at various intervals, as one faithful collaborator after another would retire to a well-earned rest, to be replaced by another of even more dazzling perfections, but the vacancy was always filled by another candidate of similar complexion, so that the harmonious balance of varieties was retained, and any type of pulchritude could always be found at a glance. Freddie blandly referred to them as his secretaries, and there is no doubt that they had left a memorable trail of scandal in every playground and every capital city in Europe and the Americas.

This was the man who said he wanted a bodyguard, and the Saint looked at him with cynical speculation.

"What's the matter?" he asked coolly. "Is somebody's husband gunning for you?"

"No, I never mess about with married women—they're too much grief." Pellman was delightfully insensitive and uninhibited. "This is serious. Look."

He dragged a crumpled sheet of paper out of his pocket and unfolded it clumsily. Simon took it and looked it over.

It was a piece of plain paper on which a cutting had been pasted. The cutting was from *Life*, and from the heading it appeared to have formed part of a layout reviewing the curtain calls in the careers of certain famous public enemies. This particular picture showed a crumpled figure stretched out on a sidewalk with two policemen standing over it in attitudes faintly reminiscent of big-game hunters posing with their kill, surrounded by the usual crowd of gaping blank-faced spectators. The caption said,

A village policeman's gun wrote finis to the career of "Smoke Johnny" Implicato, three times kidnaper and killer, after Freddie Pellman, millionaire playboy, recognised him in a Palm Springs restaurant last Christmas Day and held him in conversation until police arrived.

Underneath it was pencilled in crude capitals,

DID YOU EVER WONDER HOW JOHNNY FELT?
WELL YOU'LL SOON FIND OUT. YOU GOT IT COMING
MISTER.
A FRIEND OF JOHNNY.

Simon felt the paper, turned it over, and handed it back.

"A bit corny," he observed, "but it must be a thrill for you. How did you get it?"

"It was pushed under the front door during the night. I've rented a house here, and that's where it was. Under the front door. The Filipino boy found it in the morning. The door was locked, of course, but the note had been pushed under."

When Freddie Pellman thought that anything he had to say was important, which was often, he was never satisfied to say it once. He said it several times over, trying it out in different phrasings, apparently in the belief that his audience was either deaf or imbecile but might accidentally grasp the point of it were presented often enough from a sufficient variety of angles.

"Have you talked to the police about it?" Simon asked.

"What, in a town like this? I'd just as soon tell the Boy Scouts. In a town like this, the police wouldn't know what to do with a murderer if he walked into the station and gave them a signed confession."

"They got Johnny," Simon pointed out.

"Listen, do you know who got Johnny? I got Johnny. Who recognised him? I did. I'd been reading one of those true detective magazines in a barber shop, and there was a story about him in it. In one of those true detective magazines. I recognised him from the picture. Did you read what it said in that clipping?"

"Yes," said the Saint, but Freddie was not so easily headed off.

He took the paper out of his pocket again.

"You see what it says? *A village policeman's gun wrote finis to the career . . .*"

He read the entire caption aloud, following the lines with his forefinger, with the most careful enunciation and dramatic emphasis, to make sure that the Saint had not been baffled by any of the longer words.

"All right," said the Saint patiently. "So you spotted him and put the finger on him. And now one of his pals is sore about it."

"And that's why I need a bodyguard."

"I can tell you a good agency in Los Angeles. You can call them up, and they'll have a first-class, guaranteed, bonded bodyguard here in three hours, armed to the teeth."

"But I don't want an ordinary agency bodyguard. I want the very best man there is. I want the Saint."

"Thanks," said the Saint. "But I don't want to guard a body."

"Look," said Pellman aggressively, "will you name your own salary? Anything you like. Just name it."

Simon looked around the bar. It was starting to fill up for the cocktail session with the strange assortment of types and costumes which give Palm Springs crowds an unearthly variety that no other resort in America can approach. Everything was represented— cowboys, dudes, tourists, trippers, travelling salesmen, local business men, winter residents, Hollywood; men and women of all shapes and sizes and ages, in Levis, shorts, business suits, slack suits, sun suits, play suits, Magnin models, riding breeches, tennis outfits, swim suits, and practically nothing. This was vacation and flippancy and fun and irresponsibility for a while, and it was what the Saint had promised himself.

"If I took a job like that," he said, "it'd cost you a thousand dollars a day."

Freddie Pellman blinked at him for a moment with the intense concentration of the alcoholic.

Then he pulled a thick roll of green paper out of his pocket. He fumbled through it, and selected a piece, and pushed it into the Saint's hand. The Saint's blue eyes rested on it with a premonition of doom. Included in its decorative art work was a figure "1" followed by three zeros. Simon counted them.

"That's for today," said Freddie. "You're hired. Let's have a drink."

The Saint sighed.

"I think I will," he said.

2

One reason why there were no gray hairs on the Saint's dark head was that he never wasted any energy on vain regrets. He even had a humorous fatalism about his errors. He had stuck his neck out, and the consequences were strictly at his invitation. He felt that way about his new employment. He had been very sweetly nailed with his own smartness, and the only thing to do was to take it with a grin and see if it might be fun. And it might. After all, murder and mayhem had been mentioned, and to Simon Templar any adventure was always worth at least a glance. It might not be so dull . . .

"You'll have to move into the house, of course," Pellman said, and they drove to the Mirador Hotel to redeem the Saint's modest luggage, which had already run up a bill of some twenty dollars for the few hours it had occupied a room.

Pellman's house was a new edifice perched on the sheer hills that form the western wall of the town. Palm Springs itself lies on the flat floor of the valley that eases imperceptibly down to the sub-sea level of the Salton Sea, but on the western side it nestles tightly against the sharp surges of broken granite that soar up with precipitous swiftness to the eternal snows of San Jacinto. The private road to it curled precariously up the rugged edges of brown leaping cliffs, and from the jealously stolen lawn in front of the building you could look down and see Palm Springs spread out beneath you like a map, and beyond it the floor of the desert mottled gray-green with greasewood and weeds and cactus and smoke tree, spreading through infinite clear distances across to the last spurs of the San Bernardino mountains and widening southwards towards the broad baking spreads that had once been the bed of a forgotten sea whose tide levels were still graven on the parched rocks that bordered the plain.

The house itself looked more like an artist's conception of an oasis hideaway than any artist would have believed. It was a sprawling bungalow in the California Spanish style that meandered lazily among pools and patios as a man might have dreamed it in an idle hour—a thing of white stucco walls and bright red tile roofs, of deep cool verandahs and inconsequential arches, of sheltering palm trees and crazy flagstones, of gay beds of petunias and ramparts of oleanders and white columns dripping with the richness of bougainvillea. It was a place where an illusion had been so skilfully created that with hardly any imagination at all you could feel the gracious tempo of a century that would never come again; where you might see courtly *hacendados* bowing over slim white hands with the suppleness of velvet and steel, and hear the tinkle of fountains and the shuffle of soft-footed servants, and smell the flowers in the raven hair of laughing *señoritas* ; where at the turn of any corner you might even find a nymph—

Yes, you might always find a nymph, Simon agreed, as they turned a corner by the swimming pool and there was a sudden squeal and he had a lightning glimpse of long golden limbs uncurling and leaping up, and rounded breasts vanishing almost instantaneously through the door of the bath house, so swiftly and fleetingly that he could easily have been convinced that he had dreamed it.

"That's Esther," Freddie explained casually. "She likes taking her clothes off."

Simon remembered the much-publicised peculiarities of the Pellman ménage, and took an even more philosophical attitude towards his new job.

"One of your secretaries?" he murmured.

"That's right," Freddie said blandly. "Come in and meet the others."

The others were in the living-room, if such a baronial chamber could be correctly designated by such an ordinary name. From the inside, it looked like a Hollywood studio designer's idea of something between a Cordoban mosque and the main hall of a medieval castle. It had a tiled floor and a domed gold mosaic ceiling, with leopard and tiger skin rugs, Monterey furniture, and fake suits of armor in between.

"This is Miss Starr," Freddie introduced. "Call her Ginny. Mr Templar."

Ginny had red hair like hot dark gold, and a creamy skin with freckles. You could study all of it except about two square feet which were accidentally concealed by a green Lastex swim-suit that clung to her soft ripe figure—where it wasn't artistically cut away for better exposures—like emerald paint. She sat at a table by herself, playing solitaire. She looked up and gave the Saint a long disturbing smile, and said, "Hi."

"And this is Lissa O'Neill," Freddie said.

Lissa was the blonde. Her hair was the color of young Indiana corn, and her eyes were as blue as the sky, and there were dew-dipped roses in her cheeks that might easily have grown beside the Shannon. She lay stretched out on a couch with a book propped up on her flat stomach, and she wore an expensively simple white play suit against which her slim legs looked warmly gilded.

Simon glanced at the book. It had the lurid jacket of a Crime Club mystery.

"How is it?" he asked.

"Not bad," she said. "I thought I had it solved in the third chapter, but now I think I'm wrong. What did he say your name was?"

"She's always reading mysteries," Ginny put in. "She's our tame crime expert—Madam Hawkshaw. Every time anyone gets murdered in the papers she knows all about it."

"And why not?" Lissa insisted. "They're usually so stupid, anyone but a detective could see it."

"You must have been reading the right books," said the Saint.

"Did he say 'Templar'?" Lissa asked.

The door opened then, and Esther came in. Simon recognised her by her face, a perfect oval set with warm brown eyes and broken by a red mouth that always seemed to be whispering "*If we were alone . . .*" A softly waved mane the color of smoked chestnuts framed the face in a dark dreamy cloud. The rest of her was not quite so easily identifiable, for she had wrapped it in a loose blue robe that left a little scope for speculation. Not too much, for the lapels only managed to meet at her waist, and just a little below that the folds shrank away from the impudent obtrusion of a shapely thigh.

"A fine thing," she said. "Walking in on me when I didn't have a stitch on."

"I bet you loved it," Ginny said, cheating a black ten out of the bottom of the pack and slipping it on to a red jack.

"Do we get introduced?" said Esther.

"Meet Miss Swinburne," said Freddie. "Mr Templar. Now you know everybody. I want you to feel at home. My name's Freddie. We're going to call you Simon. All right?"

"All right," said the Saint.

"Then we're all at home," said Freddie, making his point. "We don't have to have any formality. If any of the girls go for you, that's all right too. We're all pals together."

"Me first," said Ginny.

"Why you?" objected Esther. "After all, if you'd been there to give him the first preview—"

The Saint took out his cigarette-case with as much poise as any man could have called on in the circumstances.

"The line forms on the right," he remarked. "Or you can see my agent. But don't let's be confused about this. I only work here. You ought to tell them, Freddie."

The Filipino boy wheeled in the portable bar, and Pellman threaded his way over to it and began to work.

"The girls know all about that threatening letter. I showed it to them this morning. Didn't I, Lissa? You remember that note I showed you?" Reassured by confirmation, Freddie picked up the cocktail shaker again and said, "Well, Simon Templar is going to take care of us. You know who he is, don't you? The Saint. That's who he is," said Freddie, leaving no room for misunderstanding.

"I thought so," said Lissa, with her cornflower eyes clinging to the Saint's face. "I've seen pictures of you." She put her book down and moved her long legs invitingly to make some room on the couch. "What do you think about that note?"

Simon accepted the invitation. He didn't think she was any less potentially dangerous than the other two, but she was a little more quiet and subtle about it. Besides, she at least had something else to talk about.

"Tell me what you think," he said. "You might have a good point of view."

"I thought it sounded rather like something out of a cheap magazine."

"There you are!" exclaimed Freddie triumphantly, from the middle distance. "Isn't that amazing? Eh, Simon? Listen to this, Ginny. That's what she reads detective stories for. You'll like this. D'you know what Simon said when I showed him that note? What did you say, Simon?"

"I said it sounded a bit corny."

"There!" said Freddie, personally vindicated. "That's the very word he used. He said it was corny. That's what he said as soon as he read it."

"That's what I thought too," said Esther, "only I didn't like to say so. Probably it's just some crackpot trying to be funny."

"On the other hand," Simon mentioned, "a lot of crackpots have killed people, and plenty of real murders have been pretty corny. And whether you're killed by a crackpot or the most rational person in the world, and whether the performance is corny or not, you end up just as dead."

"Don't a lot of criminals read detective stories?" Lissa asked.

The Saint nodded.

"Most of them. And they get good ideas from them, too. Most writers are pretty clever, in spite of the funny way they look, and when they go in for crime they put in a lot of research and invention that a practising thug doesn't have the time or the ability to do for himself. But he could pick up a lot of hints from reading the right authors."

"He could learn a lot of mistakes not to make, too."

"Maybe there's something in that," said the Saint. "Perhaps the stupid criminals you were talking about are only the ones who don't read books. Maybe the others get to be so clever that they never get caught, and so you never hear about them at all."

"Brrr," said Ginny. "You're giving me goose-pimples. Why don't you just call the cops?"

"Because the Saint's a lot smarter than the cops," said Freddie. "That's what I hired him for. He can run rings round the cops any day. He's been doing it for years. Lissa knows all about him, because she reads things. You tell them about him, Lissa."

He came over with clusters of Manhattans in his hands, poured out in goblets that would have been suitable for fruit punch.

"Let her off," said the Saint hastily. "If she really knows the whole story of my life she might shock somebody. Let's do some serious drinking instead."

"Okay," said Freddie amiably. "You're the boss. You go on being the mystery man. Let's all get stinking."

The fact that they did not all get stinking was certainly no fault of Freddie Pellman's. It could not be denied that he did his generous best to assist his guests to attain that state of ideal ossification. His failure could only be attributed to the superior discretion of the company, and the remarkably high level of resistance which they seemed to have in common.

It was quite a classic performance in its way. Freddie concocted two more Manhattans, built on the same scale as milk shakes. There was then a brief breathing spell while they went to their rooms to change. Then they went to the Doll House for dinner. They had two more normal-sized cocktails before the meal, and champagne with it. After that they had brandy. Then they proceeded to visit all the other bars up and down the main street, working from north to south and back again. They had Zombies at the Luau, Planter's Punches at the Cubana, highballs at the Chi Chi, and more highballs at Bil-Al's. Working back, they freshened up with some beer at Happy's, clamped it down with a Collins at the Del Tahquitz, topped it with Daiquiris at the Royal Palms, and discovered tequila at Claridge's. This brought them back to the Doll House for another bottle of champagne. They were all walking on their own feet and talking intelligibly, if not profoundly. People have received medals for less notable feats. It must be admitted nevertheless that there had been a certain amount of cheating. The girls, undoubtedly educated by past experiences, had contrived to leave a respectable number of drinks unfinished, and Simon Templar, who had also been around, had sundry legerdemains of his own for keeping control of the situation.

Freddie Pellman probably had an advantage over all of them in the insulating effect of past picklings, but Simon had to admit that the man was remarkable. He had been alcoholic when Simon met him, but he seemed to progress very little beyond that stage. Possibly he navigated with a little more difficulty, but he could still stand upright; possibly his speech became a little more slurred, but he could still be understood; certainly he became rather more glassy-eyed, but he could still see what was going on. It was as if there was a definite point beyond which his calloused tissues had no further power to assimilate liquid stimulus: being sodden already, the overflow washed over them without depositing any added exhilaration.

He sat and looked at his glass and said, "There must be some other joints we haven't been to yet."

Then he rolled gently over sideways and lay flat on the floor, snoring.

Ginny gazed down at him estimatingly and said, "That's only the third time I've seen him pass out. It must be catching up with him."

"Well, now we can relax," said Esther, and moved her chair closer to the Saint.

"I think we'd better get him home," Lissa said.

It seemed like a moderately sound idea, since the head waiter and the proprietor were advancing towards the scene with professional restraint.

Simon helped to hoist Freddie up, and they got him out to the car without waking him. The Saint drove them back to the house, and the lights went up as they stopped at the door. The Filipino boy came out and helped phlegmatically with the disembarcation. He didn't show either surprise or disapproval. Apparently such homecomings were perfectly normal events in his experience.

Between them they carried the sleeper to his room and laid him on the bed.

"Okay," said the boy. "I take care of him now."

He began to work Freddie expertly out of his coat.

"You seem to have the touch," said the Saint. "How long have you been in this job?"

"'Bout six months. He's all right. You leave him to me, sir. I put him to bed."

"What's your name?"

"Angelo, sir. I take care of him. You want anything, you tell me."

"Thanks," said the Saint, and drifted back to the living-room.

He arrived in the course of a desultory argument which suggested that the threat which had been virtually ignored all evening had begun to seem a little less ludicrous with the arrival of bedtime.

"You can move in with me, Ginny," Lissa was saying.

"Nuts," said Ginny. "You'll sit up half the night reading, and I want some sleep."

"For a change," said Esther. "I'll move in with you, Lissa."

"You snore," said Lissa candidly.

"I don't!"

"And where does that leave me?" Ginny protested.

"I expect you'll find company," Esther said sulkily. "You've been working for it hard enough."

Simon coughed discreetly.

"Angelo is in charge," he said, "and I'm going to turn in."

"What, so soon?" pouted Esther. "Let's all have another drink first. I know, let's have a game of strip poker."

"I'm sorry," said the Saint. "I'm not so young as I was this afternoon. I'm going to get some sleep."

"I thought you were supposed to be a bodyguard," said Ginny.

The Saint smiled.

"I am, darling. I guard Freddie's body."

"Freddie's passed out. You ought to keep us company."

"It's all so silly," Lissa said. "I'm not scared. We haven't anything to be afraid of. Even if that note was serious, it's Freddie they're after. Nobody's going to do anything to us."

"How do you know they won't get into the wrong room?" Esther objected.

"You can hang a sign on your door," Simon suggested, "giving them directions. Goodnight, pretty maidens."

He made his exit before there could be any more discussion, and went to his bedroom.

The bedrooms trailed away from the house in a long L-shaped wing. Freddie's room was at the far end of the wing, and his door faced down the broad, screened verandah by which the rooms were reached. Simon had the room next to it, from which one of the girls had been moved; their rooms were now strung around the angle of the L towards the main building. There was a communicating door on both sides of his room. He tried the one which should have opened in to Freddie's room, but he found that there was a second door backing closely against it, and that one was locked. He went around by the verandah, and found Angelo preparing to turn out the lights.

"He sleep well now," said the Filipino with a grin. "You no worry."

Freddie was neatly tucked into bed, his clothes carefully folded over a chair. Simon went over and looked at him. He certainly wasn't dead at that point—his snoring was stertorously alive.

The Saint located the other side of the communicating door, and tried the handle. It still wouldn't move, and there was no key in the lock.

"D'you know how to open this, Angelo?" he asked.

The Filipino shook his head.

"Don't know. Is lock?"

"Is lock."

"I never see key. Maybe somewhere."

"Maybe," Simon agreed.

It didn't look like a profitable inquiry to pursue much further, and Simon figured that it probably didn't matter. He still hadn't developed any real conviction of danger over-shadowing the house, and at that moment the idea seemed particularly far-fetched. He went out of the room, and the Filipino switched off the light.

"Everything already lock up, sir. You no worry. I go to sleep now."

"Happy dreams," said the Saint.

He returned to his own room, and undressed and rolled into bed. He felt in pretty good shape, but he didn't want to start the next day with an unnecessary headache. He was likely to have enough other headaches without that. Aside from the drinking pace and the uninhibited feminine hazards, he felt that a day would come when Freddie Pellman's conversational style would cease to hold him with the same eager fascination that it created at the first encounter. Eventually, he felt, a thousand dollars a day would begin to seem like a relatively small salary for listening to Freddie talk. But that was something that could be faced when the time came. Maybe he would be able to explain it to Freddie and get a raise . . .

With that he fell asleep. He didn't know how long it lasted, but it was deep and relaxed. And it ended with an electrifying suddenness that was as devastating as the collapse of a tall tower of porcelain. But the sound was actually a little different. It was a shrill shattering scream that brought him wide awake in an instant and had him on his feet while the echo was still ringing in his ears.

3

There was enough starlight outside for the windows to be rectangles of silver, but inside the room he was only just able to find his dressing-gown without groping. His gun was already in his hand, for his fingers had closed on it instinctively where the butt lay just under the edge of the mattress at the natural length of his arm as he lay in bed. He threw the robe on and whipped a knot into the belt, and was on his way to the door within two seconds of waking.

Then the scream came again, louder now that he wasn't hearing it through a haze of sleep, and in a way more deliberate. And it came, he was certain, not from the direction in which he had first automatically placed it, without thinking, but from the opposite quarter—the room on the opposite side of his own.

He stopped in mid-stride, and turned quickly back to the other communicating door. This one was not locked. It was a double door like the one to Freddie's room, but the second handle turned smoothly with his fingers. As he started to open it, the door outlined itself with light; he did the only possible thing, and threw it wide open quickly but without any noise, and stepped swiftly through and to one side, with his gun balanced for instant aiming in any direction.

He didn't see anything to aim at. He didn't see anyone there except Lissa.

She was something to see, if one had the time. She was sitting upright in bed, and she wore a filmy flesh-colored nightgown with white overtones. At least, that was the first impression. After a while, you realised that it was just a filmy white nightgown and the flesh color was Lissa. She had her mouth open, and she looked exactly as if she was going to scream again. Then she didn't look like that any more.

"Hullo," she said, quite calmly. "I thought that'd fetch you."

"Wouldn't there have been a more subtle way of doing it?" Simon asked.

"But there was someone here, really. Look."

Then he saw it—the black wooden hilt of a knife that stood up starkly from the bedding close beside her. The resignation went out of his face again as if it had never been there.

"Where did he go?"

"I don't know—out of one of the doors. If he didn't go into your room, he must have gone out on to the porch or into Ginny's room."

Simon crossed to the other door and stepped out on to the verandah. Lights came on as he did so, and he saw Freddie Pellman swaying in the doorway at the dead end of the L.

"Whassamarrer?" Freddie demanded thickly. "What goes on?"

"We seem to have had a visitor," said the Saint succinctly. "Did anybody come through your room?"

"Anybody come through my room? I dunno. No. I didn't see anybody. Why should anybody come through my room?"

"To kiss you goodnight," said the Saint tersely, and headed in the other direction.

There was no other movement on the verandah. He knocked briefly on the next door down, and opened it and switched on the light. The bed was rumpled but empty, and a shaft of light came through the communicating door. All the bedrooms seemed to have communicating doors, which either had its advantages or it didn't. Simon went on into the next room. The bed in there had the covers pulled high up, and appeared to be occupied by a small quivering hippopotamus. He went up to it and tapped it on the most convenient bulge.

"Come on," he said. "I just saw a mouse crawl in with you."

There was a stifled squeal, and Esther's head and shoulders and a little more jumped into view in the region of the pillow.

"Go away!" she yelped inarticulately. "I haven't done anything—"

Then she recognised him, and stopped abruptly. She took a moment to straighten her dark hair. At the same time the other half of the baby hippopotamus struggled up beside her, revealing that it had a red-gold head and a snub nose.

"Oh, it's you," said Ginny. "Come on in. We'll make room for you."

"Well, make yourselves at home," said Esther. "This just happens to be my room—"

"Little children," said the Saint, with great patience, "I don't want to spoil anybody's fun, but I'm looking for a hairy thug who seems to be rushing around trying to stick knives into people."

They glanced at each other in a moment's silence.

"Wh-who did he stick a knife into?" Ginny asked.

"Nobody. He missed. But he was trying. Did you see him?"

She shook her head.

"Nobody's been in here," said Esther, "except Ginny. I heard a frightful scream, and I jumped up and put the light on, and the next minute Ginny came rushing in and got into my bed."

"It was Lissa," said Ginny. "I'm sure it was. The scream sounded like it was right next door. So I ran in here. But I didn't see anyone." She swallowed, and her eyes grew big.

"Is Lissa—?"

"No," said the Saint bluntly. "Lissa's as well as you are. And so is Freddie. But somebody's been up to mischief tonight, and we're looking for him. Now will you please get out of bed and pull yourselves together, because we're going to search the house."

"I can't," said Esther. "I haven't got anything on."

"Don't let it bother you," said the Saint tiredly. "If a burglar sees you he'll probably swoon on the spot, and then the rest of us will jump on him and tie him up."

He took a cigarette from a package beside the bed, and went on his way. It seemed as if he had wasted a lot of time, but actually it had scarcely been a minute. Out on the verandah he saw that the door of Lissa's room was open, and through it he heard Freddie Pellman's obstructed croak repetitiously imploring her to tell him what had happened. As he went on towards the junction of the main building, lights went on in the living-room and a small mob of chattering figures burst out and almost swarmed over him as he opened the door into the arched alcove that the bedroom wing took off from. Simon spread out his arms and collected them in a sheaf.

"Were you going somewhere, boys?"

There were three of them, in various interesting costumes. Reading from left to right, they were: Angelo, in red, green, and purple striped pyjamas, another Filipino in a pair of very natty bright blue trousers, and a large gentleman in a white nightshirt with spiked moustaches and a Vandyke.

Angelo said, "We hear some lady scream, so we come to see what's the matter."

Simon looked at him shrewdly.

"How long have you worked for Mr Pellman?"

"About six months, sir."

"And you never heard any screaming before?"

The boy looked at him sheepishly, without answering.

The stout gentleman in the nightshirt said with some dignity: "Ziss wass not ordinairy screaming. Ziss wass quite deefairent. It sounds like somebody iss in trouble. So we sink about ze note zat Meestair Pellman receive, and we come to help."

"Who are you?" asked the Saint.

"I am Louis, sir. I am ze chef."

"Enfin, quand nous aurons pris notre assassin, vous aurez le plaisir de nous servir ses rognons, légèrement grillés."

The man stared at him blankly for a second or two, and finally said, "I'm sorry, sir, I don't ondairstand."

"You don't speak French?"

"No, sir."

"Then what are you doing with that accent?"

"I am Italian, sir, but I lairn this accent because she iss good business."

Simon gave up for the time being.

"Well, let's get on with this and search the house. You didn't see any strangers on your way here?"

"No, sir," Angelo answered. "Did anyone get hurt?"

"No, but we seem to have had a visitor."

"I no understand," the Filipino insisted. "Everything lock up, sir. I see to it myself."

"Then somebody opened something," said the Saint curtly. "Go and look."

He went on his own way to the front door. It was locked and bolted. He opened it and went outside.

Although there seemed to have been a large variety of action and dialogue since Lissa's scream had awakened him, it had clicked through at such a speed that the elapsed time was actually surprisingly short. As he stood outside and gave his eyes a moment to adjust themselves to the darkness he tried to estimate how long it had been. Not long enough, he was sure, for anyone to travel very far . . . And then the night cleared from his eyes, and he could see almost as well as a cat could have seen there. He went to the edge of the terrace in front of the house, and looked down. He could see the private road which was the only vehicular approach to the place dropping and winding away to his left like a gray ribbon carelessly thrown down the mountainside, and there was no car or moving shadow on it. Most of the street plan at the foot of the hill was as clearly visible also as if he had been looking down on it from an airplane, but he could see nothing human or mechanical moving there either. And even with all his delays, it hardly seemed possible that anything or anyone could have travelled far enough to be out of sight by that time—at least without making a noise that he would have heard on his way through the house.

There were, of course, other ways than the road. The steep slopes both upwards and downwards could have been negotiated by an agile man. Simon walked very quietly around the building and the gardens, scanning every surface that he could see. Certainly no one climbing up or down could have covered a great distance: on the other hand, if the climber had gone only a little way and stopped moving he would have been very hard to pick out of the ragged patchwork of lights and shadows that the starlight made out of tumbles of broken rock and clumps of cactus and incense and grease-wood. By the same token, a man on foot would be impossibly dangerous game to hunt at night: he only had to keep still, whereas the hunter had to move, and thereby give his quarry the first timed deliberate shot at him.

The Saint could be reckless enough, but he had no suicidal inclinations. He stood motionless for several minutes in different bays of shadow, scanning the slopes with the unblinking patience of a head-hunter. But nothing moved, and presently he went back in by the front door and found Angelo.

"Well?" he said.

"I no find anything, sir. Everything all lock up. You come see yourself."

Simon made the circuit with him. Where there were glass doors they were all metal framed, with sturdy locking handles and bolts in addition. All the windows were screened, and the screen frames fastened on the inside. None of them showed a sign of having been forced or tampered with in any way, and the Saint was a good enough burglar in his own right to know that doors and casements of that type could not have been fastened from outside without leaving a sign that any such thing had been done—particularly by a man who was trying to depart from the premises in a great hurry.

His tour ended back in Lissa's room, where the rest of the house party was now gathered. He paused in the doorway.

"All right, Angelo," he said. "You can go back to your beauty sleep . . . Oh, yes, you could bring me a drink first."

"I've got one for you already," Freddie called out.

Simon went on in.

"That's fine." He stood by the portable bar, which had already been set up for business, and watched Freddie manipulating a bottle. It was a feat which Freddie could apparently perform in any condition short of complete unconsciousness. All things considered, he had really staged quite a comeback. Of course, he had had some sleep. The Saint looked at his watch, and saw that it was a few minutes after four. He said, "I think it's so nice to get up early and catch the best part of the morning, don't you?"

"Did you find out anything?" Freddie demanded.

"Not a thing," said the Saint. "But that might add up to quite something."

He took the highball that Freddie handed him, and strolled over to the windows. They were the only ones in the house he had not yet examined. But they were exactly like the others—the screens latched and intact.

Lissa still sat up in the bed, the covers huddled up under her chin, staring now and again at the knife driven into the mattress, as if it were a snake that somebody was trying to frighten her with and she wasn't going to be frightened. Simon turned back and sat down beside her. He also looked at the knife.

"It looks like a kitchen knife," he remarked.

"I wouldn't let anyone touch it," she said, "on account of fingerprints."

Simon nodded and smiled, and took a handkerchief from the pocket of his robe. Using the cloth for insulation, he pulled the knife out and held it delicately while he inspected it. It was a kitchen knife—a cheap piece of steel with a riveted wooden handle, but sharp and pointed enough to have done all the lethal work of the most expensive blade.

"Probably there aren't any prints on it," he said, "but it doesn't cost anything to try. Even most amateurs have heard about fingerprints these days, and they all wear gloves. Still, we'll see if we have any luck."

He wrapped the knife carefully in the handkerchief and laid it on a Carter Dickson mystery on the bedside table.

"You're going to get tired of telling the story," he said, "but I haven't heard it yet. Would you like to tell me what happened?"

"I don't really know," she said. "I'd been asleep. And then suddenly for no reason at all I woke up. At least I thought I woke up, but maybe I didn't, anyway it was just like a nightmare. But I just knew there was somebody in my room, and I went cold all over, it was just as if a lot of spiders were crawling all over me, and I didn't feel as if I could move or scream or anything, and I just lay there hardly breathing and my heart was thumping away till I thought it would burst."

"Does that always happen when somebody comes into your room?" Ginny asked interestedly.

"Shut up," said the Saint.

"I was trying to listen," Lissa said, "to see if I couldn't hear something. I mean if he was really moving or if I'd just woken up with the frights and imagined it, and my ears were humming so that it didn't seem as if I could hear anything. But I did hear him. I could hear him breathing."

"Was that when you screamed?"

"No. Well, I don't know. It all happened at once. But suddenly I knew he was awful close, right beside the bed, and then I knew I was wide awake and it wasn't just a bad dream, and then I screamed the first time and tried to wriggle out of bed on the other side from where he was, to get away from him, and he actually touched my shoulder, and then there was a sort of thump right beside me—that must have been the knife—and then he ran away and I heard him rush through one of the doors, and I lay there and screamed again because I thought that would bring you or somebody, and besides if I made enough noise it would help to scare him and make him so busy trying to get away that he wouldn't wait to have another try at me."

"So you never actually saw him at all?"

She shook her head.

"I had the shades drawn, so it was quite dark. I couldn't see anything. That's what made it more like a nightmare. It was like being blind."

"But when he opened one of these doors to rush out—there might have been a little dim light on the other side—"

"Well. I could just barely see something, but it was so quick, it was just a blurred shadow and then he was gone. I don't think I've even got the vaguest idea how big he was."

"But you call him 'he,'" said the Saint easily, "so you saw that much, anyway."

She stared at him with big round blue eyes.

"I didn't," she said blankly. "No, I didn't. I just naturally thought it was 'he.' Of course it was 'he.' It had to be." She swallowed, and added almost pleadingly, "didn't it?"

"I don't know," said the Saint, flatly and dispassionately.

"Now wait a minute," said Freddie Pellman, breaking one of the longest periods of plain listening that Simon had yet known him to maintain. "What is this?"

The Saint took a cigarette from a package on the bedside table and lighted it with care and deliberation. He knew that their eyes were all riveted on him now, but he figured that a few seconds' suspense would do them no harm.

"I've walked around outside," he said, "and I didn't see anyone making a getaway. That wasn't conclusive, of course, but it was an interesting start. Since then I've been through the whole house. I've checked every door and window in the place. Angelo did it first, but I did it again to make sure. Nothing's been touched. There isn't an opening anywhere where even a cat could have got in and got out again. And I looked in all the closets and under the beds too, and I didn't find any strangers hiding around."

"But somebody was here!" Freddie protested. "There's the knife. You can see it with your own eyes. That proves that Lissa wasn't dreaming."

Simon nodded, and his blue eyes were crisp and sardonic.

"Sure it does," he agreed conversationally. "So it's a comfort to know that we don't have to pick a prospective murderer out of a hundred and thirty million people outside. We know that this is strictly a family affair, and you're going to be killed by somebody who's living here now."

4

It was nearly nine o'clock when the Saint woke up again, and the sun, which had been bleaching the sky before he got back to bed, was slicing brilliantly through the Venetian blinds. He felt a lot better than he had expected to. In fact, he decided, after a few minutes of lazy rolling and stretching, he felt surprisingly good. He got up, sluiced himself under a cold shower, brushed his hair, pulled on a pair of swimming trunks and a bath robe, and went out in search of breakfast.

Through the French windows of the living-room he saw Ginny sitting alone at the long table in the patio beside the barbecue. He went out and stood over her.

"Hullo," she said.

"Hullo," he agreed. "You don't mind if I join you?"

"Not a bit," she said. "Why should I?"

"We could step right into a Van Druten play," he observed.

She looked at him rather vaguely. He sat down, and in a moment Angelo was at his elbow, immaculate and impassive now in a white jacket and a black bow tie.

"Yes, sir?"

'Tomato juice," said the Saint. "With Worcestershire sauce. Scrambled eggs, and ham. And coffee."

"Yes, sir."

The Filipino departed, and Simon lighted a cigarette and slipped the robe off his shoulders.

"Isn't this early for you to be up?"

"I didn't sleep so well." She pouted, "Esther does snore. You'll find out."

Before the party broke up for the second time, there had been some complex but uninhibited arguments about how the rest of the night should be organised with a view to mutual protection, which Simon did not want revived at that hour.

"I'll have to thank her," he said tactfully. "She's saved me from having to eat breakfast alone. Maybe she'll do it for us again."

"You could wake me up yourself just as well," said Ginny. The Saint kept his face noncommittal and tried again. "Aren't you eating?"

She was playing with a glass of orange juice as if it were a medicine that she didn't want to take.

"I don't know. I sort of don't have any appetite."

"Why?"

"Well . . . you are sure that it was someone in the house last night, aren't you?"

"Quite sure."

"I mean—one of us. Or the servants, or somebody."

"Yes."

"So why couldn't we just as well be poisoned?"

He thought for a moment, and chuckled.

"Poison isn't so easy. In the first place, you have to buy it. And there are problems about that. Then, you have to put it in something. And there aren't so many people handling food that you can do that just like blowing out a match. It's an awfully dangerous way of killing people. I think probably more poisoners get caught than any other kind of murderer. And any smart killer knows it."

"How do you know this one is smart?"

"It follows. You don't send warnings to your victims unless you think you're pretty smart—you have to be quite an egotist and a show-off to get that far—and anyone who thinks he's really smart usually has at least enough smartness to be able to kid himself. Besides, nobody threatened to kill you."

"Nobody threatened to kill Lissa."

"Nobody did kill her."

"But they tried."

"I don't think we know that they were trying for Lissa."

"Then if they were so half-way smart, how did they get in the wrong room?"

"They might have thought Freddie would be with her."

"Yeah?" she scoffed. "If they knew anything, they'd know he'd be in his own room. He doesn't visit. He has visitors."

Simon felt that he was at some disadvantage. He said with a grin, "You can tie me up, Ginny, but that doesn't alter anything. Freddie is the guy that the beef is about. The intended murderer has very kindly told us the motive. And that automatically establishes that there's no motive for killing anyone else. I'll admit that the attack on Lissa last night is pretty confusing, and I just haven't got any theories about it yet that I'd want to bet on, but I still know damn well that nobody except Freddie is going to be in much danger unless they accidentally find out who the murderer is, and personally I'm not going to starve myself until that happens."

He proved it by taking a healthy sip from the glass of tomato juice which Angelo set in front of him, and a couple of minutes later he was carving into his ham and eggs with healthy enthusiasm.

The girl watched him moodily.

"Anyway," she said, "I never can eat anything much for breakfast. I have to watch my figure."

"It looks very nice to me," he said, and was able to say it without the slightest effort.

"Yes, but it has to stay that way. There's always competition."

Simon could appreciate that. He was curious. He had been very casual all the time about the whole organisation and mechanics of the ménage, as casual as Pellman himself, but there just wasn't any way to stop wondering about the details of a set-up like that. The Saint put it in the scientific category of post-graduate education. Or he was trying to.

He said, leading her on with a touch so light and apparently disinterested that it could have been broken with a breath: "It must be quite a life."

"It is."

"If I hadn't seen it myself, I wouldn't have believed it was really possible."

"Why not?"

"It's just something out of this world."

"Sheiks and sultans do it."

"I know," he said delicately. "But their women are brought up differently. They're brought up to look forward to a place in a harem as a perfectly normal life. American girls aren't."

One of her eyebrows went up a little in a tired way.

"They are where I came from. And probably most everywhere else, if you only knew. Nearly every man is a wandering wolf at heart, and if he's got enough money there isn't much to stop him. Nearly every woman knows it. Only they don't admit it. So what? You wouldn't think there was anything freakish about it if Freddie kept us all in different apartments and visited around. What's the difference if he keeps us all together?"

The Saint shrugged.

"Nothing much," he conceded. "Except, I suppose, a certain amount of conventional illusion."

"Phooey," she said. "What can you do with an illusion?"

He couldn't think of an answer to that.

"Well," he said, "it might save a certain amount of domestic strife."

"Oh, sure," she said. "We bicker and squabble a bit."

"I've heard you."

"But it doesn't often get too serious."

"That's the point. That's what fascinates me, in a way. Why doesn't anybody ever break the rules? Why doesn't anybody try to ride the others off and marry him, for instance?"

She laughed shortly.

"That's two questions. But I'll tell you. Nobody goes too far because they wouldn't be here if they did. Or they'd only do it once. And then—out. No guy wants to live in the middle of a mountain feud, and after all, Freddie's the meal ticket. He's got a right to have some peace for his money. So everybody behaves pretty well. As for marrying him—that's funny."

"Guys have been married before."

"Not Freddie Pellman. He can't afford to."

"One thing that we obviously have in common," said the Saint, "is a sense of humor."

She shook her head.

"I'm not kidding. Didn't you know about him?"

"No. I didn't know about him."

"There's a will," she said. "All his money is in a trust fund. He just gets the income. I guess Papa Pellman knew Freddie pretty well, and so he didn't trust him. He sewed everything up tight. Freddie never will be able to touch most of the capital, but he gets two or three million to play with when he's thirty-five. On one condition. He mustn't marry before that. I guess Papa knew all about girls like me. If Freddie marries before he's thirty-five, he doesn't get another penny. Ever. Income or anything. It all goes to a fund to feed stray cats or something like that."

"So." The Saint poured himself some coffee. "I suppose Papa thought that Freddie would have attained a certain amount of discretion by that time. How long does that keep him safe for, by the way?"

"As a matter of fact," she said, "it's only a few more months."

"Well, cheer up," he said. "If you can last that long you may still have a chance."

"Maybe by that time I wouldn't want it," she said, with her disturbing eyes dwelling on him.

Simon lighted a cigarette and looked up across the patio as a door opened and Lissa and Esther came out. Lissa carried a book, with her forefinger marking a place: she put it down open on the table beside her, as if she was ready to go back to it at any moment. She looked very gay and fresh in a play suit that matched her eyes.

"Have you and Ginny solved it yet?" she asked.

"I'm afraid not," said the Saint. "As a matter of fact, we were mostly talking about other things."

"I'll take two guesses," said Esther.

"Why two?" snapped Ginny. "I thought there was only one thing you could think of."

The arrival of Angelo for their orders fortunately stopped that train of thought. And then, almost as soon as the Filipino had disappeared again and the cast were settling themselves and digging their toes in for another jump, Freddie Pellman made his entrance.

Like the Saint, he wore swimming trunks and a perfunctory terry-cloth robe. But the exposed portions of him were not built to stand the comparison. He had pale blotchy skin and the flesh under it looked spongy, as if it had softened up with inward fermentation. Which was not improbable. But he seemed totally unconscious of it. He was very definitely himself, even if he was nothing else.

"How do you feel?" Simon asked unnecessarily.

"Lousy," said Freddie Pellman, no less unnecessarily. He sank into a chair and squinted blearily over the table. Ginny still had some orange juice in her glass. Freddie drank it, and made a face. He said, "Simon, you should have let the murderer go on with the job. If he'd killed me last night, I'd have felt a lot better this morning."

"Would you have left me a thousand dollars a day in your will?" Simon inquired.

Freddie started to shake his head. The movement hurt him too much, so he clutched his skull in both hands to stop it.

"Look," he said. "Before I die and you have to bury me, who is behind all this?"

"I don't know," said the Saint patiently. "I'm only a bodyguard of sorts. I didn't sell myself to you as a detective."

"But you must have some idea."

"No more than I had last night."

A general quietness came down again, casting a definite shadow as if a cloud had slid over the sun. Even Freddie Pellman became still, holding his head carefully in the hands braced on either side of his jawbones.

"Last night," he said soggily, "you told us you were sure it was someone inside the house. Isn't that what he said, Esther? He said it was someone who was here already."

"That's right," said the Saint. "And it still goes."

"Then it could only be one of us—Esther or Lissa or Ginny."

"Or me. Or the servants."

"My God!" Freddie sat up. "It isn't even going to be safe to eat!"

The Saint smiled slightly.

"I think it is. Ginny and I were talking about that. But I've eaten . . . Let's take it another way. You put the finger on Johnny Implicato last Christmas. That's nearly a year ago. So anybody who wanted to sneak in to get revenge for him must have sneaked in since then. Let's start by washing out anybody you've known more than a year. How about the servants?"

"I hired them all when I came here this season."

"I was afraid of that. However. What about anybody else?"

"I only met you yesterday."

"That's quite true," said the Saint calmly. "Let's include me. Now what about the girls?"

The three girls looked at each other and at Freddie and at the Saint. There was an awkward silence. Nobody seemed to want to speak first; until Freddie scratched his head painfully and said, "I think I've known you longer than anyone, Esther, haven't I?"

"Since last New Year's Eve," she said. "At the Dunes. You remember. Somebody had dared me to do a strip tease—"

"—never dreaming you'd take them up on it," said Ginny.

"All right," said the Saint. "Where did you come in?"

"In a phone booth in Miami," said Ginny. "In February. Freddie was passed out inside, and I had to make a phone call. So I lugged him out. Then he woke up, so we made a night of it."

"What about you, Lissa?"

"I was just reading a book in a drug store in New York last May. Freddie came in for some Bromo-Seltzer, and we just got talking."

"In other words," said the Saint, "any one of you could have been a girlfriend of Johnny's, and promoted yourselves in here after he was killed."

Nobody said anything.

"Okay," Freddie said at last. "Well, we've got fingerprints, haven't we? How about the fingerprints on that knife?"

"We can find out if there are any," said the Saint.

He took it out of the pocket of his robe, where he had kept it with him still wrapped in his handkerchief. He unwrapped it very carefully, without touching any of the surfaces, and laid it on the table. But he didn't look at it particularly. He was much more interested in watching the other faces that looked at it.

"Aren't you going to save it for the police?" asked Lissa.

"Not till I've finished with it," said the Saint. "I can make all the tests they'd use, and maybe I know one or two that they haven't heard of yet. I'll show you now, if you like."

Angelo made his impassive appearance with two glasses of orange juice for Lissa and Esther, and a third effervescent glass for Freddie. He stood stoically by while Freddie drained it with a shudder.

"Anything else, Mr Pellman?"

"Yes," Freddie said firmly. "Bring me a brandy and ginger ale. And some waffles."

"Yes, sir," said the Filipino, and paused, in the most natural and expressionless way, to gather up three or four plates, a couple of empty glasses, and, rather apologetically, as if he had no idea how it could have arrived there, the kitchen knife that lay in front of the Saint with everyone staring at it.

5

And that, Simon reflected, was as smooth and timely a bit of business as he had ever seen. He sat loose-limbed on his horse and went on enjoying it even when the impact was more than two hours old.

It had a superb simplicity of perfection which appealed to his sardonic sense of humor. It was magnificent because it was so completely incalculable. You couldn't argue with it or estimate it. There was absolutely no percentage in claiming, as Freddie Pellman had done, in a loud voice and at great length, that Angelo had done it on purpose. There wasn't a thing that could be proved one way or the other. Nobody had told Angelo anything. Nobody had asked Angelo to leave the knife alone, or spoken to him about fingerprints. So he had simply seen it on the table, and figured that it had arrived there through some crude mistake, and he had discreetly picked it up to take it away. The fact that by the time it had been rescued from him, with all the attendant panic and excitement, any fingerprints that might have been on the handle would have been completely obscured or without significance, was purely a sad coincidence. And that was the literal and ineluctable truth. Angelo could have been as guilty as hell or as innocent as a newborn babe: the possibilities were exactly that, and if Sherlock Holmes had been resurrected to take part in the argument his guess would have been worth no more than anyone else's.

So the Saint hooked one knee over the saddle horn and admired the pluperfect uselessness of the whole thing, while he lighted a cigarette and let his horse pick its own serpentine trail up the rocky slope towards Andreas Canyon.

The ride had been Freddie's idea. After two more brandies and ginger ale, an aspirin, and a waffle, Freddie Pellman had proclaimed that he wasn't going to be scared into a cellar by any goddam gangster's friends. He had hired the best goddam bodyguard in the world, and so he ought to be able to do just what he wanted. And he wanted to ride. So they were going to ride.

"Not me," Lissa had said. "I'd rather have a gangster than a horse, any day. I'd rather lie out by the pool and read."

"All right," Freddie said sourly, "You lie by the pool and read. That makes four of us, and that's just right. We'll take lunch and make a day of it. You can stay home and read."

So there were four of them riding up towards the cleft where the gray-green tops of tall palm trees painted the desert sign of water. Simon was in the lead, because he had known the trail years before and it came back to him as if he had only ridden it yesterday. Freddie was close behind him. Suddenly they broke over the top of the ridge, and easing out on to the dirt road that had been constructed since the Saint was last there to make the canyon more accessible to pioneers in gasoline-powered armchairs. But bordering the creek beyond the road stood the same tall palms, skirted with the dry drooped fronds of many years, but with their heads still rising proudly green and the same stream racing and gurgling around their roots. To the Saint they were still ageless beauty, unchanged, a visual awakening that flashed him back with none of the clumsy encumbrances of time machines to other more leisured days and other people who had ridden the same trail with him, and he reined his horse and thought about them, and in particular about one straight slim girl whom he had taken there for one stolen hour, and they had never said a word that was not casual and unimportant, and they had never met again, and yet they had given all their minds into each other's hands, and he was utterly sure that if she ever came there again she would remember, exactly as he was remembering . . . So that it was like the shock of a cold plunge when Freddie Pellman spurred up beside him on the road and said noisily: "Well, how's the mystery coming along?"

The Saint sighed inaudibly and tightened up, and said, "What mystery?"

"Oh, go on," Freddie insisted boisterously. "You know what I'm talking about. The mystery."

"So I gathered," said the Saint. "But I'm not so psychic after a night like last night. And if you want to know, I'm just where I was last night. I just wish you were more careful about hiring servants."

"They had good references."

"So had everybody else who ever took that way in. But what else do you know about them?"

"What else do I know about them?" Freddie echoed, for the sake of greater clarity. "Nothing much. Except that Angelo is the best houseboy and valet I ever had. The other Filipino—Al, he calls himself—is a pal of his. Angelo brought him."

"You didn't ask if they'd ever worked for Smoke Johnny?"

"No." Freddie was surprised. "Why should I?"

"He could have been nice to them," said the Saint. "And Filipinos can be fanatically loyal. Still, that threatening letter seems a little bit literate for Angelo. I don't know. Another way of looking at it is that Johnny's friends could have hired them for the job . . . And then, did you know that your chef was an Italian?"

"I never thought about it. He's an Italian, is he? Louis? That's interesting," Freddie looked anything but interested. "But what's that got to do with it?"

"So was Implicato," said the Saint. "He might have had some Italian friends. Some Italians do."

"Oh," said Freddie.

They turned over the bridge across the stream, and there was a flurry of hoofs behind them as Ginny caught up at a gallop. She rode well, and she knew it, and she wanted everyone else to know. She reined her pony up to a rearing sliding stop, and patted its damp neck.

"What are you two being so exclusive about?" she demanded.

"Just talking," said the Saint. "How are you doing?"

"Fine." She was fretting her pony with hands and heels, making it step nervously, showing off. "Esther isn't so happy, though. Her horse is a bit frisky for her."

"Don't worry about me," Esther said, coming up. "I'm doing all right. I'm awful hot, though."

"Fancy that," said Ginny.

"Never mind," said the Saint tactfully. "We'll call a halt soon and have lunch."

They were walking down towards a grove of great palms that rose like columns in the nave of a natural cathedral, their rich tufted heads arching over to meet above a cloister of deep whispering shade. They were the same palms that Simon had paused under once before, years ago; only now there were picnic tables at their feet, and at some of them a few hardy families who had driven out there in their automobiles were already grouped in strident fecundity, enjoying the unspoiled beauties of Nature from the midst of an enthusiastic litter of baskets, boxes, tin cans, and paper bags.

"Is this where you meant we could have lunch?" Freddie asked rather limply.

"No. I thought we'd ride on over to Murray Canyon—if they haven't built a road in there since I saw it last, there's a place there that I think we still might have to ourselves."

He led them down through the trees, and out on a narrow trail that clung for a while to the edge of a steep shoulder or hill. Then they were out on an open rise at the edge of the desert, and the Saint set his horse to an easy canter, threading his way unerringly along a trail that was nothing but a faint crinkling in the hard earth where other horses had followed it before.

It seemed strange to be out riding like that, so casually and inconsequentially, when only a few hours before there had been very tangible evidence that a threat of death to one of them had not been made idly. Yet perhaps they were safer out there than they would have been anywhere else. The Saint's eyes had never stopped wandering over the changing panoramas, behind as well as ahead, and although he knew how deceptive the apparently open desert could be, and how even a man on horseback, standing well above the tallest clump of scrub, could vanish altogether in a hundred yards, he was sure that no prospective sniper had come within sharp-shooting range of them. Yet . . .

He stopped his horse abruptly, after a time, as the broad flat that they had been riding over ended suddenly at the brink of a sharp cliff. At the foot of the bluff, another long column of tall silent palms bordered a rustling stream. He lighted a cigarette, and wondered cynically how many of the spoiled playboys and playgirls who used Palm Springs for their wilder weekends, and saw nothing but the smooth hotels and the Racquet Club, even realised that the name was not just a name, and that there really were Palm Springs, sparkling and crystal clear, racing down out of the overshadowing mountains to make hidden nests of beauty before they washed out into the extinction of the barren plain . . .

Freddie Pellman reined in beside him, looked the landscape over, and said, tolerantly, as if it were a production that had been offered for his approval: "This is pretty good. Is this where we eat?"

"If everybody can take it," said the Saint, "there's a pool further up that I'd like to look at again."

"I can take it," said Freddie, comprehensively settling the matter.

Simon put his horse down the steep zigzag, and stopped at the bottom to let it drink from the stream. Freddie drew up beside him again—he rode well enough, having probably been raised to it in the normal course of a millionaire's son's upbringing—and said, still laboring with the same subject: "Do you really think one of the girls could be in on it?"

"Of course," said the Saint calmly. "Gangsters have girlfriends. Girlfriends do things like that."

"But I've known all of them for some time at least."

"That may be part of the act. A smart girl wouldn't want to make it too obvious—meet you one day, and bump you off the next. Besides, she may have a nice streak of ham in her. Most women have. Maybe she thinks it would be cute to keep you in suspense for a while. Maybe she wants to make an anniversary of it, and pay off for Johnny this Christmas."

Freddie swallowed.

"That's going to make some things—a bit difficult."

"That's your problem," Simon said cheerfully.

Freddie sat in his saddle unhappily and watched Ginny and Esther coming down the grade. Ginny came down it in a spectacular avalanche, like a mountain cavalry display, and swept off her Stetson to ruffle her hair back with a bored air while her pony dipped its nose thirstily in the water a few yards downstream. Esther, steering her horse down quietly, joined her a little later.

"But this is wonderful!" Ginny called out, looking at the Saint. "How do you find all these marvelous places?" Without waiting for an answer, she turned to Esther and said in a solicitous undertone which was perfectly pitched to carry just far enough: "How are you feeling, darling? I hope you aren't getting too miserable."

Simon was naturally glancing towards them. He wasn't looking for anything in particular, and as far as he was concerned Esther was only one of the gang, but in those transient circumstances, he felt sorry for her. So for that one moment he had the privilege of seeing one woman open her soul in utter stark sincerity to another woman. And what one woman said to another, clearly, carefully, deliberately, quietly, with serious premeditation and the intensest earnestness, was "You bitch."

"Let's keep a-goin'," said the Saint hastily, in a flippant drawl, and lifted his reins to set his horse at the shallow bank on the other side of the stream.

He led them west towards the mountains with a quicker sureness now, as the sense of the trail came back to him. In a little while it was a track that only an Indian could have seen at all, but it seemed as if he could have found it at the dead of night. There was even a place where weeds and spindly clawed scrub had grown so tall and dense since he had last been there that anyone else would have sworn that there was no trail at all, but he set his horse boldly at the living wall and smashed easily through into a channel that could hardly have been trodden since he last opened it . . . so that presently they found the creek again at a sharp bend, and he led them over two deep fords through swift-running water, and they came out at last in a wide hollow ringed with palms where hundreds of spring floods had built a broad open sandbank gouged out a deep sheltered pool beside it.

"This is lunch," said the Saint, and swung out of the saddle to moor his bridle to a fallen palm log where his horse could rest in the shade.

They spread out the contents of their saddlebags on the sandbank and ate cold chicken, celery, radishes, and hard-boiled eggs. There had been some difficulty when they set out over convincing Freddie Pellman that it would have been impractical as well as strictly illegal to take bottles of champagne on to the reservation, but the water in the brook was sweet and ice-cold.

Esther drank it from her cupped hands, and sat back on her heels and gazed meditatively at the pool.

"It's awful hot," she said, suggestively.

"Go on," Ginny said to Simon. "Dare her to take her clothes off and get in. That's what she's waiting for."

"I'll go in if you will," Esther said sullenly.

"Nuts," said Ginny. "I can have a good time without that."

She was leaning against the Saint's shoulder for a backrest, and she gave a little snuggling wriggle as she spoke which made her meaning completely clear.

Freddie Pellman locked his arms around his knees and scowled. It had been rather obvious for some time that all the current competition was being aimed at the Saint, even though Simon had done nothing to try and encourage it, and Freddie was not feeling so generous about it as he had when he first invited the girls to take Simon into the family.

"All right," Freddie said gracelessly. "I dare you."

Esther looked as if a load had been taken off her mind.

She pulled off her boots and socks. She stood up, with a slight faraway smile, and unbuttoned her shirt and took it off. She took off her frontier pants. That left her in a wisp of sheer close-fitting scantiness. She took that off, too.

She certainly had a beautiful body.

She turned and walked into the pool, and lowered herself into it until the water lapped her chin. It covered her as well as a sheet of glass. She rolled, and swam lazily up to the far end, and as the water shallowed she rose out again and strolled on up into the low cascade where the stream tumbled around the next curve. She waded on up through the falls, under the palms, the sunlight through the leaves making glancing patterns on her skin, and disappeared around the bend, very leisurely. It was quite an exit.

The rustle of the water seemed very loud suddenly, as if anyone would have had to shout to be heard over it. So that it was surprising when Ginny's voice sounded perfectly easy and normal.

"Well, folks," she said, "don't run away now, because there'll be another super-colossal floor show in just a short while." She nestled against the Saint again and said, "Hullo."

"Hullo," said the Saint restrainedly.

Freddie Pellman got to his feet.

"Well," he said huffily, "I know you won't miss me, so I think I'll take a walk."

He stalked off up the stream the way Esther had gone, stumbling and balancing awkwardly on his high-heeled boots over the slippery rounded boulders.

They watched him until he was out of sight also.

"Alone at last," said Ginny emotionally.

The Saint reached for a cigarette.

"Don't you ever worry about getting complicated?" he asked.

"I worry about not getting kissed," she said.

She looked up at him from under her long sweeping lashes, with bright impudent eyes and red lips tantalisingly parted. The Saint had been trying conscientiously not to look for trouble, but he was not made out of ice cream and bubble gum. He was making good progress against no resistance when the crash of a shot rattled down the canyon over the chattering of the water and brought him to his feet as if he had actually felt the bullet.

6

He ran up the side of the brook, fighting his way through clawing scrub and stumbling over boulders and loose gravel. Beyond the bend, the stream rose in a long twisting stairway of shallow cataracts posted with the same shapely palms that grew throughout its length. A couple of steps further up he found Freddie.

Freddie was not dead. He was standing up. He stood and looked at the Saint in a rather foolish way, with his mouth open.

"Come on," said the Saint encouragingly. "Give." Freddie pointed stupidly to the rock behind him. There was a bright silver scar on it where a bullet had scraped off a layer of lead on the rough surface before it ricocheted off into nowhere.

"It only just missed me," Freddie said.

"Where were you standing?"

"Just here."

Simon looked at the scar again. There was no way of reading from it the caliber or make of gun. The bullet itself might have come to rest anywhere within half a mile. He tried a rough sight from the mark on the rock, but within the most conservative limits it covered an area of at least two thousand square yards on the other slope of the canyon.

The Saint's spine tingled. It was a little like the helplessness of his trip around the house the night before—looking up at that raw muddle of shrubs and rocks, knowing that a dozen sharpshooters could lie hidden there, with no risk of being discovered before they had fired the one shot that might be all that was necessary . . . "Maybe we should go home, Freddie," he said.

"Now wait." Freddie was going to be obstinate and valiant after he had found company. "If there's someone up there—"

"He could drop you before we were six steps closer to him," said the Saint tersely. "You hired me as a bodyguard, not a pall-bearer. Let's move."

Something else moved, upwards and a little to his left. His reflexes had tautened instinctively before he recognised the flash of movement as only a shifting of bare brown flesh.

From a precarious flat ledge of rock five or six yards up the slope, Esther called down: "What goes on?"

"We're going home," Simon called back.

"Wait for me."

She started to scramble down off the ledge. Suddenly she seemed much more undressed than she had before. He turned abruptly.

"Come along, then."

He went back, around the bend, past the pool, past Ginny, to where they had left the horses, hearing Freddie's footsteps behind him but not looking back. There were no more shots, but he worked quickly checking the saddles and tightening the cinches. The place was still just as picturesque and enchanting, but as an ambush it had the kind of topography where he felt that the defending team was at a great disadvantage.

"What's the hurry?" Ginny complained, coming up beside him, and he locked the buckle he was hauling on and gave the leather a couple of rapid loops through the three-quarter rig slots.

"You heard the shot, didn't you?"

"Yes."

"It just missed Freddie. So we're moving before they try again."

"Something's always happening," said Ginny resentfully, as if she had been shot at herself.

"Life is like that," said the Saint, untying her horse and handing the reins to her.

As he turned to the next horse Esther came up. She was fully dressed again, except that her shirt was only half buttoned, and she looked smug and sulky at the same time.

"Did you hear what happened, Ginny?" she said. "There was a man hiding up in the hills, and he took a shot at Freddie. And if he was where Simon thought he was, he must have seen me sunbathing without anything on."

"Tell Freddie that's what made him miss," Ginny suggested. "It might be worth some new silver foxes to you."

A dumb look came into Esther's beautifully sculptured face. She gazed foggily out at the landscape as the Saint cinched her saddle and thrust the reins into her limp hands.

She said, "Simon."

"Yes?"

"Didn't you say something last night about—about being sure it was someone in the house?"

"I did."

"Then . . . then just now—you were with Ginny, so she couldn't have done anything. And Lissa isn't here. But you know I couldn't . . . you know I couldn't have hidden a gun anywhere, don't you?"

"I don't know you well enough," said the Saint.

But it was another confusion that twisted around in his mind all the way home. It was true that he himself was an alibi for Ginny—unless she had planted one of those colossally elaborate remote-control gun-firing devices beloved of mystery writers. And Esther couldn't have concealed a gun, or anything else, in her costume—unless she had previously planted it somewhere up the stream. But both those theories would have required them to know in advance where they were going, and the Saint had chosen the place himself . . . It was true he had mentioned it before they started, but mentioning it and finding it were different matters. He would have sworn that not more than a handful of people besides himself had ever discovered it, and he remembered sections of the trail that had seemed to be completely overgrown since they had last been trodden. Of course, with all his watchfulness, they might have been followed. A good hunter might have stayed out of sight and circled over the hills—he could have done it himself . . .

Yet in all those speculations there was something that didn't connect, something that didn't make sense. If the theoretical sniper in the hills had been good enough to get there at all, for instance, why hadn't he been good enough to try a second shot before they got away? He could surely have had at least one more try, from a different angle, with no more risk than the first . . . It was like the abortive attack on Lissa—it made sense, but not absolute sense. And to the Saint's delicately tuned reception that was a more nagging obstacle than no sense at all . . .

They got back to the stables, and Freddie said, "I need a drink. Let's beat up the Tennis Club before we go home."

For once, the Saint was not altogether out of sympathy with the exigencies of Freddie's thirst.

They drove out to the club, and sat on the balcony terrace looking down over the beautifully terraced gardens, the palm-shaded oval pool, and the artificial brook where imported trout lurked under spreading willows and politely awaited the attention of pampered anglers. The rest of them sipped Daiquiris, while Freddie restored himself with three double brandies in quick succession. And then, sauntering over from the tennis courts with a racquet in her hand, Lissa O'Neill herself came up to them. She looked as cool and dainty as she always seemed to look, in one of those abbreviated sun suits that she always seemed to wear which some clairvoyant designer must have invented exclusively for her slim waist and for long tapered legs like hers, in pastel shades that would set off her clear golden skin. But it seemed as if all of them drew back behind a common barrier that made them look at her in the same way, not in admiration, but guardedly, waiting for what she would say.

She said, "Fancy meeting you here."

"Fancy meeting you," said the Saint. "Did you get bored with your book?"

"I finished it, so I thought I'd get some exercise. But the pro has been all booked up for *hours.*"

It was as if all of them had the same question on their lips, but only the Saint could handle his voice easily enough to say, quite lazily, "Hours?"

"Well, it must have been two hours or more. Anyway, I asked for a lesson as soon as I got here, and he was all booked up. He said he'd fit me in if anybody cancelled, but I've been waiting around for ages and nobody's given me a chance . . ."

A part of the Saint's mind felt quite detached and independent of him, like an adding machine clicking over in a different room. The machine tapped out: she should have known that the pro would be booked up. And of course he'd say that he'd be glad to fit her in if he had a cancellation. And the odds are about eight to one that he wouldn't have a cancellation. So she could make him and several other people believe that she'd been waiting all the time. She could always find a chance to slip out of the entrance when there was no one in the office for a moment—she might even arrange to clear the way without much difficulty. She only had to get out. Coming back, she could say she just went to get something from her car. No one would think about it. And if there had been a cancellation, and the pro had been looking for her—well, she'd been in the johnny, or the showers, or at the bottom of the pool. He just hadn't found her. She'd been there all the time. A very passable casual alibi, with only a trivial percentage of risk.

But she isn't dressed to have done what must have been done.

She could have changed.

She couldn't have done it anyway.

Why not? She looks athletic. There are good muscles under that soft golden skin. She might have been sniping revenooers in the mountains of Kentucky since she was five years old, for all you know. What makes you so sure what she could do and couldn't do?

Well, what were Angelo and his pal, and Louis the Italian chef, doing at the same time? You can't rule them out.

Any good reader would rule them out. The mysterious murderer just doesn't turn out to be the cook or the butler any more. That was worked to death twenty years ago.

So of course no cook or butler in real life would ever dream of murdering anyone anymore, because they'd know it was just too corny.

"What's the matter with you all?" Lissa asked. "Wasn't the ride any good?"

"It was fine," said the Saint. "Except when your last night's boyfriend started shooting at Freddie."

Then they all began to talk at once.

It was Freddie, of course, who finally got the floor . . . He did it principally by saying the same things louder and oftener than anyone else. When the competition had been crushed he told the story again, challenging different people to substantiate his statements one by one. He was thus able to leave a definite impression that he had been walking up the canyon when somebody shot at him.

Simon signalled a waiter for another round of drinks and put himself into a self-preservative trance until the peak of the verbal flood had passed. He wondered whether he should ask Freddie for another thousand dollars. He felt that he was definitely earning his salary as he went along.

". . . Then that proves it must be one of the servants," Lissa said. "So if we can find out which of them went out this afternoon—"

"Why does it prove that?" Simon inquired.

"Well, it couldn't have been Ginny, because she was talking to you. It couldn't have been me—"

"Couldn't it?"

She looked at him blankly. But her brain worked. He could almost see it. She might have been reading everything that had been traced through his mind, a few minutes ago, line by line.

"It couldn't have been me," Esther insisted plaintively. "I didn't have a stitch on. Where could I have hidden a gun?"

Ginny gazed at her speculatively.

"It'll be interesting to see how the servants can account for their time," Simon said hastily. "But I'm not going to get optimistic too quickly. I don't think anything about this business is very dumb and straightforward. It's quite the opposite. Somebody is being so frantically cunning that he must be practically tying himself—or herself—in a knot. So if it is one of the servants, I bet he has an alibi too."

"I still think you ought to tell the police," Ginny said.

The drinks arrived. Simon lighted a cigarette and waited until the waiter had gone away again.

"What for?" he asked. "There was a guy in Lissa's room last night. Nobody saw him. He didn't leave any muddy footprints or any of that stuff. He used one of our own kitchen knives. If there ever were any fingerprints on it, they've been ruined. So—nothing . . . This afternoon somebody shot at Freddie. Nobody saw him. He didn't leave his gun, and nobody could ever find the bullet. So nothing again. What are the police going to do? They aren't magicians . . . However, that's up to you, Freddie."

"They could ask people questions," Esther said hopefully.

"So can we. We've been asking each other questions all the time. If anybody's lying, they aren't going to stop lying just because a guy with a badge is listening. What are they going to do—torture everybody and see what they get?"

"They'd put a man on guard, or something," said Ginny.

"So what? Our friend has waited quite a while already. I'm sure he could wait some more. He could wait longer than any police department is going to detail a private cop to nursemaid Freddie. So the scare blows over, and everybody settles down, and sometime later, maybe somewhere else, Freddie gets it. Well, personally I'd rather take our chance now while we're all warmed up."

"That's right," Freddie gave his verdict. "If we scare whoever it is off with the police, they'll only come back another time when we aren't watching for them. I'd rather let them get on with it while we're ready for them."

He looked rather proud of himself for having produced this penetrating reasoning all on his own.

And then his mind appeared to wander, and his eyes changed their focus.

"Hey," he said in an awed voice. "Look at that, will you?" They looked, as he pointed. "The babe down by the pool. In the sarong effect. Boy, is that a chassis! Look at her!"

She was, Simon admitted, something to look at. The three girls with them seemed to admit the same thing by their rather strained and intent silence. Simon could feel an almost tangible heaviness thicken into the air.

Then Ginny sighed, as if relief had reached her rather late.

"A blonde," she said. "Well, Lissa, it's nice to have known you."

Freddie didn't even seem to hear it. He picked up his glass, still staring raptly at the vision. He put the glass to his lips.

It barely touched, and he stiffened. He took it away and stared at it frozenly. Then he pushed it across the table towards the Saint.

"Smell that," he said.

Simon put it to his nostrils. The hackneyed odor of bitter almonds was as strong and unmistakable as any mystery-story fan could have desired.

"It doesn't smell like prussic acid," he said, with commendable mildness. He put the glass down and drew on his cigarette again, regarding the exhibit moodily. He was quite sure now that he was going to collect his day's wages without much more delay. And probably the next day's pay in advance, as well. At that, he thought that the job was poorly paid for what it was. He could see nothing in it at all to make him happy. But being a philosopher, he had to cast around for one little ray of sunshine. Being persistent, he found it. "So anyway," he said, "at least we don't have to bother about the servants anymore."

7

It was a pretty slender consolation, he reflected, even after they had returned to the house and he had perfunctorily questioned the servants, only to have them jointly and severally corroborate each other's statements that none of them had left the place that afternoon.

After which, they had all firmly but respectfully announced that they were not used to being under suspicion, that they did not feel comfortable in a household where people were frequently getting stabbed at, shot at, and poisoned at; that in any case they would prefer a less exacting job with more regular hours; that they had already packed their bags; and that they would like to catch the evening bus back to Los Angeles, if Mr Pellman would kindly pay them up to date.

Freddie had obliged them with a good deal of nonchalance, being apparently not unaccustomed to the transience of domestic help.

After which the Saint went to his room, stripped off his riding clothes, took a shower, wrapped himself in a bath robe, and lay down on the bed with a cigarette to contemplate the extreme sterility of the whole problem.

"This ought to learn you," he told himself, "to just say No when you don't want to do anything, instead of making smart cracks about a thousand dollars a day."

The servants weren't ruled out, of course. There could be more than one person involved, taking turns to do things so that each would have an alibi in turn.

But one of the girls had to be involved. Only one of them could have poisoned Freddie's drink at the Tennis Club. And any one of them could have done it. The table had been small enough, and everybody's attention had been very potently concentrated on the sarong siren. A bottle small enough to be completely hidden in the hand, tipped over his glass in a casual gesture—and the trick was done.

But why do it then, when the range of possible suspects was so sharply limited?

Why do any of the other things that had happened?

He was still mired in the exasperating paradoxes of partial sense, which was so many times worse than utter nonsense. Utter nonsense was like a code: there was a key to be found somewhere which would make it clear and coherent in an instant, and there was only one exact key that would do it. You knew that you had it or you hadn't. The trouble with partial sense was that while you were straightening out the twisted parts you never knew whether you were distorting the straight ones . . .

And somewhere beyond that point he heard the handle of his door turning, very softly.

His hand slid into the pocket of his robe where his gun was, but that was the only move he made. He lay perfectly still and relaxed, breathing at the shallow even rate of a sleeper, his eyes closed to all but a slit through which he could watch the door as it opened. Esther came in.

She stood in the doorway hesitantly for a few seconds, looking at him, and the light behind her showed every line of her breath-taking body through the white crepe negligée she was wearing. Then she closed the door softly behind her and came a little closer. He could see both her hands, and they were empty. He opened his eyes. "Hullo," she said.

"Hullo." He stretched himself a little.

"I hope I didn't wake you up."

"I was just dozing."

"I ran out of cigarettes," she said, "and I wondered if you had one."

"I think so."

It was terrific dialogue.

He reached over to the bedside table, and offered her the package that lay there. She came up beside him to take it. Without rising, he struck a match. She sat down beside him to get the light. The negligée was cut down to her waist in front, and it opened more when she leaned forward to the flame.

"Thanks." She blew out a deep inhalation of smoke. She could have made an exit with that, but she didn't. She studied him with her dark dreamy eyes and said, "I suppose you were thinking."

"A bit."

"Have you any ideas yet?"

"Lots of them. Too many."

"Why too many?"

"They contradict each other. Which means I'm not getting anywhere."

"So you still don't know who's doing all these things?"

"No."

"But you know it isn't any of us."

"No, I don't."

"Why do you keep saying that? Ginny was with you all the time this afternoon, and I couldn't have had a gun on me, and Lissa couldn't have followed us and been at the Tennis Club too."

"Therefore there must be a catch in it somewhere, and that's what I'm trying to find."

"I'm afraid I'm not very clever," Esther confessed.

He didn't argue with her.

She said at last, "Do you think I did it?"

"I've been trying very conscientiously to figure out how you could have."

"But I haven't done anything."

"Everybody else has said that too."

She gazed at him steadily, and her lovely warm mouth richened with pouting.

"I don't think you really like me, Simon."

"I adore you," he said politely.

"No, you don't. I've tried to get on with you. Haven't I?"

"You certainly have."

"I'm not awfully clever, but I try to be nice. Really. I'm not a cat like Ginny, or all brainy and snooty like Lissa. I haven't any background, and I know it. I've had a hell of a life. If I told you about it, you'd be amazed."

"Would I? I love being amazed."

"There you go again. You see?"

"I'm sorry. I shouldn't kid you."

"Oh, it's all right. I haven't got much to be serious about. I've got a pretty face and a beautiful body. I know I've got a beautiful body. So I just have to use that."

"And you use it very nicely, too."

"You're still making fun of me. But it's about all I've got, so I have to use it. Why shouldn't I?"

"God knows," said the Saint. "I didn't say you shouldn't." She studied him again for a while.

"You've got a beautiful body, too. All lean and muscular. But you've got brains as well. I'm sorry. I just like you an awful lot."

"Thank you," he said quietly.

She smoked her cigarette for a few moments.

He lighted a cigarette himself. He felt uncomfortable and at a loss. As she sat there, and with everything else in the world put aside, she was something that no man with a proper supply of hormones could have been cold to. But everything else in the world couldn't be put aside quite like that . . .

"You know," she said, "this is a hell of a life."

"It must be," he agreed.

"I've been watching it. I can think a little bit. You saw what happened this afternoon. I mean—"

"The blonde at the Tennis Club?"

"Yes . . . Well, it just happened that she was a blonde. She could just as well have been a brunette."

"And then—Esther starts packing."

"That's what it amounts to."

"But it's been fun while it lasted, and maybe you take something with you."

"Oh, yes. But that isn't everything. Not the way I mean. I mean . . ."

"What do you mean?"

She fiddled with a seam in her negligée for a long time.

"I mean . . . I know you aren't an angel, but you're not just like Freddie. I think you'd always be sincere with people. You're sort of different, somehow. I know I haven't got anything much, except being beautiful, but—that's something, isn't it? And I do really like you so much. I'd . . . I'd do anything . . . If I could only stay with you and have you like me a little."

She was very beautiful, too beautiful, and her eyes were big and aching and afraid.

Simon stared at the opposite wall. He would have given his day's thousand dollars to be anywhere the hell out of there.

He didn't have to.

Freddie Pellman's hysterical yell sheared suddenly through the silent house with an electrifying urgency that brought the Saint out of bed and up on to his feet as if he had been snatched up on wires. His instinctive movement seemed to coincide exactly with the dull slam of a muffled shot that gave more horror to the moment. He leapt towards the communicating door, and remembered as he reached it that while he had meant to get it unlocked that morning the episode of the obliterated fingerprints had put it out of his mind. Simultaneously, as he turned to the outer door, he realised that the sound of a door slamming could have been exactly the same, and he cursed his own unguardedness as he catapulted out on to the screened verandah.

One glance up and down was enough to show that there was no other person in sight, and he made that survey without even a check in his winged dash to Freddie's room.

His automatic was out in his hand when he flung the door open, to look across the room at Freddie Pellman, in black trousers and unbuttoned soft dress shirt, stretched out on the davenport, staring with a hideous grimace of terror at the rattlesnake that was coiled on his legs, its flat triangular head drawn back and poised to strike.

Behind him, the Saint heard Esther stifle a faint scream, and then the detonation of his gun blotted out every other sound.

As if it had been photographed in slow motion, Simon saw the snake's shattered head splatter away from its body, while the rest of it kicked and whipped away in a series of reflex convulsions that spilled it still writhing spasmodically on to the floor.

Freddie pulled himself shakily up to his feet.

"Good God," he said, and repeated it. "Good God—and it was real! Another second, and it'd have had me!"

"What happened?" Esther was asking shrilly.

"I don't know. I was starting to get dressed—you see?—I'd got my pants and shirt on, and I sat down and had a drink, and I must have fallen asleep. And then that thing landed on my lap!"

Simon dropped the gun back into his pocket.

"Landed?" he said.

"Yes—just as if somebody had thrown it. Somebody must have thrown it. I felt it hit. That was what woke me up. I saw what it was, and of course I let out a yell, and then the door slammed, and I looked round too late to see who it was. But I didn't care who it was, then. All I could see was that Goddamn snake leering at me. I almost thought I was seeing things again. But I knew I couldn't be. I wouldn't have felt it like that. I was just taking a nap, and somebody came in and threw it on top of me!"

"How long ago was this?"

"Just now! You don't think I lay there for an hour necking with a snake, do you? As soon as it fell on me I woke up, and as soon as I woke up I saw it, and of course I let out a yell at once. You heard me yell, didn't you, Esther? And right after that the door banged. Did you hear that?"

"Yes, I heard it," said the Saint.

But he was thinking of something else. And for that once at least, even though she had admitted that she was not so bright, he knew that Esther was all the way there with him. He could feel her mind there with him, even without turning to find her eyes fastened on his face, even before she spoke.

"But that *proves* it, Simon! You must see that, don't you? I couldn't possibly have done it, could I?"

"Why, where were you?" Freddie demanded.

She drew herself up defiantly and faced him.

"I was in Simon's room."

Freddie stood hunched and stiff and staring at them. And yet the Saint realised that it wasn't any positive crystallising of expression that made him look ugly. It was actually the reverse. His puffy face was simply blank and relaxed. And on that sludgy foundation, the crinkles of unremitting feverish bonhomie, the lines and bunchings of laborious domineering enthusiasm, drained of their vital nervous activation, were left like a mass of soft sloppy scars in which the whole synopsis of his life was hieroglyphed.

"What is it now?" Lissa's voice asked abruptly.

It was a voice that set out to be sharp and matter-of-fact, and failed by an infinitesimal quantity that only such ceaselessly critical ears as the Saint's would catch.

She stood in the doorway, with Ginny a little behind her.

Freddie looked up at her sidelong from under his lowered brows.

"Go away," he said coldly. "Get out."

And then, almost without a pause or a transition, that short-lived quality in his voice was only an uncertain memory.

"Run along," he said. "Run along and finish dressing. Simon and I want to have a little talk. Nothing's the matter. We just had a little scare, but it's all taken care of. I'll tell you presently. Now be nice children and go away and don't make a fuss. You, too, Esther."

Reluctantly, hesitantly, his harem melted away.

Simon strolled leisurely across to a side table and lighted himself a cigarette as Freddie closed the door. He genuinely wasn't perturbed, and he couldn't look as if he was.

"Well," Freddie said finally, "how does it look now?"

His voice was surprisingly negative, and the Saint had to make a lightning adjustment to respond to it.

He said, "It makes you look like quite a bad risk. So do you mind if I collect for today and tomorrow? Two Gs, Freddie. It'd be sort of comforting."

Freddie went to the dressing-table, peeled a couple of bills out of a litter of green paper and small change, and came back with them. Simon glanced at them with satisfaction. They had the right number of zeros after the 1.

"I don't blame you," said Freddie. "If that snake had bitten me—"

"You wouldn't have died," said the Saint calmly. "Unless you've got a very bad heart, or something like that. That's the silly part of it. There are doctors within phone call, there's sure to be plenty of serum in town, and there's a guy like me on the premises who's bound to know the first aid. You'd have been rather sick, but you'd have lived through it. So why should the murderer go through an awkward routine with a snake when he had you cold and could've shot you or slit your throat and made sure of it? . . . This whole plot has been full of silly things, and they're only just starting to add up and make sense."

"They are?"

"Yes, I think so."

"I wish I could see it."

Simon sat on the arm of a chair and thought for a minute, blowing smoke-rings.

"Maybe I can make you see it," he said.

"Go ahead."

"Our suspects were limited to six people the first night, when we proved it was someone in the house. Now, through various events, every one of them has an alibi. That would make you think of a partnership. But none of the servants could have poisoned your drink this afternoon, and it wasn't done by the waiter or the bartender—they've both been at the club for years, and you could bet your shirt on them. Therefore somebody at the table must have been at least part of the partnership, or the whole works if there never was a partnership at all. But everyone at the table has still been alibied, somewhere in the story."

Freddie's brow was creased with the strain of following the argument.

"Suppose two of the girls were in partnership?"

"I thought of that. It's possible, but absolutely not probable. I doubt very much whether any two women could collaborate on a proposition like this, but I'm damned sure that no two of these girls could."

"Then where does that get you?"

"We have to look at the alibis again. And one of them has to be a phony."

The corrugations deepened on Freddie's forehead. Simon watched him silently. It was like watching wheels go round. And then a strange expression came into Freddie's face. He looked at the Saint with wide eyes.

"My God!" he said. "You mean—Lissa . . ."

Simon didn't move.

"Yes," Freddie muttered. "Lissa. Ginny's got a perfect alibi. She couldn't have shot at me. You were with her yourself. Esther might have done it if she'd hidden a gun there before. But she was in your room when somebody threw that snake at me. She couldn't have faked that. And the servants have all gone . . . The only alibi Lissa has got is that she was the first one to be attacked. But we've only got her word for it. She could have staged that so easily." His face was flushed with the excitement that was starting to obstruct his voice. "And all that criminology of hers . . . of course . . . she's the one who's always reading these mysteries—she'd think of melodramatic stuff like that snake— she'd have the sort of mind . . ."

"I owe you an apology, Freddie," said the Saint, with the utmost candor. "I didn't think you had all that brain."

8

He was alone in the house. Freddie Pellman had taken the girls off to the Coral Room for dinner, and Simon's stall was that he had to wait for a long-distance phone call. He would join them as soon as the call had come through.

"You'll have the place to yourself," Freddie had said when he suggested the arrangement, still glowing from his recent accolade. "You can search all you want. You're bound to find *something*. And then we'll have her."

Simon finished glancing through a copy of *Life*, and strolled out on the front terrace. Everything on the hillside was very still. He lighted a cigarette, and gazed out over the thin spread of sparkling lights that was Palm Springs at night. Down below, on the road that led east from the foot of the drive, a rapidly dwindling speck of red might have been the tail light of Freddie's car.

The Saint went back into the living-room after a little while and poured himself a long lasting drink of Peter Dawson. He carried it with him as he worked methodically through Esther's and Ginny's rooms.

He wasn't expecting to find anything in either of them, and he didn't. But it was a gesture that he felt should be made.

So after that he came to Lissa's room.

He worked unhurriedly through the closet and the chest of drawers, finding nothing but the articles of clothing and personal trinkets that he had found in the other rooms. After that he sat down at the dresser. The center drawer contained only the laboratory of creams, lotions, powders, paints, and perfumes without which even a modern goddess believes that she has shed her divinity. The top right-hand drawer contained an assortment of handkerchiefs, scarves, ribbons, clips, and pins. It was in the next drawer down that he found what he had been waiting to find.

It was quite a simple discovery, lying under a soft pink froth of miscellaneous underwear. It consisted of a .32 automatic pistol, a small blue pharmacist's bottle labeled "*Prussic Acid*—POISON," and an old issue of *Life*. He didn't really need to open the magazine to know what there would be inside, but he did it. He found the mutilated page, and knew from the other pictures in the layout that the picture which had headed the letter that Freddie had shown him at their first meeting would fit exactly into the space that had been scissored out of the copy in front of him.

He laid the evidence out on the dresser top and considered it while he kindled another cigarette.

Probably any other man would have felt that the search ended there, but the Saint was not any other man. And the strange clairvoyant conviction grew in his mind that that was where the search really began.

He went on with it more quickly, with even more assurance, although he had less idea than before what he was looking for. He only had that intuitive certainty that there should be something— something that would tie the last loose ends of the tangle together and make complete sense of it. And he did find it, after quite a short while.

LESLIE CHARTERIS

It was only a shabby envelope tucked into the back of a folding photo frame that contained a nicely glamorised portrait of Freddie. Inside the envelope were a savings bank pass book that showed a total of nearly five thousand dollars, and a folded slip of paper. It was when he unfolded the slip of paper that he knew that the search was actually over and all the questions answered, for he had in his hands a certificate of marriage issued in Yuma ten months before . . .

"Are you having fun?" Lissa asked.

She had been as quiet as a cat, for he hadn't heard her come in, and she was right behind him. And yet he wasn't surprised. His mind was filling with a great calm and quietness as all the conflict of contradictions settled down and he knew that the last act had been reached.

He turned quite slowly, and even the small shining gun in her hand, aimed squarely at his chest, didn't surprise or disturb him.

"How did you know?" he drawled.

"I'm not so dumb. I should have seen it before I went out if I'd been really smart."

"You should." He felt very detached and unrealistically balanced. "How did you get back, by the way?"

"I just took the car."

"I see."

He turned and stood up to face her, being careful not to make any abrupt movement, and keeping his hands raised a little, but she still backed away a quick step.

"Don't come any closer," she said sharply.

He was just over an arm's length from her then. He measured it accurately with his eye. And he was still utterly cool and removed from it all. The new stress that was building up in him was different from anything before. He knew now, beyond speculation, that murder was only a few seconds away, and it was one murder that he particularly

164

wanted to prevent. But every one of his senses and reflexes would have to be sharper and surer than they had ever been before to see it coming and to forestall it . . . Every nerve in his body felt like a violin string that had been tuned to within an eyelash weight of breaking—

And when it came, the warning was a sound so slight that at any other time he might never have heard it—so faint and indeterminate that he was never absolutely sure what it actually was, if it was the rustle of a sleeve or a mere slither of skin against metal or nothing but an unconsciously tightened breath.

It was enough that he heard it, and that it exploded him into action too fast for the eye to follow—too fast even for his own deliberate mental processes to trace. But in one fantastic flow of movement it seemed that his left hand plunged at the gun that Lissa was holding, twisted it aside as it went off, and wrenched it out of her hand and threw her wide and stumbling while another shot from elsewhere chimed into the tight pile-up of sound effects; while at the same time, quite independently, his right hand leapt to his armpit holster in a lightning draw that brought his own gun out to bark a deeper note that practically merged with the other two . . . And that was just about all there was to it.

The Saint clipped his own gun back in its holster, and dropped Lissa's automatic into his side pocket. It had all been so fast that he hadn't even had time to get a hair of his head disarranged.

"I'm afraid you don't have a very nice husband," he said.

He stepped to the communicating door and dragged the drooping figure of Freddie Pellman the rest of the way into the room and pushed it into a chair.

9

"He'll live, if you want him," said the Saint casually. "I only broke his arm."

He picked up the revolver that Freddie had dropped, spilled the shells out, and laid it with the other exhibits on the dresser while Freddie clutched at his reddening sleeve and whimpered. It seemed as if the whole thing took so little time that Lissa was still recovering her balance when he turned and looked at her again.

"The only trouble was," he said, "that you married him too soon. Or didn't you know about the will then?"

She stared at him, white-faced, without speaking.

"Was he drunk when you did it?" Simon asked.

After a while she said, "Yes."

"One of those parties?"

"Yes. We were both pretty high. But I didn't know he was that high."

"Of course not. And you didn't realise that he wouldn't mind framing you into a coffin to keep his gay playboy integrity."

She looked at the collection of exhibits on her dresser, at Freddie, and at the Saint. She didn't seem to be able to get everything coordinated quickly. Simon himself showed her the marriage certificate again.

"This is what I wasn't supposed to find," he said. "In fact I don't think Freddie even imagined you'd have it around. But it made quite a difference. How much were you going to shake him down for, Lissa?"

"I only asked him for two hundred thousand," she said. "I'd never have said anything. I just didn't want to be like some of the others—thrown out on my ear to be a tramp for the rest of my life."

"But you wanted too much," said the Saint. "Or he just didn't trust you, and he thought you'd always be coming back for more. Anyhow, he figured this would be a better way to pay off."

His cigarette hadn't even gone out. He picked it up and brightened it in a long peaceful draw that expressed all the final settling down of his mind.

"The mistake that all of us made," he said, "was not figuring Freddie for a moderately clever guy. Because he was a bore, we figured he was moderately stupid. Which is a rather dangerous mistake. A bore isn't necessarily stupid. He doesn't necessarily overrate his own intelligence. He just underrates everyone else. That makes him tedious, but it doesn't make him dumb. Freddie isn't dumb. He just sounds dumb because he's talking down to how dumb he thinks the rest of us are. As a matter of fact, he's quite a lively lad. He put a lot of gray matter into this little scheme. As soon as he heard that I'd arrived in town, he had the inspiration that he'd been waiting for. And he didn't waste a day in getting it started. He wrote himself the famous threatening letter at once—it was quite a coincidence, of course, that there was that last Christmas party to hang it on, but if there hadn't been that he'd certainly have thought of something else almost as good. He only had to establish that he was being menaced, and get me into the house to protect him. Then he had to put you in the middle of the first situation, in a set-up that would look swell in the beginning but would get shakier and shakier as things went on. That wasn't difficult either."

The only sound when he paused was Freddie Pellman's heavy sobbing breathing.

"After that, he improvised. He only had to stage a series of incidents that would give everyone else in turn an absolutely ironclad alibi that would satisfy me. It wasn't hard to do—it was just a matter of being ready with a few props to take advantage of the opportunities that were bound to arise. Perhaps he was a bit lucky in having so many chances in such a short space of time, but I don't know. He couldn't go wrong anyway. Everything had to work in for him, once the primary idea was planted. Even an accident like Angelo picking up the knife was just a break for him—there weren't any fingerprints on it, of course, and it just helped the mystery a little . . . And this evening he was able to finish up in style with the snake routine. It wasn't exactly his fault that the routine fitted in just as well with another pattern that was gradually penetrating into my poor benighted brain. That's just one of the natural troubles with trying to create artificial mysteries—when you're too busy towing around a lot of red herrings, you don't realise that you may be getting a fishy smell on your own fingers . . . That was what Freddie did. He was being very clever about letting it work out that your alibi was the only flimsy one, but he forgot that when I had to start questioning alibis it might occur to me that there was one other person whose alibis were flimsier still. And that was him."

Simon drew on his cigarette again.

"Funnily enough, I was just leading up to telling him that when he made his first major mistake. You see, I had an idea what was going on, but I was going nuts trying to figure out why. There didn't seem to be any point to the whole performance, except as a terrific and ponderous practical joke. And I couldn't see Freddie with that sort of humor. So

I was just going to come out flatly and face him with it and see what happened. It's a shock technique that works pretty well sometimes. And then he took all the wind out of my sails by insisting on helping me to see how it all pointed to you. That's what I mean about him underrating other people's intelligence. He was just a little too anxious to make quite sure that I hadn't missed any of the points that I was supposed to get. But it had just the opposite effect, because I happened to know that your alibi must have been genuine. So then I knew that the whole plot didn't point to you—it was pointed at you. And when Freddie went a little further and helped me to think of the idea of staying behind tonight and searching your room, I began to guess that the climax would be something like this. I suppose he got hold of you privately and told you he'd started to get suspicious of what I was up to—maybe I was planning to plant some evidence and frame one of you?"

"Yes."

"So he suggested that the two of you sneak off and see if you could catch me at it?" She nodded.

"Then," said the Saint, "you peeked in through the window and saw me with the exhibits on the dressing-table, and he said 'What did I tell you?' . . . And then he said something like, 'Let's really get the goods on him now. You take this gun and walk in on him and keep him talking. If he thinks you're alone he'll probably say enough to hang himself. I'll be listening, and I'll be a witness to everything he says.' Something like that?"

"Something like that," she said huskily.

"And then the stage was all set. He only had to wait a minute or two, and shoot you. I was supposed to have suspected you already. I'd found a lot of incriminating evidence in your room. And then you'd walked in on me with a gun . . . While of course his story would have been that he was suspicious when you sneaked off, that he followed you home, and found you holding me up, and you were just about to give me the works when he popped his pistol and saved my life. Everyone would have said that 'of course' you must have been Smoke Johnny's moll at some time, and nobody would ever have been likely to find the record of that marriage in Yuma unless they were looking for it—and why should they look for it? So you were out of the way, and he was in the clear, and I'd personally be his best, solid, hundred-per-cent witness that it was justifiable homicide. It would have made one of the neatest jobs that I ever heard of—if it had worked. Only it didn't work. Because just as I knew you had a good alibi all the time, I knew that all this junk in your drawer had been planted there, and so I knew that I still had something else to look for—the real motive for all these things that were going on. Maybe I was lucky to find it so quickly. But even so, from the moment when you walked in, something exciting was waiting to happen . . . Well, it all worked out all right—or don't you think so, Freddie?"

"You've got to get me a doctor," Freddie said hoarsely.

"Do I have all the right answers?" Simon asked relentlessly.

Freddie Pellman moaned and clutched his arm tighter and raised a wild haggard face.

"You've got to get me a doctor," he pleaded in a rising shout. "Get me a doctor!"

'Tell us first," insisted the Saint soothingly. "Do we know all the answers?"

Pellman tossed his head, and suddenly everything seemed to disintegrate inside him.

"Yes!" he almost screamed. "Yes, damn you! I was going to fix that little bitch. I'll do it again if I ever have the chance. And you, too! . . . Now get me a doctor. Get me a doctor, d'you hear? D'you want me to bleed to death?"

The Saint drew a long deep breath, and put out the stub of his cigarette. He took a pack from his pocket and lighted another. And with that symbolic action he had put one more episode behind him, and the life of adventure went on.

"I don't really know," he said carelessly. "I don't think there'd be any great injustice done if we let you die. Or we might keep you alive and continue with the shakedown. It's really up to Lissa."

He glanced at the girl again curiously.

She was staring at Freddie in a way that Simon hoped no woman would ever look at him, and she seemed to have to make an effort to bring herself back to the immediate present. And even then she seemed to be a little behind.

She said, "I just don't get one thing. How did you know all that stuff had been planted in my drawer? And why were you so sure that my flimsy alibi was good?"

He smiled.

"That was the easiest thing of all. Aren't you the detective-story fan? You might have gotten good ideas from some of your mysteries, but you could hardly have picked up such bad ones. At least you'd know better than to keep a lot of unnecessary incriminating evidence tucked away where anyone with a little spare time could find it. And you'd never have had the nerve to pull an alibi like that first attack on yourself if it was a phony, because you'd have known that anyone else who'd ever read a mystery too would have spotted it for a phony all the time. About the only thing wrong with Freddie is that he had bright ideas, but he didn't read the right books."

"For Christ's sake," Freddie implored shrilly, "aren't you going to get me a doctor?"

"What would they do in a Saint story?" Lissa asked.

Simon Templar sighed.

"I imagine they'd let him call his own doctor, and tell the old story about how he was cleaning a gun and he didn't know it was loaded. And I suppose we'd go back to the Coral Room and look for Ginny and Esther, because they must be getting hungry, and I know I still am. And I expect Freddie would still pay off in the end, if we all helped him to build up a good story . . ."

Lissa tucked her arm under his.

"But what are the rest of us going to do tonight?"

"The Hays Office angle on that bothers the hell out of me," said the Saint.

HOLLYWOOD

INTRODUCTION

It is not remarkable that a writer of such catholic scope as myself should have finally succumbed to the temptation of offering his own fictional slant on Hollywood, but it is almost phenomenal that he should have waited so long to do it.

Such records as I have indicate that this story was written some time in 1941, or at least eight years after I first displayed my open mouth in a booth at a Brown Derby.

It would be nice to say that this unprecedented pause for station identification was solely due to an impregnable integrity which would not permit me to go off on any subject at half cock.

Unfortunately, that same impregnable integrity forbids me to make any such claim. The plain truth of the matter is that for eight years I resisted the temptation, clinging fanatically to some ethereal hope that I might go to my grave with that one esoteric epitaph: "At least he never wrote a line about Hollywood." Having failed to die during that unconscionable time, this harmless fancy seemed to become more tired with every passing year. It finally reversed itself so that it seemed almost mandatory for me to write something about Hollywood, however half-baked, before I appeared actually eccentric.

This then is my superficial version of Hollywood, a town about which I think I know much less today than I thought I knew in 1933.

—Leslie Charteris (1946)

1

It was not to be expected that Simon Templar could have stayed in Hollywood in an ordinary way. Nothing that ever happened to him was really ordinary—it was as if from the beginning he had had some kind of fourth-dimensional magnetism that attracted adventure and strange happenings, or else it may have been because nothing to him was entirely commonplace or unworthy of expectant curiosity, that he had a gift of uncovering adventure where duller people would have passed it by without ever knowing that it had been within reach. But as the saga of perilous, light-hearted buccaneering lengthened behind him past inevitable milestones of newspaper headlines, it became even more inescapable that adventure would never let him alone, for unordinary people went out of their way to drag him into their unordinary affairs. In the most platitudinous and yet exciting and fateful way, one thing simply led to another, and he was riding a tide that only slackened enough to let him catch his breath before it was off on another irresistible lunge.

It was like that in Hollywood, where he was eating his first breakfast of that visit when the telephone rang in his apartment at the Château

Marmont, which he had chosen precisely because he thought that he might attract less attention there than he would have at one of the large fashionable hotels with a publicity agent hungrily scrutinising every guest for possible copy.

"Mr Simon Templar?" said a girl's voice.

It was a businesslike and efficient voice, but it had a nice quality of sound, a freshness and a natural feeling of friendliness that made him feel interested in talking to it some more. So he admitted hopefully that he was Simon Templar.

"Just a moment," she said. "Mr Ufferlitz is calling."

Simon was not quite sure whether he caught the name right, but it didn't sound like any name among his acquaintances. In any case, he had arrived late the night before, and hadn't yet told anyone he knew that he was in town. Of course, it was possible that some shining light of the local Police Department was already leaping on to his trail, afire with notions of importance and glory—that was an almost monotonous habit of shining lights of local Police Departments, even in much more out-of-the-way places, whenever Simon Templar paused in his travels, although none of them had ever achieved the importance and glory to which their zeal would have entitled them in a world less hidebound by the old-fashioned rules of evidence. But Simon also felt sure that no Police Department employed telephone girls with such friendly voices. It would have disrupted the whole system . . .

"Hullo, Mr Templar," said the telephone. "This is Byron Ufferlitz."

"Baron who?" Simon queried.

"Byron," said the new voice. "Byron Ufferlitz."

This voice was not fresh and provocative, although it was apparently trying to be friendly. It sounded as if it was rather overweight and wore a diamond ring and had a cigar in its mouth. It also appeared to think that its name should be recognised immediately and inspire awe in the hearer.

"Have we ever met?" Simon asked.

"Not yet," said the voice jovially. "But I want to put that right. Will you have lunch with me?"

There were times when Simon's directness left the Emily Post School of Social Niceties out of the cosmos.

"What for?" he inquired, with the utmost detachment.

"I'm going to give you a job."

'Thank you. What is it?"

"I'll tell you all about it at lunch."

"Did anyone tell you I was looking for a job?"

"Oh, I know all about you," said Mr Ufferlitz confidently. "Been watching you for a long time. That was a great thing you did in Arizona. And that funny business in Palm Springs—I read all about it. So I know what you cost. You asked Pellman for a thousand dollars a day, didn't you? Well, I'll pay you the same. Only I don't want a bodyguard."

"How do you know I can do what you want?"

"Look," said Mr Ufferlitz, "you're Simon Templar, aren't you?"

"Yes."

"You're the fellow they call the Saint."

Something like the faintest whisper of distant music seemed to touch the Saint's eardrums with no more substance than the slipstream of a passing butterfly.

"Well," he admitted cautiously, "I've heard the name."

"You're what they call the Robin Hood of modern crime. You're the greatest crook that ever lived, and you've put more crooks away than all the detectives who keep trying to hang something on you. You're always on the side of the guy who's up against it, and you're always busting up some graft or dirty work, and all the gals are nuts about you, and you can jump through windows like Doug Fairbanks used to and knock guys cold like Joe Louis and shoot like Annie Oakley and figure things out like Sherlock Holmes and . . . and—"

"Catch airplanes in my teeth like Superman?" Simon suggested.

"No kidding," said Mr Ufferlitz. "You're the greatest proposition that ever hit this town. I've got all the angles worked out. Tell you all about it at lunch. Let's say the Vine Street Derby at one o'clock. Okay?"

"Okay," said the Saint tolerantly.

It was exactly why and because he was Simon Templar, the Saint, that things always happened to him. The last few sentences of Mr Ufferlitz had given him a sudden and fairly clear idea of what sort of proposition Mr Ufferlitz would consider "great," and what kind of angles Mr Ufferlitz would have worked out—even before he turned to the telephone directory and found an entry under Ufferlitz Productions, Inc. Anyway, he had nothing else to do and no other plans for lunch, and Mr Ufferlitz could always provide comic relief.

He was right about that, but he also had no inkling whatever of a number of quite unfunny things that were destined to cross his path as a direct result of his amused acceptance of that invitation.

During the morning he called a friend of his, an agent, and after they had exchanged a suitable amount of nonsense he inquired further about Mr Ufferlitz.

"Byron Ufferlitz?" repeated Dick Halliday. "He's quite an up-and-coming producer these days. A sort of cross between Sammy Click and Al Capone. I don't suppose you'd know about it, but he bobbed up only a little over a year ago with some wildcat Studio Employees Union that he'd invented, and somehow he got so many studio employees to join it and made such a nuisance of himself with a few well-timed strikes that finally they had to buy him off."

"By suddenly discovering that he was a production genius?"

"Something like that. The Government tried to get him for extortion, but the witnesses called it off, and he was supposed to be wanted in New Orleans on some old charge of sticking up a bank, but nothing came of that either. Now he's quite the white-haired boy. He brought in a picture for about fifty thousand dollars, and surprisingly enough it wasn't bad. What does he want you to do—sell him your life story or bump somebody off?"

"I'm going to find out," said the Saint, and went to his appointment with even a shade more optimism.

The Brown Derby on Vine Street—smarter offspring of the once famous hat-shaped edifice on Wilshire Boulevard—was unchanged since he had last been there. Even the customers looked exactly the same—the same identifiable people, even with different names and faces, labeled as plainly as if they had worn badges. The actors and actresses, important and unimportant. The bunch of executives. The writers and directors. The agent with the two sides of a possible deal. The radio clan. The film colony surgeon and the film colony attorney. The humdrum business men and the visiting firemen. The unmistakable tourists, working off this item of their itinerary, trying hard to look like unimpressionable natives but betraying themselves by the greedy wandering of their eyes.

In this clear-cut patchwork of types the Saint acquired a puzzling neutrality. He stood scanning the room with interest, but he was quite positively not a tourist. Yet the tourists and the non-tourists stared at him alike, as if he were someone they should have known and were trying to place. With the casual elegance of his clothes and his dark handsome face he could have been some kind of romantic actor, only that his good looks didn't seem to have any of the weaknesses of a romantic actor—they had a sinewy recklessness of fundamental structure that belonged more to the character that a romantic actor would try to play than to the character of the impersonator. But he was quite unactorishly unaware of attracting that sort of interest at all, and was satisfied when he caught the eye of a man who was waving frantically at him from a booth half-way down the room, who could only have been Mr Byron Ufferlitz.

For Mr Ufferlitz looked just like his voice. He was rather overweight, and he wore a diamond ring, and he had a cigar in his mouth. The rest of him fitted those features in with the picture that Simon had constructed from Dick Halliday's comments. He had thick shoulders and thick black hair, and his face had a quality of actual physical toughness that was totally different from the thin-lipped affectation of a tough guy behind a mahogany desk.

"Have a drink," said Mr Ufferlitz, who had already been passing the time with a highball.

"Cleopatra," said the Saint.

"What's that?" asked Ufferlitz, as the waiter repeated it and moved away.

"One of the best dry sherries."

It was as if Ufferlitz opened a filing cabinet in his mind, punched a card, and put it away. But he did it without the flicker of a muscle in his face, and sat back to make a cold-blooded inventory of the Saint's features.

"You're all right," he announced. "You're swell. I recognised you as soon as you came in. From your pictures, of course. But I couldn't tell from them whether they'd just caught you at a good angle."

"This is a great relief to me," Simon remarked mildly.

A flash bulb popped at close quarters. Simon looked up, blinking, and saw the photographer retreating with an ingratiating grin.

"That's just a beginning," explained Mr Ufferlitz complacently. "We'll get plenty more pictures later, of course. But there's no harm grabbing anything that comes along."

"Would you mind," asked the Saint, "telling me just what this is all about?"

"Your build-up. Of course I know you're a celebrity already, but a little extra publicity never hurt anyone. I've got the best press-agent in town working on you already. Want you to meet him this afternoon . . . We got you all fixed up for tonight, by the way."

"You have?" Simon said respectfully.

"Yep. It was in Louella Parsons this morning. I shot it in last night, soon as I knew you'd arrived. Didn't you see it?"

"I'm afraid I was too busy reading the subsidiary part of the paper. You know—the part where there's a war going on."

Mr Ufferlitz thumbed through a bulging wallet and extracted a clipping. It had a sentence ringed in red pencil.

. . . Simon Templar ("The Saint," of course) will be in town today, and the glamor girls have a new feud on. But his first date is April Quest, whom he will squire to Giro's tonight. They met in Yellowstone last summer . . .

"It's wonderful," said the Saint admiringly. "A whole new past opens behind me."

"You'll be crazy about her," said Mr Ufferlitz. "Face like a dream. Chassis like those girls in *Esquire*. And intelligent! She's been all through college and she reads books."

"Does she remember Yellowstone too?"

For the first time, a slight cloud passed over Mr Ufferlitz's open features.

"She'll cooperate. She's a real trouper. You gotta cooperate too. Hell, I'm paying you six G a week, ain't I?"

"Are you?" said the Saint interestedly. "I don't remember that we fixed it definitely. It might help if you told me what you wanted me to do."

"All I want you to do," said Ufferlitz expansively, "is be yourself."

"There's a catch in it," said the Saint. "I do that most of the time for free."

"Well, there's a difference . . ."

The revelation of the difference had to wait while they gave their lunch order. Then Mr Ufferlitz put his elbows on the table and leaned forward.

"This is the greatest idea there's ever been in pictures," he stated modestly. "They've done plenty of movies about modern heroes—Edison—Rockne—Sergeant York—all the rest of 'em. But there's always something phony about it to me. I can't look at Spencer Tracy and think he's Edison, because I know he's Spencer Tracy. I can't see Tyrone Power building the Panama Canal or the Pyramids or whatever it was. Now when the Duke of Windsor walked out of Buckingham Palace I had a great idea. Let him play himself in his own story. It was a natural. I wrote to Sam Goldwyn about it—I was in business in Chicago then—but he was too dumb to see it. Would ya believe that?"

"Amazing," said the Saint.

"But this is even better," said Mr Ufferlitz, cheering up. "You're plenty hot yourself, right now, and some ways you got more on the ball. Everything you've done was on your own. And you can still do it. Sergeant York couldn't play himself because he's an old man now, but you're just right. And are you photogenious? Hell, the fans'll go nuts about you!"

Simon Templar took a long mouthful of Cleopatra.

"Wait a minute," he said. "Do I get the idea that this earth-shaking idea of yours is a scheme to make a movie star out of me?"

"*Make* a star?" echoed Mr Ufferlitz indignantly. "You are a star! All I want you to do is help me out with one picture. We'll make it a sort of composite of your life, ending up with that Pellman business in Palm Springs. I got a coupla writers working on it already—they'll have a first draft for me tomorrow. You'll play yourself in your own biography. I had the idea all worked out for a fiction character—Orlando Flane was going to do it for me—but this is ten times hotter. We can easily fix up the story."

His face was bright with the autogenous energy of its own enthusiasm. And then, as if a switch had been flipped over, the theatrical lighting was gone. The professional illumination which he had picked up somewhere in his career went away from him, and there was only the heavy-boned face that had kicked an independent union together and made it stick.

"Of course," he said, "there are plenty of people who'd hate to see me make a hit with this idea. One or two of 'em would go a long ways to wreck it. That's why I couldn't try it with anyone but you. I guess you can take care of yourself. But if you're scared, we can call it off and you won't get hurt."

2

She was everything that her voice had promised. Beyond that, she had golden-brown hair and gray eyes with a sense of humor. She looked as if she could take care of herself without hurting anyone else. She had a slim figure in a navy blue sweater that brought her out in the right places. She was taller than he had expected, incidentally. Long legs and neat ankles.

Simon said, "By the way, what's your name?"

"Peggy Warden," she told him. "What now?"

"While the attorneys haggle over my epoch-making contract, you're supposed to introduce me to the writing talent."

"The third door on the left down the passage," she said. "Don't let them get your goat."

"My goat is in cold storage for the duration," said the Saint. "See you later."

He went to the third door down the passage and knocked on it. A voice like that of a hungry wolf bawled *"Yeow?"* The Saint accepted that as an invitation, and went in.

Two men sat around the single battered desk. Both of them had their feet on it. The desk looked as if it had learned to think nothing of that sort of treatment. The men had an air of proposing that the desk should like it, or else.

One of them was broad and stubby, with a down-turned mouth and hair turning gray. The other was taller and thinner, with gold-rimmed glasses and a face that looked freshly scrubbed, like the greeting of a Fuller Brush Man. They inspected the Saint critically while he closed the door behind him, and looked at each other as if their heads pivoted off the same master gear.

"I thought he'd have a machine-gun stuck down his pants leg," said the gray-haired one.

"They didn't put the chandelier back in time," countered the Fuller Brush Man, "or he could swing on it. Or am I thinking of somebody else?"

"Excuse me," said the Saint gravely. "I'm supposed to be taking an inventory of this circus. Are you the performing seals?"

They looked at each other again, grinned, and stood up to shake hands.

"I'm Vic Lazaroff," said the gray-haired man. "This is Bob Kendricks. Consider yourself one of us. Sit down and make yourself unhappy."

"How are you getting on with the epic?" Simon inquired.

"Your life story? Fine. Of course, we've had a lot of practice with it. It started off to be a costume piece about Dick Turpin. Then we had to make it fit a soldier of fortune in the International Brigade in Spain. That was when Orlando Flane was getting interested. Then we took it to South America when everyone was on the goodwill rampage. We worked in a lot of stuff that they threw out of one of the Thin Man pictures, too."

"Were you ever befriended by a Chinese laundryman when you were a starving orphan in Limehouse?" Kendricks asked.

"I'm afraid not," Simon confessed. "You see—"

"That's too bad; because it ties in with a terrific routine where you're flying for the Chinese Government and the Japs have captured one of the guerrilla chieftains and they're going to have a ceremonial execution, and you find out that this chieftain is the guy who once saved your life with chop suey, and you set out for practically certain death to try and save him. Flane thought it was swell."

"I think it's swell too," said the Saint soothingly. "I was only mentioning that it didn't happen."

"Look here," said Lazaroff suspiciously, "are you trying to set us right about your life?"

"We've got to have some dramatic license," explained Kendricks. "But we'll do right by you. You'll see. We'll give you the best life story any guy ever had."

"As Byron is always saying," insisted Lazaroff, "you gotta cooperate. Aren't you going to cooperate?"

Simon added his feet to the collection on the desk, and lighted a cigarette.

"Tell me more about the great Byron," he said.

Lazaroff ruffled his untidy gray locks.

"What, his life story? He changes it every time he tells it. Actually he's a retired racketeer. Well, not retired, but he's changed his racket. Now his strong-arm men don't walk in and say 'How about buyin' some protection, bud?' They say, 'How about lendin' us your yacht for a coupla days for some location shots?'—in the same tone of voice."

"Byron Ufferlitz is his real name, too," supplied Kendricks. "It's on his police record."

"It's on our checks every Saturday," said Lazaroff, "and the bank honors it. That's all we have to worry about."

"How do you get on with him?"

"I get on fine with anyone who gives me a check every Saturday. In this town, you have to, if you want to eat. He isn't any more ignorant than a lot of other producers we've worked for who didn't have police records. We rib him plenty, and he doesn't get too sore. Just now and again he gets a look in his eye as if he's just ready to say 'Okay, wise guy, howja like to get taken for a ride?' Then we lay off him for a bit. But we don't have to steal anything more illegal than ideas, so what the hell? At that, I'd rather work with him than Jack Groom."

"The trouble is," said Kendricks, "we don't have the choice. We have to work with both of 'em."

"Who's Jack Groom?" Simon asked.

"The genius who's going to condescend to direct this epic. Art with a capital 'F.' You'll meet him."

Simon did, a little later.

Mr Groom was tall and thin and stoop-shouldered. He had pale hollow cheeks and lank black hair that fell forward to meet his thick black brows. He had a rich deep voice that never seemed as if it could be produced by such a sepulchral creature.

He inspected Simon with complete detachment, and said, "Could you grow a moustache in ten days?"

"I should think so," said the Saint. "But what would I do with it? Is there a market for them?"

"You should have a moustache in this picture. And your hair should be slicked down more. It'll give you a smoother appearance."

"I used to slick it down once," said the Saint, "but I got tired of it. And I never have worn a moustache, except in character."

Mr Groom shook his head, and swept his forelock back with long tired fingers. It promptly fell down again.

"The Saint would wear a moustache," he stated impregnably. "I've got a feeling about it."

"You remember me?" said the Saint, with a slight floating sensation. "I'm the Saint."

"Yes," said Mr Groom patiently. "I visualise you with a moustache. Get one started right away, won't you? Thanks."

He waved a limp hand and drifted away, preoccupied with many responsibilities.

Eventually Simon found his way back to Byron Ufferlitz's outer office, where Peggy Warden looked up from a clatter of typewriting with her fresh friendly smile.

"Well," she said cheerfully, "did you meet everybody?"

"I don't know," said the Saint. "But if there are any more of them, I'll wait till tomorrow. I don't want to spoil the flavor by being gluttonous. The Wardrobe Department will probably want to check the cut of my jockstrap, and I expect the Prop Department will tell me what sort of gun I prefer."

"We'll find out about that as soon as we make the breakdowns."

"That's a cheering thought," Simon murmured. "I'll be the easiest breakdown you ever saw."

"Is there anything I could do to make you happy?"

"Yes. Tell me what you're doing tonight?"

"You're forgetting. You've got a date."

"Have I?"

"Miss Quest. You pick her up at her house at seven o'clock. Here's the address."

"What would Byron and I do without you?" Simon pocketed the typewritten slip. "Let's go out and get a drink now, anyway."

"I'm sorry," she said, laughing. "I punch a time clock. And Mr Ufferlitz mightn't like it if I just walked out . . . You'll come back, won't you? Mr Ufferlitz wanted to see you again before you left. I think he wants to tell you how to act with Miss Quest. In case you can't find out for yourself."

"You know," said the Saint, "I like you."

"Don't commit yourself until after tonight," she said.

Byron Ufferlitz, of course, as he had carefully explained to the Saint, was too smart to have fallen for a salaried producer's job at one of the major studios. What he had negotiated for himself was a major release—he did his own financing, and saved the terrific standard mark-up for "overhead" of ordinary studio production. He had his offices and rented facilities at Liberty Studios, a new outfit on Beverly Boulevard which catered to independent producers. Opposite the entrance there was a cocktail lounge whimsically named The Front Office, which would unmistakably have suffered a major depression if a hole had opened across the street and Liberty Studios had dropped in. But ephemeral as its position may have been in the economic system, it fulfilled the Saint's immediate requisites of supply and demand, and he settled himself appreciatively on a chrome-legged stool and relaxed into the glass-panelled décor without any active revulsion.

He had a little difficulty in getting service, because the lone bartender, who looked like a retired stunt man and was actually exactly that, was having a little dialogue trouble with the only other customer at that intermediate hour, who had obviously been a customer with more enthusiasm than discretion.

"He can't do that to me," declared the customer, propping his head in his hands and staring glassy-eyed between his fingers.

"Of course not," said the bartender. "Take it easy."

"You know what he said to me, Charlie?"

"No. What did he say to you?"

"He said, 'You stink!'"

"He did?"

"Yeah."

"Take it easy."

"You know what I'm gonna do, Charlie?"

"What you gonna do?"

"I'm gonna tell that son of a bitch where he gets off."

"Take it easy, now."

"He can't do that to me."

"Of course not."

"I'm gonna tell him right now."

"Now take it easy. It's not that bad."

"I'll kill the son of a bitch before he can get away with that."

"Why don't you go out and get something to eat first? You'll feel better."

"I'll show him where he gets off."

"Take it easy."

"I'm gonna show him right now." The customer lurched up, staggered, found his balance, and said, "Goo'bye."

"Goodbye," said the bartender. "Take it easy."

The customer navigated with careful determination to the door, and vanished—an almost ridiculously good-looking young man, with features so superficially perfect that he could easily have stepped straight out of a collar advertisement if he had been a little less dishevelled.

"Yes, sir?" said the bartender, facing the Saint with the combination of complete aplomb, extravagant apology, comradely amusement, genial discretion, and sophisticated deprecation which is the heritage of all good bartenders.

"A double Peter Dawson and plain water," said the Saint. "Is there something about the air around here which drives people to drink?"

"It's too bad about him," said the bartender tolerantly, pouring meanwhile. "When he's sober, he's as nice a fellow as you could meet. Just like you'd think he would be from his pictures."

A vague identification in the Saint's mind suddenly came into surprising focus.

"I get it," he said. "Of course. Orlando Flane—the heartthrob of the Hemisphere."

"Yeah. He really is a nice guy. Only when he's had a few drinks you gotta humor him."

"Next time," said the Saint, "you should ask him about the Chinese laundryman."

It took no little ingenuity to frustrate the bartender's professional curiosity about that unguarded remark, but it was as entertaining a way of passing the time as any other, and the Saint felt almost human again when he turned back to the white walls of Liberty Studios.

He had no lasting interest in Orlando Flane as a person at all, and might have forgotten him again altogether if they had not been literally thrown together so very shortly afterwards.

That is, to be excruciatingly specific, Orlando Flane was thrown. Or appeared to be. At any rate, he seemed to be nearing the end of a definite trajectory when Simon opened the outer door of Mr Ufferlitz's office and almost tripped over him. Only because he was prepared by a lifetime of lightning reactions, Simon adapted himself resiliently to the shock and scooped the actor up with one sinewy arm.

"Is there a lot of fun like this around here?" he inquired pleasantly, looking at Peggy Warden, who was getting up rather suddenly from her typewriter.

Then he saw that Mr Ufferlitz himself was standing in the communicating doorway to his private office, and realised exactly what certain remarks of the cynical Lazaroff were intended to convey, and why out of his own experienced judgement he had sensed long ago that Mr Ufferlitz was not merely a farcical stock character.

"Get out of here," Byron Ufferlitz was saying coldly. "And stay out, you drunken bum."

Orlando Flane might have gone back to the floor a second time, if the Saint had not been interestedly holding him up. He reeled inside the supporting semicircle of the Saint's arm, and wiped the back of his hand across his bruised lips. But he had sobered surprisingly, and there was no more alcoholic slur in his syllables than there was in the savage set of his dark long-lashed eyes as he looked back across the room.

"All right, you bastard," he said distinctly. "You can throw me out now because I'm drunk. But I can remember just as far back as you can. I've got plenty of things to settle with you, and when I fix you up you're going to stay fixed!"

3

The colored butler showed Simon into April Quest's living-room, and brought him a Martini. It was a comfortable room, modern in style, but it had the untouched impersonal feeling of an interior decorator's exhibit. Everything in it looked very new and overwhelmingly harmonious. But the chairs were large and relaxing, the sort of chairs that a man likes, and at least there were no sham-period gewgaws or laboriously exotic touches.

Simon lighted a cigarette and amused himself with some magazines which he found on a shelf under the table by the couch. Some of them were fan magazines, and one of them had her picture on the cover. He remembered now that it had caught his eye on a newsstand not long ago. Naturally it was a beautiful face, since that was part of her profession, framed in softly waved auburn hair, with a small nose and high cheekbones and large expressive eyes. But he had noticed her mouth, which was generous and yet sultry, laughing and yet wilful, as if she could be passionate in her selfishness but never cold or unkind . . . Then he looked up, and she was standing in front of him.

It was a slight shock, as if the picture had suddenly come to life. She was so exactly like it. The only thing different was her dress, and this was something formal and white and very simple. But the neck was cut down to her waist, and the material was so sheer that you would have known exactly what she wore underneath it if she had worn anything. She looked like a wayward Madonna decked out in a suitable disguise to find out what really went on in night clubs.

She said, "Sorry I wasn't ready, but I had the goddamnedest time getting dressed. Every lousy rag I put on looked like hell."

"Well," he said, "I'm glad you were able to save something out of the junk pile."

"Pretty frightening, isn't it?" she said, looking down at herself. "Brings out all the floozie in me. And everything else. Well, nobody can ever say I didn't give my All."

She had a glass in her hand, practically empty. She emptied it, and sat down beside him and tinkled a small hand-bell.

"Shall we have some more serum before we go to the rat race?"

He drained his own glass and nodded, but the acceptance was hardly necessary. The butler appeared like a watchful genie with a shaker in his hand, and proceeded to pour without any instructions.

Simon gazed at her speculatively over his cigarette.

"It's a hell of a way to get acquainted, isn't it?" he remarked. "But it's nice of you to cooperate, as Byron calls it."

"If a girl never had to cooperate any worse than this," she said, "this goddamn racket would be a breeze."

"Just how much cooperation is supposed to he ordered here?" Simon asked. "Byron left it a little vague."

She looked at him.

"It doesn't sound like Byron, to leave anything to your imagination."

"Maybe my imagination is a little slow."

"Are you kidding me, or where have you been all your life?"

"I haven't been getting an Ufferlitz-Hollywood build-up all my life."

Her eyes were curious.

"We're going to Ciro's together; in this town, that automatically means a budding romance. If we leer at each other and hold hands a bit, they'll just about have us in bed together. We don't actually have to go to bed before witnesses, because you can't print that anyway. Disappointed?"

"Not a bit," said the Saint. "It's much more fun without witnesses."

"For Christ's sake," she said pleasantly. "You didn't have to be here long to learn the routines, though."

His clear blue eyes rested on her again, and this time their lazy mockery had a different twinkle. A slow grin etched itself around his mouth.

"Thank God," he drawled, and held out his hand. She couldn't help shaking it, and smiling back at him, and suddenly they were laughing together. "Now we can have fun," he said.

So they were friends.

Simon Templar had to admit that inefficiency at least was not one of Mr Ufferlitz's failings, or at any rate of his assistants. The head waiter at Giro's, whom Simon had never seen before in his life, said "Good evening, Miss Quest," and then, "Good evening, Mr Templar!" with an air of glad surprise, as though he were greeting an old and valued customer who had been away for a long time, and ushered them to a ringside table from which he removed the RESERVED card with a flourish. He said enticingly, "A cocktail to start with?"

"Dry Martinis," said the Saint, and he bowed and beamed himself away.

"The works," said April Quest.

"So I see," murmured the Saint. "Let's pretend we're used to it."

"You're going to be an experience," she said. "Did you ever do any acting?"

"Not for the camera."

"Were you on the stage?"

He shook his head.

"Not that either. Just what you might call privately. You see, when you lead a wicked life like mine, you can't always be yourself," he explained. "According to the job in hand, you may want to pretend to be anything, from a dyspeptic poet with Communist tendencies to a retired sea-captain with white whiskers and a perpetual thirst."

She was studying him with candid interest now.

"Then some of that stuff about you must be on the level."

"Some of it," he admitted mildly.

"Most of it, I guess." She said it herself. "I ought to have known— it isn't the sort of thing that press-agents think up. But Jesus, you meet so many phonies in this business you get out of the habit of believing anything. I'm one myself, so I know."

"You?"

"What do you think you know about me?"

"Let's see. Your name's April Quest," he began cautiously. "Or is it?"

"That's about as far as you'll get, and nobody would believe that. What's a name! Even that isn't a hundred per cent, either. It was Quist on my birth certificate, but they thought Quest sounded better."

"I remember reading something about you," he recalled. "Last year, wasn't it, when you were the new sensational discovery? You were raised in the logging country up north. Your parents died when you were a kid, but you kept the old forest going. You'd never been in a city or bought a ready-made dress or worn a pair of shoes, but tough lumberjacks worshipped the ground you walked on and worked like slaves for you. You'd never seen a lipstick or a powder puff. You were the unspoiled glamor girl of the wilderness, the untamed virgin queen of the Big Trees—"

"Nuts," she said. "My father was a drunken longshoreman who got his skull cracked in a strikers' riot. I was dealing them off the arm in a truck-drivers' hash house outside Seattle when Jack Groom stopped in for a cup of coffee and offered me a trial contract at twenty-five a week. I'd just about settled on another offer to be a B-girl in San Francisco, but this looked better. And that's more than I'd tell another soul in this village. I guess I must have a feeling about you."

"That's nice," said the Saint, and meant it.

Suddenly her hand slid over his fingers, and her smile was really intoxicating.

"Darling," she said softly.

He looked at her in a quite unreasonable stillness.

A flash bulb popped.

Simon turned in time to see the photographer backing away. April Quest giggled, and let go his hand.

"Sorry," she said. "I only just saw the bastard coming in time."

"Try to warn me next time, will you?" said the Saint gently. "My heart's liable to blow a gasket when you put so much soul into your work."

A heavy hand fell on his shoulder, and he looked up and back. April mirrored his movement at the same time. Mr Byron Ufferlitz stood between them, looking heavily genial with a fat cigar in his mouth.

"That was nice cooperation, kiddies," he rumbled. "I told him to get another later on, when you're dancing. How's everything?"

"Fine," April said.

She smiled dazzlingly, but her voice sounded very faintly mechanical.

"How ya getting on with the Saint? He's all right, huh? What a profile! And that figure . . . You two are gonna make a great team.

Maybe you'll do a lotta pictures together, like Garbo and Gilbert or Colman and Banky in the old days."

"I can't afford it," said the Saint. "Earning that kind of money is too expensive these days."

"We'll take care of that," said Mr Ufferlitz jovially, if a trifle ambiguously. "Say, April, about your new hair-do, I was talkin' to Westmore just now and . . ."

Simon looked around the room and caught the raised eyebrows of Dick Halliday, who had just come in with Mary Martin. He grinned, and then he saw Martha Scott and Carl Alsop making faces at him, and they were just the first of other faces that were breaking into expressions of recognition, and he knew that he was certainly going to have to be well paid for the explanations he would have to make to some of his friends in Hollywood for his manner of arriving back among them. Then, trying to postpone that awkward moment by finding some blank direction to turn to, he looked towards the entrance from the bar and saw Orlando Flane.

Flane was looking right at them. He had a highball glass in his hand, and his feet were braced apart as if to steady himself. In spite of that he was swaying a little. His too-handsome face was flushed, and his hair and necktie had the uncomfortably rumpled look that can never be confused with any other kind of untidiness. There was no doubt that Orlando Flane was drunk again, or still drunk. The twist of his mouth was vicious.

"Well, I mustn't stay any longer," Mr Ufferlitz was saying. "Don't want to look like I was promoting this. Have yourselves a time, and don't worry about the check. It's all taken care of. 'Bye."

He clapped them on the shoulders again and moved away. Simon's eyes followed him towards the bar with interested expectations, but Orlando Flane had disappeared.

"There," said April cold-bloodedly, "goes one of the prize-winning swine of this town."

With Flane still on his mind, Simon said, "Who?"

"Ufferlitz, of course. Dear Byron."

Their drinks came belatedly, accompanied by menus, and there was an interruption for the ordering of dinner. From the wine list, Simon added a bottle of Bollinger '31.

"On Byron," he said, as the waiter removed himself. "Everyone tells me something about him. He was a stick-up man in New Orleans, but his pictures make money. He's a retired union racketeer, but he pays his slaves. Take it away."

"How much does he pay them?"

The Saint's brows levelled fractionally.

"He hasn't shown me the payroll yet," he admitted. "But two literary gents named Kendricks and Lazaroff told me his checks were okay."

"Listen," she said. "Those two clowns used to be rated one of the best writing teams in Hollywood, even though they nearly drove every producer nuts that they worked for. But last year they went too far. They got in a beef with Goldwyn, and he fired them. So they bluffed their way into his house when he was out and filled all his clothes with itching powder and left ink soap in all the bathrooms. The Producers' Association banned them and they haven't worked since—until Byron hired them. How much d'you think he had to pay them when they were in a spot like that, and why wouldn't they be goddamn glad to get it?"

This was a new angle.

"I didn't know about that," he said thoughtfully. "The deal he offered me was all right, but of course he hasn't got anything on me . . . yet," he added. "What about you?"

This was a new angle.

"He expects to rape me before we start shooting, of course, but he doesn't need much else. He got me with Jack Groom, because Jack still has my contract."

"For twenty-five a week?"

"No, a bit more than that now. I don't know what Jack's deal is, but I know he hates Byron's guts."

"I met Comrade Groom today," Simon remarked casually. "How do you get on with him?"

The exquisitely drawn green eyes measured him contemplatively, and then they were bright with laughter.

"'*The Saint Goes On,*'" she quoted. "I can see it coming. Now stop being a damn detective, will you? This is your night off. We're supposed to be having fun and romance, and we've hardly stopped being serious for a minute. Dance with me."

She stood up imperiously, and he had to join her. It wasn't hard to do. She could change her moods as quickly as light could flicker over the facets of cut crystal, and do it without seeming to leave raw edges or a sense of chill: you were not cut off or left behind, but taken with her.

They danced. And dined. And danced again. And she made it impossible to be serious any more. With all her callous cynicism and violent language, she could be a fascinating and exciting companion. The Saint found himself having a much more entertaining evening than he had expected. It was as if they instinctively recognised in each other an intense reality which in spite of all other differences made them feel as if they had known each other a hundred times longer than those few hours.

It was one o'clock when he drove her home, after a brief struggle through the regular nightly crew of autograph hunters outside.

"Come in and have a drink," she said.

Simon thought about it, while another belated car cruised by.

"Maybe not," he said.

"Why not?"

"Cooperation only goes so far."

"So what?"

"So I don't want you to call me a wolf again. But I'm human."

"My God," she said, "don't you think I know the difference? Don't you think I could . . . I'd like to buy you a drink," she said.

He kissed her, and broke it off quickly when he felt the warmth of her lips.

"Goodnight, darling," he said.

She got out, and he drove away while he still could.

When he entered his apartment at the Château Marmont there was a note in a plain envelope under the door. He opened it and frowned over the heavy sprawling hand. It seemed to have been composed very much impromptu, for it was written on a sizable blank space under the date line of *The Hollywood Reporter*—obviously torn out of one of those strange advertisements which say, in infinitely modest type, "Joe Doakes directed WOMEN IN ARMS," and buy a whole page to set it off.

> *WHATEVER TIME you get home tonight, I want you to come right out and see me. Don't tell ANYONE I sent for you. This is VERY IMPORTANT. The door will be open. Don't ring!*
>
> *BYRON UFFERLITZ*
> *(603 Claymore Drive)*

The Saint sighed, and put the note in his pocket. A few minutes later he was retracing his tracks out Sunset Boulevard.

Claymore Drive was only a couple of blocks from April Quest's house, and as he passed her street Simon smiled again over the easy way she had taken his mind from its habitual restless search for plot. She had been right, of course: so much of his life had been woven with conspiracy and dark purposes that he had long since ceased to be as interested in the solution of past mysteries as he was in anticipating mysteries that had not yet shaped themselves, and that inquiring watchfulness had become so automatic that he was apt to find himself stalking the shadow of his own imagination.

Or was he? . . . A long time had gone by since one of those hunches had last let him down. What had Ufferlitz said? *"There are plenty of people who'd hate to see me make a hit with this idea. One or two of 'em would go a long ways to wreck it . . . I guess you can take care of yourself. . ."* He had almost accepted Ufferlitz's note as just one of those regal impetuosities that Hollywood producers traditionally indulge in; the thought that it might after all be more than that gave him a sudden feeling of inward stillness as if the blood momentarily ceased to move in his veins.

He shrugged it off as he slowed down at Mr Ufferlitz's number, and yet enough of it remained to paralyse his right foot from the reflex shift from accelerator to brake. He crawled round the next corner, and in the next few yards found several cars parked outside a house where all the lights were on. He eased in among them, and walked back to 603 Claymore Drive. He grinned derisively at himself for doing it; yet it was one of those Saintly precautions that cost nothing even if they were to prove unnecessary. So was the handkerchief with which he covered his fingers when he opened the front door.

The hall itself was unlighted, but a shaft of illumination spilled from an open doorway to his left.

"Hullo there," he said quietly.

There was no answer as he crossed to the lighted doorway. As soon as he reached it he could see why. The room was Mr Ufferlitz's study, and Mr Ufferlitz was there, but it was quite obvious that no one would have to cooperate with Mr Ufferlitz anymore.

4

Mr Ufferlitz sat at his mahogany desk, which was about the size of a ping-pong table. His head was pillowed on the blotter, which had not proved sufficiently absorptive to take care of all the blood that had run out of him. Simon walked round the desk and saw that Mr Ufferlitz's back hair was a little singed around the place where the bullet had gone in, so that the gun must have been held almost touching his head; probably most of the upper part of his face had been blown out, because blood had splashed forward across the desk and there were little blobs of gray stuff and white chips of bone mixed with it.

The larger splotches of blood were still shiny, and the chewed end of a cigar that lay among them was still visibly damp. So the Saint estimated that the shot couldn't have been fired more than an hour ago. At the outside.

He looked at his watch. It showed exactly two o'clock.

The house was absolutely silent. If there were any servants in, their quarters were far enough away for them to have been undisturbed.

Simon stood very quietly and looked around the room. It had an air of having been put together according to a studio designer's idea of what an important man's study should look like. One wall was lined with bookshelves, but most of the books wore dark impressive bindings with gilt lettering, having undoubtedly been bought in sets and most probably never read. The bright jackets of a few modern novels stood out in a clash of color. There were a couple of heavy oil paintings on the walls. Scattered between them were a number of framed photographs with handwriting on them. They were all girls. One of them was April Quest, and there was another face that seemed faintly familiar, but the inscription only said *"Your Trilby."* Obviously these were symbols of Mr Ufferlitz's new career as a producer. The room itself had the same appearance—Mr Ufferlitz had hardly been in the business long enough to have built the house himself, but he had clearly selected it with an eye to the atmosphere with which he felt he ought to surround himself.

The one thing that was conspicuously lacking was any sort of clue of the type so dear to the heart of the conventional fiction writer. There might have been fingerprints, but Simon was not equipped to look for them just then. On the desk, besides the blotter and Mr Ufferlitz's head and samples of his blood, brains, and frontal bones, there was a fountain pen set, a couple of pencils, an evening paper, a couple of scripts and some loose script pages, a dentist's bill, a liquor price list, and a memorandum block on which nobody had thoughtfully borne down on the last sheet torn off with a blunt pencil so that the writing would be legible on the next page in a slanting light. On a side table by the fireplace there were some old weeklies, but no copies of *The Hollywood Reporter*—which meant nothing, because the executive subscribers to this daily record of the movie industry usually receive it at their offices. The only indication of anything unusual at all was the ashtrays. There were three of them, and they had all been used, and they were smeared with ash and carbon to prove it, but they had all been emptied—and not into the fireplace or the wastebasket.

Simon thought mechanically, like an adding machine: "A servant didn't empty them, because he'd have wiped them as well. Byron didn't do it, because he wouldn't have carried the ashes out of the room. Therefore the murderer did it, and took the debris away with him, so that his cigarette stubs wouldn't be held against him. I guess he doesn't believe in Sherlock Holmes and what he would do with a microscope and what's left in the trays. He could be right, at that . . ."

But the train of thought did suggest another. If the murderer had had to take that precaution, he must have done his share of smoking; therefore he had been there for some time; therefore he was most likely someone whom Mr Ufferlitz knew—someone who might even have talked to Mr Ufferlitz for quite a while before putting a gun to his occiput and blowing it out through his forehead.

And that suggested something else. Simon stood behind Mr Ufferlitz and sighted along the line that the bullet would probably have taken. It carried his eyes to a fresh scar gouged in the panelling opposite. He walked over to it, and had no doubt that it had been made by the spent bullet. But either the slug had not had enough force left to embed itself properly in the woodwork, or else it had been carefully pried out: it was not in the hole, or on the floor below it. There was no way to tell even the caliber of the gun which had been used. The murderer seemed to have been quite efficient.

And he had not left behind any muddy footprints, buttons, shreds of cloth, hairs, hats, scraps of paper, cigarette lighters, handkerchiefs, keys, match booklets, cuff links, spectacles, gloves, combs, wallets, rings, fraternity pins, fobs, nail files, false teeth, tie clips, overcoats, ticket stubs, hairpins, garters, wigs, or any of the other souvenirs which murderers in fiction are wont to strew around with such self-sacrificing generosity. He had just walked in and smoked a few cigarettes and fired his gun and emptied the ashtrays and walked out again, without leaving any more traces than any normal visitor would leave.

"Which is Unfair to Disorganised Detectives," said the Saint to himself. "If I knew where the guy lived I'd picket him."

But the flippancy was just a ripple on the surface of his mind, and underneath it his brain was working with the steady flow of an assembly line, putting together the prefabricated pieces that he had been collecting without knowing what they were for. If he was right, and the murderer was someone whom Mr Ufferlitz had known well enough to entertain in his study at that hour, there was at least a fair chance that it was someone whom Simon had already met. It might even be more than a chance. The Saint was probing back through the threads that he had once tried to weave together when there was nothing to tie them to. And the note in his pocket, the note that had brought him there, with its hurried scrawl and emphatic capitals, came into his mind as clearly as if he had taken it out to look at it. Had Byron Ufferlitz written it because something had happened to warn him that he would be in danger that night?

Or hadn't he written it?

Had somebody seen the Saint's entrance—literally—into the picture as the heaven-sent gift of a ready-made scapegoat, and cashed in on it without one day's delay? Had it been sent only to bring him there at the right moment, so that . . .

All at once Simon was aware of the silence again. The whole house was wrapped in an empty hush that seemed to close in on him with an intangible pressure, while he tried to strain through it for any sound that would crystallise this re-awakened vigilance. He was very cool now, utterly limber and relaxed, with the triggered stillness of a cat.

There was no sound even yet.

He went out of the study and crossed the hall, moving with the same supple noiselessness. The front door had a small glass panel in it, and he looked out through that without touching anything. There was a car parked outside now, without lights, and two dark figures stood beside it. While he looked, a flashlight beam stabbed out from one of them, swept over the lawn, flicked across the front of the house, and wavered nosily over palm trees and shrubbery. The two figures began to move up the paved walk. The Saint didn't have to see them any better to know what they were.

"Ay tank we go home," he murmured, and turned rapidly back.

He didn't hesitate for a moment over the idea of flinging the door open and congratulating them on their prompt arrival. If the police were already preparing to take an interest in the premises, they must have already received a hint that there was something there to merit their professional attention, and with the Saint's unfortunate reputation there were inclined to be certain technical complications about being caught in strange houses with dead bodies spilling their brains over the furniture. The Saint knew better than anyone how sceptical policemen could be in circumstances like that, and he had no great faith now that the note which he might have produced from his pocket to substantiate part of his story would stand up to unfriendly scrutiny.

He wrapped a handkerchief round his right hand again as he went back through the study, where he had already noticed a glazed door to the garden. It was bolted on the inside—another partial confirmation of his theory that the murderer had not crept in on Mr Ufferlitz unseen. Simon opened it, and stepped out into a paved patio, closing the door silently again behind him. A wooden gate in the wall to his left let him out on to a lawn with a swimming pool in the center. The wall around this lawn was six feet high, with no gates. Even more like a prowling cat, Simon swung himself to the top of the wall without an effort and dropped like a feather on to the lawn of the house next door. This was the corner house. He turned to the right, where the grounds were bordered by a high thick hedge. A well-aged and artistically planted elm extended a massive branch at just the right height and angle for him to catch with his hands and jackknife his long legs over the hedge.

THE SAINT GOES WEST

This time he landed on concrete, in the black shadow of the big tree, and found that he was at the side of the house around the corner, in the drive leading to the garages at the back.

As he came to the corner of the building he walked into a babble of cheerful voices that ended with a chorus of good-nights. A door closed, and he saw two couples straggling away in search of their cars. Without hesitation he set off in a brisk curve that carried him first towards them and then away from them, as though he had left the party at the same time and branched off towards his own car.

A flashlight sweeping over from some yards away touched on him as he reached the pavement.

Simon squinted at it, and turned away to call a loud "Goodnight" after the other departing guests. Then without a pause he opened the door of his car and ducked in. An automatic answering "Goodnight!" echoed back to him as he did it. And with that pleasant exchange of courtesies he drove away.

As he turned on to Sunset he had an abrupt distinct recollection of a previous goodnight, and a car that had driven slowly by while he was outside April Quest's. That could have been a coincidence, and the recent timely arrival of the police could have been another, but when they were put together it began to look as if somebody was quite anxious to make sure that Hollywood wouldn't be dull for him.

5

Simon walked into Mr Ufferlitz's outer office at eleven o'clock in the morning and said, "Hullo, Peggy."

"Hullo." Peggy Warden's smile was a little vague, and her voice didn't sound quite certain. "How are you today?"

"Fine."

"Did you have a good time last night?"

"Mm-hm." The Saint nodded. "But I still want a date with you."

"Well—"

"What about lunch?"

"I don't know—"

Her face was paler than it had been yesterday, but he gave no sign of noticing it.

"It's a date," he said, and glanced towards the communicating door. It was half open. He had seen that when he came in. "Has the Great Man arrived yet?"

"Will you go right in?"

Simon nodded, and strolled through.

A new face sat behind Mr Ufferlitz's desk. It was a lined face of indeterminate age, with a yellowish kind of tan as if it had once had a bronze which was wearing off. It had close-cropped gray-black hair and heavy black brows over a long curved nose like a scimitar. Its whole sculpture had an air of passive despondency that was a curious contrast to its bright black eyes.

"Hullo," murmured Simon amiably. "Do you work here too?"

"Condor's the name," said the face pessimistically. "Ed Condor. Yours?"

"Templar. Simon Templar."

The face moved a toothpick from one side of its mouth to the other.

"Mr Ufferlitz won't be in today," it said.

"Oh."

"In fact, Mr Ufferlitz won't be around here anymore."

"No?"

"Mr Ufferlitz is dead."

Simon allowed the faint frown of perplexity which had begun to gather on his brow to tighten up.

"What?"

"He's dead."

"Is this a gag?"

"Nope. He died last night. You won't see him any more unless you go to the morgue."

The Saint lighted a cigarette slowly, glancing back at the door through which he had just entered with the same puzzled frown deepening on his face.

It was a masterpiece of timing and restrained suggestion. If Condor was disappointed because he didn't draw one of the conventional gaffes of the "Who shot him?" variety, he didn't show it. He said, "I told her not to say anything. Wanted to see how you took it."

"I may be dumb," said the Saint, "but I think I'm missing something. Are you an undercover man for a Gallup Poll, or what is this?"

Condor flipped his lapel.

"Police," he said gloomily. "Sit down, Mr Templar."

The Saint sank into a deep leather armchair and exhaled a long drift of smoke.

"Well I'm damned," he said. "What did he die of?"

"Murder."

Simon blinked.

"Good God—how?"

"Shot through the head. From behind. In his study, at his house." Condor seemed to resign himself to the conviction that he wasn't going to catch any revelations of premature knowledge, and opened up a bit. "Sometime around half-past one. The cook thought she heard a noise about that time, but she didn't wake up properly and figured it was probably a car backfiring outside. Miss Warden was working there until about midnight, when he came in, and she says he was all right when she left about half an hour later."

Simon nodded.

"I saw him at Giro's before that."

"What time did he leave there?"

"I wouldn't know. It was probably around eight-thirty when I saw him, but I don't know how much longer he stayed. I wasn't paying much attention."

"You with anyone?"

"April Quest."

"How did Ufferlitz seem?"

"Perfectly normal . . . Are there any clues?"

"We haven't found any yet. The killer seems to have been good and careful. Even emptied the ashtrays."

Simon drew at his cigarette again and rubbed his chin thoughtfully. He found an ashtray on the small table at his right elbow and tapped his cigarette over it. The rest of the table was littered with a pile of back numbers of *The Hollywood Reporter* and *Variety*. Right on top of the pile was a *Reporter* of yesterday. So Byron Ufferlitz hadn't had it with him to scribble that note on, and if he had written it in his office before leaving he wouldn't have used the *Reporter* for paper. Of course he could have picked up another copy, but—

"The only thing is," said Condor, "Ufferlitz knew the guy who killed him. The servants didn't let anyone in, except Miss Warden, so Ufferlitz must have done it himself."

"Suppose the guy let himself in?"

"Then he couldn't have gone into the study until not more than an hour before he shot Ufferlitz. But he still smoked enough to have to empty three ashtrays. So Ufferlitz knew him well enough to keep talking to him."

Simon nodded again. It was his own old deduction, but it indicated that Ed Condor was at least not totally blind and incompetent. The Saint wondered how much more he had on the ball. Certainly he was not a man to be careless with.

"I see," Simon said. "So you sit here waiting for people who knew him to drop in."

"Yeah. I've seen two writers and the director—Groom. Now you."

"Have you had any good reactions?" Simon asked with superb audacity.

Condor nibbled his toothpick with the corners of his mouth drawn down unhappily.

"Nope. Not yet. It hasn't been anybody's morning to pull boners." He went on without any transition: "What time did you go home last night?"

"I took Miss Quest home about one o'clock."

"When were you home?"

"We talked for a while. I didn't notice the time, but I guess I was home in about half an hour . . ."

Condor's black eyes that missed nothing were fixed on him steadily, and Simon knew almost telepathically that the night elevator operator at the Château Marmont had already been consulted. But he had had several hours to remember that that would have been an inevitable routine, eventually, anyway.

". . . the first time, that is," he continued easily. "Then I went out again. I didn't have any liquor in the apartment, and I wanted another drink. I went to a joint on Hollywood Boulevard and had a drink at the bar, and went home at closing time."

"What joint was that?"

Simon told him the name of a night spot which did a roaring if not exactly exclusive trade, where he knew that nobody would be able to say positively whether he had been in or not.

"See anyone you knew there?" Condor asked nevertheless.

"No. In fact, if you want a cast-iron alibi," Simon admitted with an air of disarming candor, "I'm afraid I can't give it to you. Do I need one?"

"I dunno," Condor said glumly. "How long would it take you to drive from your apartment to Ufferlitz's?"

"I haven't the least idea," said the Saint innocently. "Where does he live?"

The detective sighed. In any other circumstances Simon could almost have felt sorry for him. He was certainly a trier, and it just wasn't doing him any good.

He said, "On Claymore, in Beverly Hills. You could drive there in ten minutes easy, even missing a few lights."

"But I thought Ufferlitz was shot at one-thirty. I was home just about then."

"You aren't sure. And the cook isn't sure either. She only thinks it was about one-thirty. She could be five minutes wrong. So could you. That makes enough difference for you to have been there. Maybe the shot wasn't at one-thirty anyway. Maybe she did hear a car backfiring, and the shooting was some other time. Like when you say you were out having a drink."

"What do the doctors say?"

"They can't fix it as close as that. You ought to know."

"I suppose not," said the Saint. "Still, you make it a bit tough for a guy. You want me to have an alibi, but you don't know what time I'm supposed to have an alibi for."

Condor removed his toothpick, inspected it profoundly, and put it back.

"I got another time," he announced finally.

"What's that?"

"Ufferlitz called the Beverly Hills police station and said he thought someone was prowling around his house, and asked for a patrol car to come by. That call was received at exactly eight minutes of two."

A subcutaneous tingle pin-pointed up between the Saint's shoulder-blades—even though he had always been sure that that patrol car had never arrived by accident. But his face showed nothing more than a rather exasperated bafflement.

"For Pete's sake," he said, "how many more times have you got to cover?"

"Just that one."

"But that makes the other time all haywire."

"Could be. I said, maybe the cook never heard the shot. She went to sleep again."

Simon consumed his cigarette meditatively for a few seconds. Then he looked at Condor again with a slight lift of one eyebrow.

"On the other hand," he remarked, "can anyone swear that Ufferlitz made that call? Maybe the murderer made it himself, just to confuse you. Maybe you ought to be very suspicious of anybody who has got a perfect alibi for eight minutes of two."

Condor stared at him for a while with unblinking intentness, and then the barest vestige of a smile moved in under his long drooping features. It literally did that, as if the surface of his face was too stiffly set in its cast of abject melancholy to relax perceptibly, and the smile had to crawl about under the skin.

"That," he said, "is the first thing you've said that sounds like some of the stuff I've heard about you."

"So far," murmured the Saint, "you've seemed to want me for a suspect more than a collaborator."

"I gotta suspect everybody."

"But be reasonable. Ufferlitz just gave me a job for a thousand dollars a day. I don't know now whether I've got a job any more. Why would I kill that sort of meal ticket? Besides, I never met him before lunch-time yesterday. I'd have to have hated him in an awful hurry to work up to shooting point by last night."

Condor wrinkled his nose.

"It seems to me," he said, "I've heard you're supposed to've killed a few people that you didn't have any particular personal feelings about. Something about being your own judge, jury, and hangman. Not that it wasn't all quite legal and accidental, of course," he added, "or it came to look that way in the end, but that's what they say. Well, from what I've heard about Ufferlitz, he's got some things in his record that might save you the trouble of hating him by yourself."

The Saint sank lower in his chair and for the first time ventured to look slightly bored.

"Here we go again," he drawled. "Are you trying to hang something on me or not? Make up your mind."

"Well . . ." Condor drew his chin back so that the toothpick drooped from his upper teeth. "I guess I do sound sort of antagonistic sometimes. Gets to be second nature. You'll have to excuse me. But I've heard plenty of complimentary things about you too. Maybe you could help me a lot, at that.

"You've given me one good idea already. I wouldn't like to be a nuisance, but if you wanted to give me any more I'd be honored."

He was as disarming as a drowsing crocodile. You felt ashamed of yourself for having misunderstood him and put him into a position where he had to defend himself. Your heart warmed with the consciousness of having put him back where he belonged, nevertheless. You felt pretty loosened up altogether. Unless you were Simon Templar.

"I'm afraid it's a little bit out of my line," said the Saint. "As a matter of fact, I go a little bit nuts over these split-second timetables. They're too confusing. And I don't believe in them, anyway. They're too much like the super-solemn kind of detective story. Nobody outside of a book is ever watching the time from minute to minute. And even if they were, their watches wouldn't be synchronised. And as soon as there's any chance of any error, you might as well give up. On top of which there are too many ways of faking, if you've read any mysteries."

"That's how I feel," Condor agreed sadly. "Personally, I'll settle for anyone who could have been there between twelve-thirty and about two-fifteen, when the patrol found him."

"What about the other people you've talked to?"

"You mean have they got alibis too?"

"Yes."

"Lazaroff and Kendricks were working on a script until about two-thirty. They share an apartment. They have a cleaning woman, but she doesn't sleep there, so there's no one to back them up. But they alibi each other."

"And Groom?"

"He was with a dame. He left her at half-past one and stopped in at the Mocambo for a couple drinks. He told me three or four people he spoke to, so he probably did."

"He could have telephoned, too," Simon observed.

Condor brooded silently, poking his toothpick about in his bicuspids.

"There's one thing I'm puzzled about," Simon said presently. "Ufferlitz must have known quite a few people outside. Why does it have to be someone from this unit?"

"It just seems a good place to start. The cook says he never had anybody home except people he was mixed up in business with, except sometimes a girl he was trying to promote. Besides, from what I hear nobody else was crazy about visiting him anyway. Then, when he came home to dinner yesterday evening, he said he wasn't in to anyone unless it was from the studio."

"What about the business he was in before this?"

"He cut himself off from all those mugs when he got to be a producer. We keep tabs on some of 'em, so I know that. But I don't know any of 'em who're sore with him."

"He played square with the racket while he was in it, did he?"

"He knew what was good for him. You can't chisel those kind of guys and keep healthy. You can only do that with high-class suckers." The detective seemed to derive some morbid satisfaction from the thought. "No—he still sees some of the mob, but he don't ask 'em home. Some of 'em think it's a big laugh, his going high-hat. But they aren't sore. Or I haven't heard about it . . . None of it's conclusive, of course, but this still looked like a good place to begin. I've found with most murders you don't have to look awful far. It's usually somebody who's been around pretty close."

Simon lighted another cigarette and drew at it for a while. Condor didn't seem to have anything more to say. He began pulling open drawers and browsing through the papers he found in them.

Presently Simon got up.

"Well, I'd better leave you to it," he said. "If I get any more brilliant ideas I'll let you know."

"Do that," said Condor earnestly. "I'll be seeing you around."

The Saint strolled out and met Peggy Warden's tentative half-apologetic smile with unruffled cheerfulness.

"Quite a business, isn't it?" he said.

She nodded.

"I felt mean about not telling you. But Lieutenant Condor told me not to say anything. I'm glad it didn't get you into trouble."

"I never get into trouble," said the Saint virtuously. "But I seem to live an awfully precarious life. Have I got a job now, or do I go back on relief?"

Her eyes strayed to some papers on her desk.

"I don't really know," she confessed. "Mr Braunberg brought your contract back yesterday evening, and Mr Ufferlitz signed it before he left the office, but you didn't sign anything yourself so I don't know what the position is."

"Braunberg—he was the attorney, wasn't he?"

"Yes. I've already spoken to him on the phone, of course, and he said he'd be in this afternoon. I'm sure he'll be able to tell you how you stand legally."

Simon picked up the contract. It was a standard printed form, about the size of a centenarian's autobiography, covering every possible contingency from telepathy and revolutions to bankruptcy and habitual drunkenness, with a couple of pages of special clauses which invalidated most of it. Simon only glanced through it casually, and turned to the signature.

He had a microphotographic eye for certain kinds of detail, and he had no need to compare it with the note that was in his pocket to know that the note was a forgery—a passable amateur job, but a long way from being expert.

Unfortunately it would be a great deal harder if not impossible to discover who had done it. He was practically resigned to discarding *The Hollywood Reporter* as a clue. Almost everybody in the movie business was a subscriber, and in addition it could be bought at any newsstand within a radius of twenty miles. It was far too much to hope that the sender of the note would be considerate enough to have kept in his possession the mutilated copy into which the Saint's torn fragment could be fitted.

The decease of Mr Ufferlitz was a mystery that looked less encouraging every time Simon Templar turned to it.

He said, "Don't forget, Peggy, you've got a date with me for lunch."

6

"No," she said. "No more cocktails. I've still got to look as if I wanted to keep a job."

The Front Office offered a choice of steaks, chops, or hamburger. They had steaks. She sniffed hers ecstatically.

"Mmm! This was a good idea. I'd almost forgotten what a real lunch could taste like."

"I heard of a studio once where they had good food in the commissary," said the Saint. "So everybody felt fine and happy every afternoon. Agents came in and sold them everything they had at enormous prices, actors broke down and begged for salary cuts, assistant directors went about their work with a smile, and writers told producers their ideas stank and they ought to go back to peddling trusses."

"What happened?"

"The other producers ganged up on them and charged them with unfair trade practices. The Government ordered them to go back to serving the same old dead food as all the other studios, and very soon they were quite normal and in receivership again."

"You've learnt a lot in a little while."

Simon finished his drink and picked up his knife and fork.

"How long have you been in this racket?" he asked.

"Only about six months."

"Where were you before?"

"In a real estate office in New York."

"You didn't know when you were well off."

"I thought I'd come out here and get educated."

"Were you with Byron all that time?"

"No. I started in the stenographic department at MGM. Then an agent took me out of there. Then Mr Ufferlitz took me away from the agent. Now I may have to go on relief with you. I expect Mr Braunberg will tell me."

The Saint nibbled a fried potato.

"My life with Byron was certainly short and sweet," he remarked. "What sort of a guy was he really?"

She finished a mouthful carefully before she said, "You must have heard something about him."

"A few things."

"Then you must have your own ideas."

"Not very good ones," said the Saint.

She shrugged.

"He was just his own kind of Hollywood producer."

"He went further than most of them, though, didn't he?" said the Saint. "I mean, he was a rather special kind. That is, if there's anything in the rumors."

"There's something in most rumors—even in Hollywood."

"I've been wondering," Simon said, carving himself another wedge of sirloin, "what Orlando Flane had on his mind yesterday. You know—during that happy homey interlude when Byron called him a drunken bum and bounced him off the carpet into my arms. Flane said he could remember as far back as Byron could. Was he referring to some other rumor, or were they just boys together?"

"It could have been both," she said cautiously.

He waited.

After a while she said, reluctantly, as if she would rather have changed the subject if she could have seen herself doing it gracefully, "You've probably heard another rumor that Mr Ufferlitz is supposed to have been in trouble with the police in New Orleans."

"Yes."

"Orlando Flane comes from New Orleans."

"I see."

"He won one of those publicity department contests three or four years ago—for somebody to be the New Rudolph Valentino, with a touch of George Raft. The story is that he was much more of a real-life George Raft type before he became a glamor boy."

"Is he really a drunken bum?"

"I think he's been drinking rather a lot lately. He's supposed to have been slipping at the box office, so there may be an excuse for him. But it just made the producers cool off faster. He hadn't had a decent part for nearly a year until Mr Ufferlitz offered him a break just a few weeks ago."

Simon raised his eyebrows.

"Then what on earth had Flane got to beef about?"

"Flane was going to star in this picture—it was called *Salute to Adventure* then. Mr Ufferlitz fired him when he decided to change the story and hire you."

The Saint concentrated on applying mustard to a piece of steak with the infinite care of a painter of miniatures. His face was impassive, but the series of obvious implications tripped through his head with the dainty footsteps of a troupe of charging elephants.

Orlando Flane had good and recent cause to hate Mr Byron Ufferlitz. Orlando Flane had openly threatened Mr Ufferlitz with permanent evidence of his dislike. Orlando Flane had a background which in spite of his slightly effeminate facial beauty might have qualified him as a cool tough hombre. And Orlando Flane had a reason to resent Simon Templar enough to be willing to round out his revenge by trying to stage it so that the Saint would take the rap for it.

Simon looked at Peggy Warden again and said, "Do you think Flane could have killed Byron?"

She stared at him as though the idea stunned her.

"Flane?" she repeated.

"Yes."

"But . . . he's an actor," she said weakly.

He chuckled.

"Most murderers have some other spare-time job, darling. Comrade Condor seems to think it could easily have been somebody from the studio. You must have heard our conversation. If it could have been a writer, a director, or me, it could have been an actor. Byron is dead. Somebody killed him."

She nodded in a bewildered way.

"Yes. I suppose so. It just doesn't seem real. I mean . . . I can't imagine Orlando Flane as a real murderer."

"He had the best motive I've come to yet."

"But a lot of other people didn't like Mr Ufferlitz."

Simon nodded. It was true, of course.

"I hear that Jack Groom didn't like him either. Do you know why that was?"

She shook her head.

"I haven't any idea."

"Was it on account of April Quest, by any chance?"

"I don't know." The girl studied him shrewdly. "Are you rather interested in that?"

"Very much," said the Saint calmly. "It's the only other angle that doesn't seem to have been gone into yet, and it's a good traditional motive. What sort of a guy was Ufferlitz with women?"

She hesitated for a few seconds before she met his eye, but then her gaze was steady and direct.

"I believe he was quite a swine," she said.

"Who with?"

"I wouldn't know that. I didn't have anything to do with his private life."

"He didn't ever take a shot at you?"

Her face chilled for barely an instant, and then she laughed a little without smiling.

"I'm a good secretary," she said, "and that's harder to find."

Simon conceded that. But on second thought he added to himself that she might also not have been Mr Ufferlitz's type. His guess was that Byron Ufferlitz's quarry would have been either ingenuous and trusting or tough and cynical. The dumb innocents could be swept off their feet by Mr Ufferlitz's self-created grandeur and overwhelmed with the old line of what he could do for them in pictures, and the hard-boiled mercenaries could be talked to in their own language and handled as they expected to be, thereby reducing the shooting schedule. But to a man of that type Peggy Warden's natural honesty and clear-eyed composure would be highly disconcerting. She could so obviously deflate baloney or bullying with equally devastating simplicity.

Simon liked her for those same qualities. It occurred to him with a sort of rueful inward humor that he really met quite a remarkable number of girls he liked. He must have possessed an inexhaustible human sympathy, or else he was very lucky. In twenty-four hours, to have drawn two out of the bag like Peggy Warden and April Quest . . .

He frowned. April Quest—there was someone that Byron Ufferlitz might easily have seen as a good prospect. And the Saint remembered that she had made no secret of what she expected Mr Ufferlitz's intentions to be and what she thought of him.

He was getting nowhere at an impressively steady pace.

"Do you get headaches?" Peggy Warden asked, several minutes later.

"Headaches?" The Saint came back a few thousand miles with a start.

"Yes. You keep your brain working so hard."

He grinned, and pushed away his plate and lighted a cigarette.

"It's a bad habit," he said. "I'm sorry."

The gray eyes were still inquiring.

"Are you really taking a professional interest?"

"You heard what Condor said. If I get any brilliant ideas, he wants to hear them."

"But why should you be interested?"

Simon meditated over his cigarette. It was a question that he had been about ready to ask himself.

"Partly because I don't have anything much else to do just at this moment," he said at length. "And this is pretty much in my lap. Partly because the guy who bumped off Byron has probably cheated me out of an amusing experience—not to mention an interesting amount of dough. Partly because it's a rather fascinating problem, in a very quiet way. A murder without clues and without alibis—so beautifully simple and so beautifully insoluble. There has to be a catch in it somewhere, and I collect catches."

"But you aren't a policeman. You're supposed to have very unconventional ideas about justice. Suppose you decided that the murderer had a thoroughly good reason to kill Mr Ufferlitz?"

"I'd still want to know who did it. It's like having to know the answer to a riddle."

He couldn't tell her that while all that was true, the most important reason was that in everything but the leaving of a skeleton Saint figure pinned to Mr Ufferlitz's back, the murder seemed to have been staged with the considered intention of having the Saint accused of it, and to Simon Templar that was a challenge which could not be let pass. The Saint had for once been minding his own inoffensive business, and somebody had gratuitously tried to get him into trouble. Therefore somebody had got to be shown what an inferior inspiration that had really been.

His financial interest was actually the least of all, but there were other reasons why he was anxious to hear the official statement of Mr Braunberg that afternoon.

The attorney arrived almost as soon as they got back, and hurried busily into the late Mr Ufferlitz's private office, calling Peggy Warden after him and closing the door.

The Saint sat on a corner of Peggy Warden's desk and eased open the nearest drawer. He knew that he would not have to look far for what he wanted, and as it happened he found it at the first try—an indexed loose-leaf book of private addresses and telephones. He could probably have asked her for the information, but it was even more convenient to get it without advertising. He copied the locations of Lazaroff and Kendricks, Orlando Flane, and Jack Groom on to a slip of paper, and he had just finished and put the directory back when Lazaroff and Kendricks came in.

Kendricks shook his hand solemnly and said, "Congratulations, pal. I knew you'd do it. What a masterful way to deal with a producer! You should have come to Hollywood sooner—it would have been a different town."

"About four weeks sooner would have suited me," said Lazaroff. "When I think of all the cooperation we put in on that lousy script—"

"Never mind," said the Saint. "You can just change it around some more and sell it to Columbia for a new *Blondie*."

Lazaroff went through the mechanical gesture of smoothing his unsmoothable hair.

"Seriously, I suppose a guy like you takes a murder like this in his stride. But I'd still like to know how you got away with it."

"With what?" Simon asked a little incredulously.

"With just being anywhere around when it happened. I should think the cops would grab a guy like you without even asking questions, and start beating you up to see what they got."

"There was a certain suspiciousness at first," Simon admitted. "But I was able to talk myself out of it. For the time being, anyway. You see, as a matter of fact I wasn't around."

"Well, you'd just come into the studio and signed up with Byron."

"But God!" said Kendricks, "if you'd been at Byron's house when it happened, or if you'd found the body—"

The Saint smiled.

"It would have been distinctly awkward," he said candidly.

At which point Peggy Warden came out and said, "Will you all go on in?"

They filed in and chose their chairs and lighted cigarettes, and there was a rather self-conscious silence. Then the door opened again and April Quest came in, with Jack Groom following her. She had a friendly smile for everyone, and if the smile that she gave the Saint had a personal and curious quality it was not to be noticed by anyone else, and even Simon might have imagined it. She sat in a chair that Lazaroff gave up, and Jack Groom sat on the arm and gave an impression of covering her with his wing.

Mr Braunberg shuffled a sheaf of papers, zipped and unzipped his briefcase, adjusted his rimless glasses, and cleared his throat. Having thus obtained the awed attention of the gathering, he put his fingertips together and launched very briskly into his speech.

"You are all naturally anxious to know how Mr Ufferlitz's death will affect you. I can tell you this very quickly."

He picked up a pencil and tapped his sheaf of papers.

"Your contracts with Mr Ufferlitz were all personal contracts with him. In his releasing contract with Paramount he merely undertakes to provide a certain number of pictures of a certain length on certain terms; all the details of cast and production were in his hands, and therefore your individual contracts with him were not included in any kind of assignment. His arrangements with his financial backers were of the same nature, so that your contracts do not revert to them either. Normally, therefore, they would pass to his heirs. Mr Ufferlitz, however, has no heirs. His will directs that the residue of his estate, if any, shall be expended on an . . . er . . . open house party which anyone and everyone employed in the motion picture industry may attend, so long as the refreshments last. I believe that it would be impossible to hold that such a party could inherit, enforce, discharge, or in any sense administer these contractual obligations. Legally, therefore, you are all free persons, subject of course to technical confirmation when Mr Ufferlitz's will is probated. I think you can safely regard that as a mere formality."

Lazaroff went over to Kendricks, who stood up. They shook hands, gravely emitted three shrill irreverent yips, bowed to each other and to Mr Braunberg, and sat down again.

Mr Braunberg frowned.

"Your salaries will be paid up to and including yesterday, on which date the estate will hold that all obligations were mutually terminated. The only difficulty arises with Mr Templar."

"Who is neither here nor there," murmured the Saint.

"Your position is a little ambiguous," Mr Braunberg conceded. "However, in the circumstances I don't think we'll need to fight over it. As Mr Ufferlitz's executor, I'm willing to offer you, say, three thousand dollars, or half a week's salary, in full settlement. That would save us both the expense of going to court over it and also a long delay in winding up the estate, and I don't think the . . . er . . . party will suffer very much from it. Mr Ufferlitz's assets, I believe, will be sufficient to take care of everything on this basis. If that's satisfactory to you?"

"Fair enough," said the Saint, who was a philosopher when there was no useful alternative.

Jack Groom leaned forward over his lantern jaw.

"You said that Mr Ufferlitz had no heirs, Mr Braunberg. Suppose some obscure relative should turn up and contest the will?"

"He'd be taken care of with the usual formula. There's a standard clause in the will which provides that everyone not specifically named is specifically excluded and if they want to argue about it the estate can settle with them for one dollar." The attorney put his fingertips together again. "Are there any further questions?"

There didn't seem to be any.

"Very well, then. It may be a week or two before I can get your checks out, but I'll take care of it as soon as I can. Thank you very much."

He stood up and began to shovel the papers into his briefcase, an efficient business man with a lot of other things to attend to. With true professional discretion, he had not even said a word about the circumstances of Mr Ufferlitz's departure from the ranks of mushroom Hollywood magnates. From his point of view as the executor of a will, the question was not involved. And Simon felt an inward quirk of sardonic amusement as he considered how rapidly and methodically a man's material affairs could be wound up, the ideas and intrigues and ephemeral importances to which he had seemed so essential . . .

The telephone began to ring then in the outer office.

Kendricks and Lazaroff had a few words with Jack Groom on their way out, and Simon caught April Quest's eye again and was moving towards her when Peggy Warden intercepted him.

"A Mr Halliday's calling you."

Simon went into the outer office and took the telephone.

"A fine thing," said Dick Halliday. "Don't you ever take a holiday?"

"I don't seem to have much chance," said the Saint.

"Now I suppose you're out of a job again."

"It looks like it. We've all just had a speech from a legal gent named Braunberg, and we're all out. But being treated right."

"That's quite a break for Lazaroff and Kendricks," Dick said. "I hear that Goldwyn has been offering all kinds of money to get them back."

A formation of butterflies looped and rolled in the Saint's stomach.

"But I thought he'd sworn they were never going to get another job in Hollywood."

"I know. But you know what this town is like. It seems that Goldwyn read a story about how Zanuck hired a man who kicked his behind and told him he was a lousy producer, so now he wants to have a sense of humor too. Besides, the last job they did for him is a terrific success right now. So he wants to forgive them and double their salary."

7

The congregation had dispersed as easily as a puff of smoke. Simon glanced up and down an empty corridor, and went rapidly on to the stairs which led him out into the stucco-reflected glare of Avenue A. He just caught a glimpse of what looked like the thin stooped back of Jack Groom vanishing into the doorway of the entrance lobby, and lengthened his stride in pursuit.

It was Groom, but April Quest had already disappeared when Simon saw him. Instead of her, Lieutenant Condor was talking to him. The detective moved slothfully out in an effective blocking movement that would have made it impossible for the Saint to pass by with a nod.

"Well, Mr Templar, what did you think of the will?"

"Interesting and original," drawled the Saint. "It should be quite a party. I suppose you knew about it already."

"Yeah—I had a preview."

"It's too bad there weren't a lot of heirs and legatees, isn't it?" Simon remarked. "It would have made everything so nice and complicated."

Condor nodded, with his toothpick wagging from his incisors.

"I guess the freed slaves will be all moved out from here tomorrow. You weren't thinking of leaving town, were you?"

"No, I think I'll stick around for a bit."

Groom had been gazing at the Saint in aloof and somber silence.

"You shaved this morning," he said at last, with an air of tired and pained discovery.

"I often do," Simon admitted.

"I thought I asked you to start a moustache for this picture."

"I know. I remember. But since there ain't gonna be no picture—"

Condor moved his large feet.

"When you shaved this morning," he said suddenly, "how did you know there wasn't going to be a picture?"

No earthquake actually took place at that moment, but Simon Templar had the same feeling in his limbs as if the ground had started to shiver under him. He felt rather like a master duellist whose flawless guard has been thrown wide by a bludgeon wielded by an unconsidered spectator. But he was only stopped for an instant. He was lighting a cigarette, and he brought the job to an unruffled completion while his reflexes used the pause to settle back into balance.

"I didn't know," he said lightly. "I was just trying to make Mr Groom see that it doesn't really matter now. As a matter of fact I still wasn't sold on the idea, and I was going to argue about it some more."

"The Saint would wear a moustache," Mr Groom insisted moodily.

His pale emaciated face seemed to be without triumph or maliciousness: he might have been quite unaware of having set a trap and caught a stumble.

"I hate to see you still worrying," said the Saint. "Didn't you hear Braunberg say that we were through with the picture?"

"He didn't say that," Groom corrected him. "He said that we were through with Mr Ufferlitz. There are still Mr Ufferlitz's backers.

They've got a certain amount of money invested, and they might want to go on. It'd be a different set-up, of course."

Condor's bright black eyes were still fixed on the Saint, and Simon knew it, but he was careful not to glance that way. He said to Groom, "Would that mean that you'd still be the director and you might step into Ufferlitz's job as well?"

"I don't know. It's possible," Groom said vaguely.

"So this murder could be quite a break for you."

The detective's eyes had changed their objective. Simon knew that, still without looking.

"What are you getting at?" said Groom.

"I'm just wondering how much this new set-up might be worth to you."

"Isn't that rather insulting?"

The Saint's smile was charming.

"Maybe," he said. "But you can't find a murderer without insulting somebody. You hated Ufferlitz, didn't you?"

"I don't know what you're talking about."

"You hated his guts," said the Saint.

The director combed his fingers through his dank forelock and turned to Condor with a baffled gesture.

"I don't know what he's trying to make out, but he must want to put me in a bad light. He's making a mountain out of a molehill."

"What was there between you and Ufferlitz?" Condor asked casually.

"If you don't want to do it," said the Saint relentlessly, "I don't mind telling him for you."

After which he held his breath.

Groom said, "It just shows what silly gossip will do. Ufferlitz and I had a bit of a fight once at the Trocadero. I got into conversation with a girl at the bar, and apparently he had a date to meet her there. He'd been drinking. He got mad and made a scene."

"And of course you beat the bejesus out of him," Simon said gently.

Two faint red spots burned on Groom's pallid cheekbones.

"It was just one of those night-club brawls. He apologised later. It was just one of those things. That ought to be obvious. Otherwise I wouldn't have been working for him afterwards."

"Do you know what I think?" asked the Saint, with such complete deliberation that the effrontery of what he was saying was almost too bland to grasp. "I think you were on the make for his girl, and you were out of luck. I think he pushed your face in in front of everyone who was there. I think you've been nursing your humiliation ever since—"

"Then why did I go to work for him?" asked Groom, with surprising self-possession.

Simon knew that he was on a tightrope. He was bluffing his head off to get information, and it had worked up to a point, but he could be knocked off his precarious elevation with a feather. But once he had started, he couldn't stop.

"What did Ufferlitz have on you?" he retorted.

"You must be crazy."

"Are you sure?"

"All right. You tell the Lieutenant this time."

Condor's inquisitive gaze switched back again.

The Saint shrugged.

"You're too clever," he said. "I don't know. Naturally. If a lot of people knew, there wouldn't have been any point in playing ball with Ufferlitz to keep him quiet. And there wouldn't have been any point in killing him to make it permanent."

The director appealed to Condor with another helpless movement of his hands.

"What on earth can I say to an insinuation like that? I took this job with Ufferlitz because I needed it quite badly, and I thought it might do me some good. I didn't have to like him especially. But now he must have been blackmailing me, and if nobody knows what I was being blackmailed with I must have murdered him."

"This girl you quarrelled about," Condor said. "Was that recently?"

"No. It was months ago—nearly a year."

"What was her name and where does she live?"

"She doesn't," said Groom.

The detective cocked his head sharply.

"What's that?"

"She died soon after. Too many sleeping tablets." Groom's voice had an almost ghoulish flatness. "She was pregnant. She was trying to get into pictures, but I guess she never got any further than the casting couch."

"Is that on record?"

"No—it's just more gossip. Ufferlitz went out with her quite a lot. However, Mr Templar will probably tell you that I murdered her too."

"What was her name?" asked the Saint.

"Trilby Andrews."

Something smooth and magnificent like a great wave rolled up over Simon Templar's head, and when it had passed he was outside the studio, alone, and the conversation had broken up and petered out in the frustrated ineffectual way that had perhaps always been doomed for it, but that didn't seem to matter anymore. It had ended with Groom sulky and sneering, and Condor turning his long predatory nose from one to the other of them like the beak of a suspicious bird; there was nothing much more that he could do, it was only talk and suggestion and leads that he could remember to follow later, but Simon hardly even noticed how the scene ended. Clear as a cameo in his mind now he had a name, a name that had been written on a photograph of a face which in some faint disturbing way had seemed as if it should have been familiar and yet was not, and now the wave rolled over and left him with a serenity of knowledge that out of all the cold threads that he had been trying to weave into patterns he had at last touched one that had a warmth and life of its own . . .

He found himself crossing the boulevard to think it over with the mild encouragement of a few drops of Peter Dawson. The interior of the Front Office was dim and soothing after the bold light outside, and he had been there for several minutes with a drink in front of him before he was aware that he was not the only customer ahead of the five o'clock stampede.

"H'lo," said the heart-shaking voice of Orlando Flane, now somewhat thickened and slurred with alcohol. "The great detective himself, in person!"

He unwound himself from the obscurity of a booth and steered a painstaking course to the bar, only tripping over his own feet once.

"Hullo," said the Saint coolly.

"The great actor, too. Going to be a big star. Have your name in lights. Women chasing you. Cheering crowds, an' everything."

"Not any more."

"Whaddaya mean?"

"My job was with Ufferlitz. No more Ufferlitz—no more job. So I have to go back to detecting, and the crowds can cheer you again."

Flane shook his head.

"Too bad."

"Isn't it?"

"Too bad, after you did such a swell job chiselling me out."

"I didn't chisel you out."

"No. You just took my part away from me. That was nice to do. Real Robin Hood stuff."

"Listen, dope," said the Saint temperately. "I never took anything away from you. You were out anyway. Ufferlitz dragged me in. When he made a deal with me I didn't know you'd ever been involved. How the hell should I?"

Flane thought it over with the soggy concentration of drunkenness.

"Thass right," he announced at last.

"I'm glad you can see it."

"You're okay."

"Thanks."

"Shake."

"Sure."

"Less have a drink."

They had a drink. Flane stared heavily at his glass.

"So here we are," he said. "Neither of us got a job."

"It's sad, isn't it?"

"My pal. You gotta get a job. I'll find you a job. Talk to my agent about you."

"I wouldn't bother, I didn't really want to be in this racket to start with. It just looked like fun and a bit of dough."

"Yeah. Dough. That's all I'm in for. I never thought I'd be in this racket either."

"What racket were you in before?"

"Lotsa things. You don't think I'm tough, do you?"

"I don't know."

"Most people don't."

"I suppose not."

"But I am tough, see? I've been around. I know what it's all about."

"Like Ufferlitz?"

"That son of a bitch."

"Was he really?"

"Threw me out of the picture. Threw me outa his office when I was drunk an' couldn't give him what he had coming."

"Yes, I was there."

"That dirty bastard."

"But you fixed him, didn't you?" Simon asked gently.

Flane stared at him dimly.

"Whatsat?"

"You said you were going to fix him."

"Yeah. So he'd stay fixed."

"You certainty did."

"Too late now," Flane said gloomily.

Simon looked at him over his glass with a slight frown.

"What d'you mean—too late?"

"Too late to fix him. He's been fixed."

"But you did it, didn't you?"

Flane steadied himself, and a smudgily truculent rigidity came over his face.

"Are you nuts?"

"No. But you said you'd fix him—"

"Are you trying to hang something on me?"

"No. It was just a natural thing to think."

"Well quit thinking."

"I might," said the Saint, "but I don't know whether the police will. After all, you were heard to threaten him."

"To hell with the police."

"Hasn't Condor talked to you yet?"

"Who?"

"Lieutenant Condor—the guy who's in charge of the case."

"Christ, no! Why should he? Annew know something? You know what I'd do if any cop came near me?"

"What would you do?"

"I'd poke him right in the eye!"

"Let's have another drink," said the Saint.

Flane picked up his drink when it came and focused on it with intense deliberation. He held it rather like a binnacle holds a ship's compass, rocking under and around it but holding it in miraculously isolated suspension.

"That son of a bitch," he said. "I coulda fixed him."

"How?"

"I coulda put him right in the can."

"What for?"

"For quail!"

Simon lighted a cigarette as if it were fragile. It was curious how coincidences always had to be repeated, and when your luck was coming in you just had to let it alone.

"You mean Trilby Andrews," he said calmly.

"Yeah. She was under age. He ditched her an' she took a sleep."

"That's just gossip."

"That's what you think. But I coulda proved it."

"Only you didn't," Simon said carefully, "because he had something even better on you."

He had a picture already of the methods and associations of the late Mr Ufferlitz which made that kind of shot in the dark look almost as good as the chance of hitting a wall from inside a room, but he was not quite prepared for the response that he got this time.

Flane put down an empty glass and turned and took hold of him by the lapels of his coat. The alcoholic slackness was crushed down in his face as if with a great effort of will, and his eyes were cold even through the obvious bleariness of his vision. For the first time since Simon had set eyes on him he really looked as if he could have been tough. He didn't raise his voice.

"Who told you that?" he said.

Simon had played this kind of poker all his life. Now he had to be good. He didn't move. The bartender was down at the far end of the bar, polishing glasses while he looked over a magazine, and he didn't seem to have been paying any attention for some time.

The Saint met Flane's straining gaze with utter confidence. He dropped his own voice even lower, and said, "Ufferlitz's attorney."

"What did he know?"

"Everything."

"Keep talking."

"You see, Ufferlitz didn't trust you. And he wasn't dumb. He took precautions. He left a letter to be opened if anything happened to him. He had quite a story about your early life."

"In New Orleans?"

"Yes."

Flane fought against the compulsion of his clouded instincts. Simon could see him doing it, and see him losing his way in the struggle.

"About the girl who got knocked off—who was a witness—"

"Yes," said the Saint, with absolute intuitive certainty now. "When you were a talent scout for a rather less glamorous business."

Flane steadied himself against Simon's lapels.

"How many other people did he tell?"

"Quite a lot. More than you could take care of now . . . You're all washed up, brother. If Condor hasn't found you yet, you'd better get ready for him. You're going to make the best headlines of your career."

"Yeah? . . . My pal!"

"Not your pal," said the Saint, "since you tried to hang the rap on me by sending me that note."

Flane blinked at him.

"What note?"

"The note you sent to put me on the spot."

"I didn't send you any note."

"Your memory needs a lot of reminding, doesn't it? But you're not helping yourself a bit. You had it all—"

The Saint's voice loosened off uncertainly. It wasn't from anything that Flane had said or done. It was from something that came up within himself: a recollection, an idea—two ideas—something that was trying to form itself in his mind against the train of his thought, that suddenly softened his own assurance and his attention at the same time.

At that instant Flane pushed lurchingly against him, and the bar stool started to topple. Off balance, the Saint made a wild attempt to get at least one foot on the ground and get a foundation from which he could hit. It was too much of a contortion even for him, Flane's fist smashed against his jaw—not shatteringly, but hard enough to put new acceleration into his fall. As he went down, the next stool hit him on the back of the head, and then for an uncertain interval there was nothing but a thunderous blackness through which large engines drove round and round . . .

8

He woke up in a surprising lucidity, as if he had only dozed for a moment—except for a throbbing ache that swelled up in waves from the base of his brain. He woke up so clearly that he could lay still for a moment and take full advantage of the wet towel that the bartender was swabbing over his face.

"Thanks," he said. "Do I look as stupid as I feel?"

"You're okay," said the bartender, and added without intention, "How d'ya feel?"

"Fine."

The Saint stood up. For a second he thought his head was going to fall off; then it righted itself.

"What happened?" asked the bartender.

"I slipped."

"He gets ugly sometimes, when he's been drinking."

"So do a lot of guys. Where did he go?"

"Out. He scrammed outa here like a bat outa hell. Maybe he was scared what you'd do to him when you got up."

"Maybe," said the Saint, appreciating the sympathy. "How long a start has he got?"

"Long enough. Now look, take it easy. Better have a drink and cool off. On the house."

"Anyway that's an idea," said the Saint.

He had a drink, which might or might not have helped the pain in his head to subside a little, and then went back across the boulevard and interviewed the studio gatekeeper.

"Lieutenant Condor? No, sir. He left right after you did. He didn't say where he was going."

Simon picked up the desk phone and dialled Peggy Warden.

"So you're still there," he said. "Didn't they fire you too?"

"I expect I'll be here till the end of the week, clearing some things up for Mr Braunberg."

"That's good."

"You left in an awful hurry."

"My feet started travelling. I had to run to catch up with them."

"You've got to give me an address where we can send your check."

"I'll be seeing you before that."

"You're not still going on being a detective, are you?"

"I am."

"I wonder what you're like when you relax?"

"You could find out."

"A dialogue writer," she said.

"Where are you going to be later?"

"Where are you going to be?"

"I don't know right now. Can I call you?"

"I'll be at home. Probably washing my last pair of silk stockings. The number's in the book."

"I don't read very well," said the Saint, "but I'll try and get someone to look it up for me."

He walked around to the parking lot and retrieved his car, and drove north towards the hills that look down across the subdivided prairie between Sunset Boulevard and the sea. Lazaroff and Kendricks lived up there, not Orlando Flane, and yet suddenly the pursuit of Orlando Flane was not so important. Flane could be found later, if he wanted to be found at all—if he didn't, he wouldn't be sitting at home. But other patterns were taking a shape from which Flane was curiously lacking. It was like stalking a circus horse in the belief that it was real, and finding it capable of separating into two identities with cloths over them . . .

The house was perched on a sharp buttress of rock high above the Strip—that strange No Man's Land of county in the middle of a city whose limits traditionally extend to the Jersey side of the Holland Tunnel. There were cars in the open garage, Simon noticed as he parked, and he rang the bell with the peaceful confidence that the wheels were meshing at last and nothing could stop them.

Kendricks himself flung the door open, looking more than ever like one of the earnest ambassadors of the House of Fuller, as if their positions ought to have been reversed and he should have been on the outside trying to get in. The sight of the Saint only took him aback for a moment, and then his face broke into a hospitable grin.

"Surprise, surprise," he said. "Superman has a nose like a bloodhound, on top of everything else. We were just starting to celebrate. Come in and help us."

"I didn't get your invitation," said the Saint genially, "so I didn't know what time to come."

"Somebody has to be first," Kendricks said.

He led the way into the Tudor bar which appeared to substitute for a living-room, and Vic Lazaroff raised his shaggy gray head from some intricate labors over a cocktail shaker.

"Welcome," he said. "You are going to study genius in its cups. We shall reciprocate by studying you in yours."

"It's a great event," Simon said.

"You bet it is. Once again the uncrowned kings of Holly wood are on the throne—"

"That's quite definite, is it?"

"Everything but the signatures, which we shall write tomorrow if we can still hold a pen."

Simon settled on the arm of a chair.

"Goldwyn must think a lot of you."

"Why shouldn't he? Look at all the publicity he can get out of us."

"But it does seem like going a bit far."

"What does?"

"Murdering Ufferlitz," said the Saint, "so he could get you back."

Neither of them spoke at once. Kendricks stood still in the middle of the room. Lazaroff carefully put down the bottle from which he had been pouring. The silence was quite noticeable.

"It's a deep gag," Kendricks said finally.

"Of course," said the Saint imperturbably, "if it wasn't so obvious that Sam Goldwyn must have bumped him off so he could get his two favorite writers back, some people might think the writers had done it to get free again."

"Very deep," said Lazaroff.

"The only thing I don't get," Simon said, "is why you thought it would be clever to hang it on me."

"We what?"

"Why you sent me that note and phoned the police about a prowler, pretending that you were Ufferlitz, so that I'd be caught in the house with his body and very probably sent to jail for a week or two for killing him."

This silence was even deeper than the last one. It grew up until Simon was conscious of making an effort to hold the implacable stillness of his face and force them to make the first movement.

At last Lazaroff made it.

He stretched up a little, as though he were lifting a weight with his hands.

"Better tell him, Bob," he said.

Kendricks stirred, and the Saint looked at him.

"I guess so," he said. "We did send you that note."

"Why?"

"For a laugh." Kendricks was like a schoolboy on the carpet. "One of those crazy things we're always doing. You could have made the front pages all day, too. Banners when you were arrested, and a double column when they found out it was all a mistake."

"And how were they going to find that out?"

"I tell you, when we planned it we didn't know Ufferlitz was going to get killed."

"So you only thought of that afterwards."

Lazaroff dragged his fingers through his hair and said, "Good God, we didn't kill him."

"You were just playing rough, and he couldn't take it."

"We never saw him."

"Then why didn't you say anything? You expected me to be there, and get caught by the police. If you were surprised to hear Ufferlitz had been murdered, weren't you surprised that I wasn't in jail?"

"We were," said Kendricks. "When I saw you in the office this afternoon I nearly fell over backwards."

"But you never said anything."

"We sort of hinted—to try and find out where you stood."

"But you didn't care whether I was in a jam."

"We didn't know. You mightn't have fallen for that note. Anything might have happened. You mightn't have gotten home at all last night—"

"But you knew I'd received the note and fallen for it," said the Saint coldly. "You saw me drop April Quest and go home. Your car drove by when we were saying goodnight." It was another fragment of the jigsaw that fitted accurately into place now. "After that you saw me arrive at Ufferlitz's. That was when you phoned the police. But you still didn't think I was in a jam."

Kendricks made a helpless movement.

"You're getting me tied up," he said. "Just like a lawyer. The whole truth is that we didn't know what had happened to you. You've got a great reputation for getting out of jams—you might have dodged that one. We didn't know. But we couldn't come out and say anything, because if the cops knew we'd framed you like that they'd naturally think what you thought—that we'd murdered Ufferlitz and tried to make it look like it was you. We were in the hell of a jam ourselves. It was a gag that fate took a hand in, or something. And we were stuck with it. We just had to shut up and hope something would happen."

"But you weren't in the house yourselves."

"Not once."

"Then how," Simon asked very placidly, "did you know, when you wrote that note, that the front door would be unlocked?"

There was stillness a third time, a stillness that had the explosive quality of a frenzied struggle gripped in immovable chains. Lazaroff finally made a frustrated gesture, as if his hand had turned into lead.

"It sounds worse and worse, but we just happened to know."

"How?"

"I heard Ufferlitz telling his secretary about working there last night. He said 'The door'll be open as usual.' She said 'Don't you ever lock your door?' and he said 'I haven't locked my house up for years. I always lose keys, and what the hell, if anybody's going to get in they'll get in anyway and leave me a busted window on top of it.' I don't suppose you'll believe that, but you can check on it."

Simon held his eyes and moved to another seat by the telephone. He picked up the directory, and found Peggy Warden's number. He put the telephone on his knee and dialled it.

Lazaroff went on looking at him steadily.

"Hullo," she said.

"This is Lieutenant Condor," said the Saint, and his voice was a perfect imitation of the detective's soured and dismal accent. "There's one thing I forgot to check with you. When you left Mr Ufferlitz's house last night, did you leave the door unlocked?"

"Why, yes. It was unlocked when I got there. He never locked it."

"Never?"

"No. He said he always lost his keys, and if a burglar really wanted to get in he'd just break a window or something."

"When did he tell you that?"

"It was only yesterday, as a matter of fact. But the door was unlocked the last time I went there, to bring him some letters."

"Had you been there often—of course, I mean on business?"

"Only once before. I just took him some letters one Sunday morning, and he signed them and I took them away with me."

"Did anyone else know about him never locking the door?"

"I don't really know, Lieutenant."

"Could anyone have heard him telling you?"

"I suppose so." She hesitated. "Those two writers had been in the office—yes, Mr Lazaroff was still there. But—"

"But what?"

"You don't really think they could have had anything to do with it, do you?"

"I can't make guesses, miss," he said. "I'm trying to get facts. Thanks for your information."

He hung up. Lazaroff and Kendricks were watching him.

"Well," he said, "she confirms your story."

"It's true," said Kendricks.

"But it only proves that you knew the door would be open—so you could be sure of putting your scheme through."

"Look, for Christ's sake. We aren't dopes. We've kicked plots around. If we'd really wanted to frame you, we could have done more than that. We could have put you in a much worse spot. We could have left your trademark drawing on Ufferlitz, if we'd killed him, so you'd really have had something to explain. Now don't do another of those lawyer tricks and ask how we know there wasn't a drawing. I'll bet there wasn't, or Condor would certainly have had you in the cooler."

It was true there had been no drawing, and it was a point. Simon took out a cigarette.

"You don't owe us anything," Lazaroff said. "We're screwballs and occasional heels and a few other things, but we've never murdered anyone or tried to put anyone in a spot like you're in. You call Condor if you want to. Tell him the whole story. Bob and I'll admit it. It won't be much fun for us, but I guess we've got it coming. Anyhow you'll be in the clear."

"You'd better do it," said Kendricks resignedly. "Get yourself out of the mess."

"And still leave it looking as if it was just a coincidence, and you guys had nothing to do with the murder."

"By God," said Lazaroff, "we didn't kill Ufferlitz! But you don't have to cover us up. Tell this guy Condor what you think. We can take it."

His square florid face was screwed up like a baby preparing to cry. All at once he looked ludicrous and defeated and curiously pathetic, and at the same time desperately sincere.

It had to be genuine; Simon realised it with a hopeless sense of relaxation. Lazaroff with a real crime on his conscience would have responded in any way but that. He wasn't a dope. He was an irresponsible practical joker and a facile professional story-weaver as well. Between the two characteristics he would have been glib or indignant or bluffingly calm or angry. He wouldn't have been deflated and frightened, as if he had pointed a supposedly unloaded gun once too often and heard it thunder in his hand.

Then—it was true. A coincidence that had gotten itself entangled with real murder, that had distorted the whole picture of plotting and motive. Now the Saint was trying to shake his head clear of all the assumptions and misconceptions that had rooted themselves into his mind because he had leapt on to the premise that two things were inseparably related when actually they had no connection at all.

"Give me that drink," he said. "I'm going to start trying to use my brain for a change."

"Let's all have one," said Lazaroff fervently. Kendricks went over and switched on the radio. A musical theme ended, and an unctuous announcer began to discourse on the merits of a popular intestinal lubricant.

"How bad a spot are you really in?" Kendricks asked.

"Not so bad yet. I was in Ufferlitz's house when the police came, but I managed to get away. Naturally I didn't tell Condor about having been there. That note would have looked like as bad an excuse for being there as your explanation sounded. So I don't want to drag you into it now, if you'll go on leaving me out."

"You bet we will. But could Condor find out any other way?"

"You never know. That's why I still want to find the murderer first."

"Haven't you any idea now who it was?" pleaded Lazaroff.

The Saint stared at his cigarette. He had to begin all over again. But now things forced themselves into the front of his mind that he had not been able to see clearly before.

The radio said, "And now, here is Ben Alexander with the news."

"Good evening, everyone," said a new voice. "Before we turn to the European headlines, here's a flash that has just come in. Orlando Flane, the movie star, shot himself at his home at Toluca Lake this afternoon. His sensational rise to world-wide fame began when he was featured in . . ."

9

April Quest poured two Martinis from the shaker and sat down beside the Saint. Her beauty still gave him that unearthly feeling of having stepped out of ordinary life into a dream—the perfect harmony of her dark copper hair, the exquisite etching of emerald eyes, the impossible sculpture of her features, the way her body flowed into every movement and disturbed the mind with its unconscious suggestion of the fulfilment of all the hungers known to all men.

She said, "Well, you louse, I suppose you've stopped feeling human so now you feel safe."

He said, "That's a sad reward for being a gentleman."

"Nuts," she said. "A gentleman is anyone who does what you want them to do when you want them to do it. A swine is the same guy who does the same thing when you don't want him to do it. Or who won't do it when you want him to."

Simon smiled and tasted his drink.

"You're a philosopher too, darling. Was that why you wouldn't talk to me this afternoon?"

"I didn't want to talk to you in front of all those jerks."

"That's nice. But afterwards—"

"Then you were on the phone."

"You must have been in an awful hurry."

"If you wanted to see me, you knew where to find me. I-I was hoping you would."

The Saint lighted her a cigarette, and one for himself. He watched the smoke drifting away, and said, "April, what do you think about Ufferlitz getting bumped off?"

"I haven't thought much," she said. "It's just something that happened. He might have caught pneumonia jumping out of a warm bed."

"Doesn't it make any difference to you professionally?"

"Not very much. I told you I was under contract to Jack Groom. He gets half of what he can sell me for, after he's reimbursed himself for what he's paid me when I haven't been working. So he'll get me another job, just to make his half good."

"He sort of hinted to me," Simon said, "that Ufferlitz's backers might give him Ufferlitz's job. Then I suppose he might be able to make a better deal for both of you."

"He might be."

She was quite disinterested.

"Don't you care?"

"Christ," she said, "why should I get any gray hairs? If he makes a better deal, okay. If he doesn't, I won't starve. I'm pretty lucky. I've got a beautiful puss and a beautiful body, and not too much talent and goddam little sense. I'm never going to be a Bette Davis, and I'm not going to screw up my life trying to be a prima donna. I can eat. And that means plenty."

"You don't care about seeing Jack Groom get ahead?"

"Why the hell should I? He can take care of himself. Don't let that spiritual-hammy act of his fool you. He knows all the angles. He can play politics and connive and lick boots in the best company."

"I asked you last night," said the Saint, "but you wouldn't tell me. So I was still wondering if there was anything personal between you."

It was amazing that such a face could be so passionless and detached.

"He took me to Palm Springs one weekend, and he was lousy. He'll never have the nerve to try it again. But I've been a good business proposition, and that's a lot in his life."

Simon tapped his cigarette over the ashtray.

"Then—you wouldn't kill anyone on account of him?"

"God, no."

"Then why did you kill Ufferlitz?"

She was an actress. She sat and looked at him, without any exaggerated response.

"This should be good," she said. "Go on."

"By the way," he said, "did you hear the news a little while ago? On the radio?"

"I heard some of it."

"Did you hear about Orlando Flane bumping himself off?"

"Yes. Did I do that too?"

"I don't know. Can you think of any reason why he should kill himself?"

"Several. And he's all of them. He was a bastard from away back. And he was pretty well washed up in this town. He didn't have anything to live for for months, except Ufferlitz almost gave him a break."

"And what do you think about Trilby Andrews?"

"I never heard of her. Who is she?"

"She isn't. She was."

She leaned back with her glass in her hand.

"*Hawkshaw Rides Again,*" she said. "Go on. You do the talking. I told you last night I could see it coming. I'm not a detective. Tell me how it works."

He took another cigarette and lighted it from the stub of one that was only half finished. He refilled both their glasses from the shaker. Then he relaxed beside her and gazed up at the ceiling. He felt very calm now.

"I'm a lousy detective," he said. "I never really wanted to be one . . . Maybe all detectives are lousy. They only get anywhere because the suspects are lousy too, and it doesn't matter how many mistakes a detective makes. You just blunder around and wait for something to pop . . . That's all I've been doing. I've thrown accusations all over the place, and been sure I'd strike a spark somewhere. You rush around and jump to conclusions and have kittens over every flash, and get gorgeously master-minded and confused . . . But in the end I've started to think."

He was thinking now, while he talked, picking up the loose ends that his driving imagination had so blithely pushed aside.

"Byron Ufferlitz was shot through the back of his head, in his study, in his home, by somebody that he presumably knew pretty well—at least well enough to give an opportunity like that to. That gives the first list of suspects. None of them have very good alibis, but on the other hand nobody except the murderer knows exactly when it was done, so alibis aren't so important. I could have done it myself. So could you."

"And you've decided that I did."

"There wasn't any clue," said the Saint. "No clue at all. Every clue had been very carefully cleaned up. And I was too busy to see that the first clue might be there."

"You'll have to explain that."

"When you leave clues, you don't necessarily book yourself to the gas chamber. But when you clean up clues, you may do just that.

Because the blank spaces show your own guilty conscience. A clue isn't a death warrant, because it's only circumstantial. If I dropped in here and killed you and went out again, I might leave a lot of clues—and none of them would mean anything. A scientific detective might sweep the carpet and put the dust under a microscope and find celluloid dust in it, and say, 'Ha! Someone has been here who's been in contact with motion picture film; therefore the villain is someone from a studio.' So what? So are hundreds of people . . . Or I might leave a book of matches from the House of Romanoff, and the inspirational detective would say, 'Ha! This is a man of such and such a type who goes to such and such places'—regardless of the fact that I might have bummed the matches from a chauffeur who bummed them from somebody else's chauffeur whose boss left them in the car. I might never have been in the House of Romanoff in my life . . . Now I don't know what was cleaned off Ufferlitz's carpet, or what matches were taken away, or anything else, but I do know one clue that was cleaned up that tells a story."

"This is fascinating," she said. "Go on."

"The ashtrays were emptied," he said.

She sipped her Martini.

"There might have been fingerprints on the cigarettes. Or . . . or the make of cigarette would tell who'd been there—"

"I'm not such an expert, but I wouldn't want the job of trying to get fingerprints from old cigarette butts. They aren't held right—you might get bits of three fingers, but never one complete impression. On top of which they'd be smudged and crushed and probably fogged up with ash. It's a million to one you couldn't get an identification. As for telling anything from the brand of cigarette—that may have worked for Sherlock Holmes, but you can't think of a brand today that isn't smoked by thousands of people. And most of them change brands pretty freely, too. But one thing could have stood out on those cigarettes, one thing that nobody could miss, that even the dumbest amateur would have had to do something about."

"What was that?"

He said, "Lipstick."

It was very quiet in the room. It was as if a section of the world enclosed between four walls and a floor and ceiling had been moved out into unrelated space. Ice settled in the shaker with a startling collapse like an avalanche.

"Of course," she said.

"So it had to be a woman," he said. "It couldn't be Trilby Andrews, because she's dead. But it might very likely be someone that he'd treated the same way, who reacted differently. She killed herself, but a different kind of girl might prefer to kill him. Or, it could be someone who was squaring accounts for Trilby."

"Either way," she said, "you came to me."

He just looked at her.

She put out her cigarette and looked at the red tip where her lips had left their color. Then she turned to him again. Her eyes were strangely hard to read.

"So you're still a great detective," she said. "Now what happens?"

"We could have another drink."

"Do you think I should give myself up, or would you rather turn me in and get some glory?"

"Neither. I may be a detective, but I'm not a policeman. I can be my own grand jury. From what I've found out about Ufferlitz since I began meddling with this, I'd just as soon leave everything as it is."

A bell chimed somewhere in the house.

"Tell me the strings," she said. "Go on. I'm grown up."

"There are no strings, April," he answered. "I feel rather satisfied about Ufferlitz getting killed. You see, some of those stories about me are still true. Once upon a time, before the Hays Office got hold of me, I might easily have killed him myself."

Her eyes suddenly blurred in front of him.

"'Saint,'" she said, and her voice gave the word new meaning. But she didn't finish.

The butler came in on padded feet, and said, "Lieutenant Condor is asking for Mr Templar."

Simon stood up.

Her eyes never left him as she stood up too.

"I'll try and take him away," he said. "May I come back and finish my drink later?"

Without waiting for an answer he strolled out into the hall to greet the hungry lugubrious figure of Lieutenant Condor. The Saint's smile was genial and carefree.

"Well, well, well!" he murmured. "The never-sleeping bloodhound. How did you know I was here?"

"I figured you'd be with somebody," Condor said rather cryptically. "I just tried one or two places, and this was it. Do you want to talk here or shall we go outside?"

"Let's go outside."

They went out into the dark that had fallen outside, and sauntered over the lawn towards the sidewalk where Condor's police car was parked. A street lamp shone down on it like a dull white moon among the palms. Simon saw the driver stick his head out and watch them.

"You get on pretty well with her?" Condor asked, with matter-of-fact impersonality.

"Very well."

"Was she helping you work out another alibi for when Flane was shot?"

Simon slowed his step, with his hands in his pockets, and said quite amiably, "If you're serious about that, I'd like an official warning and we'll talk it over with the District Attorney and my own lawyer. Otherwise you'd better go easy with those cracks. I can't let you go on like this indefinitely. Now do I really need an alibi or what?"

"I'm afraid not," Condor admitted lugubriously. He sighed. "This time you seem to be in the clear. Do you know anything about it?"

"Only what I heard on the radio."

"Flane rushed into his home, quite cockeyed apparently, and went straight to his bedroom. His housekeeper was trying to ask him about something, but he just didn't pay any attention. He must have grabbed a gun out of a drawer and shot himself, bang, just like that. She rushed right in and there he was, falling down, with a gun in his hand."

"That's quite a relief to me," said the Saint. "So now why did you want me?"

"I thought you might have done some more figuring since it happened."

The police driver opened the car door and got out, as they stopped on the pavement. He kept moving towards them with short awkward steps, his face fixed and staring.

"If it happened the way you say it did," Simon observed, "it might have been a genuine suicide. In fact, I should say it must have been. So it's no use dreaming about your murderer following up to cover himself."

"Unless he's a genius," said Condor.

The driver was right with them now. He was still staring at the Saint, his eyes popping a little. Suddenly his hand settled on to his gun.

"Is this Templar?" he interrupted hoarsely.

"Yes," Condor said, glancing at him.

The driver's mouth worked.

"Well, I saw him last night! I was circlin' round to cover the back, an' I had my flashlight right on him. I thought he'd come out of another house where they was havin' a party. He musta bin at Ufferlitz's when we got there!"

10

"This had better be good," said Condor dispassionately.

He sat beside the Saint with a fresh toothpick between his teeth and a gun in the hand on his knee, while Simon zigzagged his big Buick down on to Beverly Boulevard. He glanced once over his shoulder at the lights following behind them, and added: "Dunnigan's right on your trail, so I hope you weren't thinking of pulling any fast ones."

"I'm hoping to save you a hell of a stink and a lawsuit for false arrest," said the Saint. "Have you read that note?"

Condor looked at it again under the dashboard lights.

"And this is supposed to be why you went there."

"That's why I went there."

"When did you write it?"

"I knew you'd say that. That's why I got the hell out. I walked in, and there was Ufferlitz with his brains all over the desk. Then the cops came. I knew I was being framed, so I went away quickly."

"You didn't even say anything about it when I talked to you this morning."

"Of course not. Nothing had been changed. You'd still have thought I was trying to put over a clever story. But you can check on it yourself now. I did. According to the night man at the Château Marmont, that note was delivered by a medium-sized man in a buttoned-up tweed overcoat and a bushy red beard. A disguise, of course. And of course it sounds phony as hell. I could just as well have done it myself, with my knees bent to cut my height down. I knew you'd think that, and I'd have been crazy if I'd told you."

Condor chewed audibly on his flake of timber.

"I like having my mind put straight for me," he said. "So you played secrets. Did you know who the murderer was then?"

"No," said the Saint honestly. "I had to get away and think and investigate for a bit. But I had to find him. I had to find him before he got me into some more trouble that I wouldn't be able to get out of so easily. I knew it must have been somebody who hated my guts. Somebody who was tough enough to kill Ufferlitz in the first place, and vicious enough to try and frame me for it. A guy with two motives."

"And you found him all by yourself."

"Yes," said the Saint. "Orlando Flane."

They stopped for a traffic light. Simon shifted into low gear and held the clutch out. He kept his eyes ahead, but he knew Condor was still watching him.

"You tell it," said Condor. "It's your story."

"There wasn't much to it. I'd taken a part away from Flane. He was on the skids, and that part might have saved him, but I took it away. I didn't mean to. It was Ufferlitz's idea. Flane was just letters in lights to me. But he didn't understand that. His brain was all rotten with alcohol, anyway. He was drunk at Giro's last night when we were there. You can check on that, too. And I guess he was just too mad to have any sense."

"But why did he kill Ufferlitz?"

"Because Ufferlitz was blackmailing him. Flane wasn't always a glamor boy for cameras. There was a time in New Orleans when he was charming feminine hearts for a much less romantic racket. He was in a bad spot once, and there was a girl who was a witness. She died—very conveniently. But Ufferlitz had the goods on him."

"How do you know that?"

"You forget," said the Saint gently. "Crime is my business. And I've got a rather phenomenal memory. Only sometimes it's a little bit slow. But you don't have to take my word for it. You can confirm it with New Orleans."

They were rolling eastwards on the boulevard again.

"Why didn't you tell me that this morning?"

"It just hadn't come into my head then. I got it after I left you this afternoon. Going off on a wrong tack after Groom—that business about the girl . . . girls . . . dirty work with girls—and suddenly the gates were open and it all poured in. I was in the Front Office then, and by God, Flane was there. Well, I'm just not a good citizen. I never could see why policemen should have all the fun. I just have to stick my own nose in. So I did. I told Flane I was wise to him. I told him the whole story, and invented what I wasn't sure of. But I made it good. Just to see if I could make him break."

"And then—"

"Then he broke. I don't have to try and convince you about that. Here's my first witness."

He braked the car to a stop outside the neon façade of the Front Office, and the prowl car slid tightly in behind. Simon opened his door and got out with careful leisureliness, and the detective put his gun away and got out after him.

They went into the crepuscular discretion of the bar, where a sizeable clientele was now dispersed through shadowy corners, and Simon beckoned the bartender over.

"Will you tell Mr Condor what happened this afternoon?"

The bartender looked surprised to see the Saint again so soon, and along with his surprise there was a habitual wariness.

"About what?" he said innocently.

"About Flane," said the Saint.

"It's all right," Condor put in soothingly. "There's no beef. Mr Templar just wanted me to hear it." The bartender wiped his hands on his apron.

"I guess Mr Flane had just had one too many," he said.

"He was talking to this gentleman, and I couldn't hear what they were saying. Then it looked as if Mr Flane was getting tough—he does that sometimes, when he's had a drink—or I should say he used to do it—"

"Go on," Condor said.

"Well, I tried to hear something then, but I couldn't hear anything, and then he must have slugged Mr Whatyoucalledhim, because he fell off his stool, and Mr Flane beat it out of here, an' I got the gentleman up again an' bought him a drink an' he went out. That's all I know."

"Thank you," said Condor.

Then they were outside again.

"After that," said the Saint, "I went back to the studio to see if you were still there, but you'd left. We can walk over and you can check that. If the same gatekeeper isn't on now, he'll know where we can find the guy I spoke to."

Condor gazed moodily across the street, like a dyspeptic crocodile on a river bank watching succulent game cavorting on the other side.

"I'll believe you," he said. "You wouldn't want me to check it if I wouldn't get the right answers. But why didn't you call me at Headquarters?"

"I meant to," said the Saint. "But I . . . well, I had a date. You know how it is. And I got drinking, and sort of put it off. Then I heard the news on the radio. Then I was just scared to stick my neck out. I figured the case was washed up anyhow. I'd as good as told Flane he was sunk, and he'd bumped himself off. So—justice was done, even if nobody got any medals."

Condor massaged his long melancholy nose.

"You want me to believe a helluva lot," he said. "And a guy in my job eats medals."

"Don't believe any more than you want to," Simon nonchalantly. "Just convince yourself. Flane had it in for Ufferlitz. He'd threatened him before—"

"He had?"

"Right in that bar. The first time I ever saw him. He was drunk, and he was shooting off his mouth about how Ufferlitz couldn't do things to him and he was going to show him where he got off. The bartender was trying to calm him down. Go back and ask him."

The detective shook his head.

"If you had that bartender primed with one story, you'd have him rehearsed in all of 'em," he said unenthusiastically. "Who else heard Flane say he'd get Ufferlitz?"

The Saint thought, and a picture came into his mind.

"Ufferlitz's secretary heard him—Ufferlitz threw him out of his office yesterday, and Flane said then that he'd fix him. Didn't she tell you?"

"No."

"She should have. She was there."

Condor hunched his shoulders.

"We'll see if she's home," he said.

So they were in the Saint's car again, heading north across Hollywood Boulevard to an address that they looked up in the phone book in the corner drug store. The prowl car followed behind them like a shadow.

But the Saint was hardly aware of it any more. Certainly it had no more sinister implications. Condor was sold, even though he hadn't admitted it aloud. It was only a question of a little more time and some routine verifications. The detective's mournful passivity and the dejected downward angle of the toothpick in his mouth were their own acknowledgments. In the end it had been as simple as that. And Simon was only wondering why he had never thought of that scene before, when Flane had come hurtling out of Ufferlitz's office and the Saint had picked him up and steadied him while he made his threat—the scene that Peggy Warden had omitted to tell Condor about. Simon thought he had been very slow about that. But it was all taken care of now . . .

And they were in Peggy Warden's apartment, and she was a little frightened and wide-eyed, but she said, "Yes, Mr Flane did say that, but—"

And Condor said, "Do you remember his words?"

"It was something like—" She wrinkled her brow. "Something like 'When I fix you, you're going to stay fixed.'"

"That was it," said the Saint.

She said, "But he was drunk—he didn't really know what he was saying—"

Condor turned away from her with a movement of glum separation whose superficial rudeness had less to do with any deliberate intention than with his congenital inability to loosen his official armor.

His bright black eyes circled down on to the Saint like tired dead crows.

"Okay, Saint," he said. "You're good. I don't know how good yet, but good."

"Then what happens?"

"I can't say. I just work for a living. It'll all have to go to the DA. Probably the Big Shots'll go to work on him to push it away without any scandal. Another Hollywood mystery dies a natural death. That's my guess. I'm only a cop."

"But you're satisfied?"

"I'm going to have to be. I'll do some more checking up, but if you're as good as you sound it won't make any difference." His mouth turned down one-sidedly. "If you're not worried any more, you don't need to be."

The Saint sat down in the nearest chair and prepared himself a cigarette with unwontedly deliberate fingers.

"I think," he remarked judicially, "that I could use a drink."

"I've got some Scotch," said the girl.

"With ice," said the Saint, "and plain water."

"What about you, Lieutenant?"

Condor shook his head.

"Thanks, miss. I've got to worry about my report. I won't take any more of your time." He looked at the Saint. "You've got your car, so I'll be on my way."

He pulled the toothpick out of his teeth, inspected it, and thrust it back. He didn't seem to be able to make a good exit. His eyes were still watchful, as they always would be, as they would always be searching and challenging, but without the conscience-created menace behind them they were just awkward and lonely and disillusioned. He was just a guy who'd been trying to do a job. And when the job wasn't there any more he was no more frightening or perhaps just as frightening as a man who had rung the bell to try and sell a vacuum cleaner and been told that there were no customers for vacuum cleaners. He said at last: "Well, next time don't forget that some of us need medals."

"I won't," said the Saint.

He sat and watched the door close, and drew slowly and introspectively at his cigarette, and waited while Peggy Warden brought him a highball and put it into his hand. He smiled his thanks at her and oscillated the glass gently so that the liquid circulated coolingly around the ice cubes.

She had a drink herself. She sat down opposite him, and he admired her again in his mind, the fresh clean trimness of her, so fearless and clean-cut, and quietly lovely too, with the natural golden brown of her hair and the steady gray of her eyes. It was a face that one would never remember vividly for any unique lines, and yet it had something independent of conformation that would puzzle the memory and yet always be haunting—as it was haunting him now.

"I've been very stupid, Peggy," he said. "But the case is closed now, as you heard Condor say, and it's all right the way it is. I just lose sleep over loose ends. Tell me why you killed Byron Ufferlitz."

11

She couldn't answer at first. It was as if all the answers were there in her mind, but she couldn't talk.

He helped her after a little while, and his voice and body were very lazy and peaceful, without any urgency or eagerness. They had a hypnotic quality, unassumed and unthinkably comforting.

"It was for Trilby Andrews, wasn't it?" he said.

Her eyes drew all their life from his face.

"Andrews—Warden," he said. "It's practically an anagram. But I almost missed it. And then the signed photograph in his study. I knew it was familiar—it kept worrying me. But I was looking at it the wrong way. I kept thinking it had to be somebody, and so I never could place it. It took a long time before I realised that it was just like somebody. Like somebody else . . . What was she?"

"My sister," she said.

It was as if speech were a strange thing, as if she had never spoken before.

He nodded.

"Yes, of course."

"When did you know?" she asked, still with that curious preciseness, as if the forming of words was a conscious performance.

"It sort of came gradually. I was all wrong most of the time. Eventually I knew it must have been a woman, because all the ashtrays were emptied. So there wouldn't be any cigarette-ends with lipstick on them. But then I had the wrong woman. It all hit me together when I found out that you'd never said anything about that scene in the office that I walked in on—when Flane told Ufferlitz he was going to fix him. Naturally that should have been the first thing you'd think of, if you were just an ordinary person. But you never said a word about it."

"How could I?" she said. "I'd done it, and I didn't want to be caught, but I didn't want anyone else to get in a jam because of me."

He drew again at his cigarette.

"Do you want to tell me the rest of it?"

"There isn't much else. She was younger than me, and . . . maybe she was stupid. I don't know. But she thought she could go places. She might have. She was really beautiful . . . She came out here, and she met Ufferlitz. I got that from her letters, when she wrote sometimes. But she met a lot of other people too. She never said who it was. But . . . when she was in trouble, it sounded like Ufferlitz. And then she was dead . . . I had to find out. I came out here, got a job at MGM, and made contacts and waited until I could get with Ufferlitz. Then I waited. I had to be sure. And I still didn't know what I could do. But I went to his house once, and there was a picture . . . After that I bought a gun. I still didn't know what I'd do with it. But I had it with me last night . . . Then he came in, and—I suppose I'd been thinking too much. It just ran away with me."

"You were sure then?"

"He'd been drinking," she said. "He wasn't drunk, but he'd been drinking. Enough for him to let down his hair. He'd never been like that with me before. He tried to make love to me. He said 'You remind me of somebody.' I asked him if it was the girl in the photograph. He said 'She was a dumb cluck.' I asked him why. He said 'She didn't know what it was all about, and she lost her head.' . . . That was when I lost my head. I went around behind him and pretended I was still making up to him, and said 'Was she just a little bit pregnant?'—as if I thought it was funny. He said 'Yeah, the damn fool. I'd have taken care of her. But she lost her head.' . . . Then I picked up my bag and took the gun out. It was just like being drunk. I said 'She was probably making a sucker out of you. How did she know it was you?' He said 'Jesus Christ, it was me all right, but she didn't have any sense. I never let a girl down in my life, baby'—and then I knew it was him, I didn't think any more, but I knew it was him, and he'd let anybody down, but he had his line off by heart, and she might have listened to the same words I was listening to, and I just didn't think any more, but I put the gun against the back of his head and pulled the trigger and I was glad about it."

Simon moved his glass after a while, and she lighted a cigarette and shook the match out, and it was as if her mind had been washed clear at last as a shower washes the sky.

"So," she said, "then I knew what I'd done, but I didn't feel any different about it. I just tried to be very careful. I gathered up the papers I'd been working on, and emptied the ashtrays because they were so obvious—though I didn't stop to think then that I was supposed to have been there anyway—and I dug the bullet out of the panelling. And all the time it didn't seem like me. I'd done something and I thought it was right, but I knew it was dangerous, and I didn't see why I should be punished. I just tried to think of everything. I even drove home all the way round by Malibu Lake, and threw the gun and the bullet in . . . Now you know it all."

"I've forgotten already," he said.

She still seemed to be wondering where she really was.

"Do you . . . do you think Condor was really satisfied?"

"I believe him," said the Saint. "The case is closed. Flane shot himself. So he had a gun. His gun could have killed Ufferlitz, and if he'd dug out the bullet and got rid of it there wouldn't have been any more evidence."

"But I still don't know why Flane shot himself."

"I drove him into it," said the Saint. "I was just blundering on, annoying everybody and waiting for a fish to rise. Well, Orlando rose. I knew Ufferlitz must have had something on him, since that seems to have been Ufferlitz's technique with almost everybody, and I just bluffed it out of him. It was something quite ugly, so we don't need to feel sorry for him. But I let him think that Ufferlitz had pretty well broadcast it with one of those voice-from-the-grave messages. It was something that would have sold him out of pictures for good and all. So—he just rang his own curtain down. It was a big help, though, because then I was able to come out with a nice solution and make Condor happy and make sure that the case was all tied up and put away."

She got up and went to the window and looked out, and presently when she came back he knew that the world had begun again for her as if it had never stopped moving.

"There's no reason why you should do all that for me," she said.

"I didn't do it for you," he said brutally. "I just did it. I like to see puzzles worked out to the right solution. I don't mean the correct solution. That's dull pedantic stuff. I mean the right one. Which means the right one for all concerned, as well as I can see it. Don't try to put too many haloes on me."

"You've already got one, haven't you?"

He finished his drink, and peeled himself out of the chair, the whole whipcord length of him, and stretched himself with the physical luxury of a cat, so that suddenly it seemed as if his world also began again; only this was a world which began again every day, and would never cease to begin again, and everything in the past was only a holiday. She saw his face dark and debonair in the shaded lamplight, and the ageless amusement in his blue eyes, and already she had the feeling that he was only a legend that had paused for a few hours.

"Don't ever be sure of it," he said.

He thought about her some more as he drove west again on Sunset, but there was someone else on his mind too, so that his thought became somewhat confused. Only a little while ago he had been falsely accusing April Quest, and he realised now that once she recovered her poise she had been quietly leading him on—for mischief, or because she had to know what he would propose to do about his belief? Or perhaps some of both . . . Well, he'd still given the right answer . . . So now there was a threat of another unwanted halo hanging over his head, and a few more pitfalls between them. But nothing, he hoped, that the drink he had asked her to save for him wouldn't cure. Or at least the drink after that.

PUBLICATION HISTORY

The stories in this volume, the twenty-third book, were written specifically for the book and have, unusually for Charteris, very little history outside of this book. They were written at a time when Charteris was well established in America; he'd been there off and on for many years, was living and working on the west coast and was married to his second wife, Barbara, an American.

The book was first published in June 1942 by Doubleday in the USA, with a UK edition following in August that same year; just ten years later Hodder were on their seventeenth imprint, suggesting it was yet another strong seller for the Saint and Leslie Charteris. Things got complicated though, when Avon started publishing a paperback edition in America in 1948, for they decided—for no clear reason—to omit the first story, Arizona. Subsequent American paperbacks, right up to the 1982 Ace Charter edition, followed suit, despite the fact that references to the Saint's Arizona adventure remain in the story "Hollywood."

Leslie's introduction to the story explains some of the history of the Saint's adventures in "Palm Springs" and it's worth highlighting, purely for clarity, that the 1941 film *The Saint in Palm Springs*, starring George Sanders as the Saint, owes absolutely nothing to the story in this book. But the 1960 French film, *Le Saint mène la danse*, which starred Felix Marten as the Saint, was loosely based on the story in this book, however it was so bad that Leslie Charteris wouldn't let it be released in any English-speaking country.

Both "Arizona" and "Hollywood" were adapted for *The Saint* with Roger Moore; "Hollywood" as "Starring the Saint," which first aired on 26 September 1963, whilst "Arizona" formed the basis of "The Sign of the Claw," which first aired on 4 February 1965.

First off the mark to translate the book were the Swedes who released *Helgonet i Hollywood* in 1946 (but what about Arizona and Palm Springs?); the French published *Le Saint au Far-West* in 1947 whilst the Dutch opted for *De Saint trekt westwaarts* and the Portuguese went for *O Santo vai para o Oeste*, both in 1950.

ABOUT THE AUTHOR

I'm mad enough to believe in romance. And I'm sick and tired of this age—tired of the miserable little mildewed things that people racked their brains about, and wrote books about, and called life. I wanted something more elementary and honest—battle, murder, sudden death, with plenty of good beer and damsels in distress, and a complete callousness about blipping the ungodly over the beezer. It mayn't be life as we know it, but it ought to be.

—*Leslie Charteris in a 1935 BBC radio interview*

Leslie Charteris was born Leslie Charles Bowyer-Yin in Singapore on 12 May 1907.

He was the son of a Chinese doctor and his English wife, who'd met in London a few years earlier. Young Leslie found friends hard to come by in colonial Singapore. The English children had been told not to play with Eurasians, and the Chinese children had been told not to play with Europeans. Leslie was caught in between and took refuge in reading.

"I read a great many good books and enjoyed them because nobody had told me that they were classics. I also read a great many bad books which nobody told me not to read . . . I read a great many popular scientific articles and acquired from them an astonishing amount of general knowledge before I discovered that this acquisition was supposed to be a chore."[1]

One of his favourite things to read was a magazine called *Chums*. "The Best and Brightest Paper for Boys" (if you believe the adverts) was a monthly paper full of swashbuckling adventure stories aimed at boys, encouraging them to be honourable and moral and perhaps even "upright citizens with furled umbrellas."[2] Undoubtedly these types of stories would influence his later work.

When his parents split up shortly after the end of World War I, Charteris accompanied his mother and brother back to England, where he was sent to Rossall School in Fleetwood, Lancashire. Rossall was then a very stereotypical English public school, and it struggled to cope with this multilingual mixed-race boy just into his teens who'd already seen more of the world than many of his peers would see in their lifetimes. He was an outsider.

He left Rossall in 1924. Keen to pursue a creative career, he decided to study art in Paris—after all, that was where the great artists went—but soon found that the life of a literally starving artist didn't appeal. He continued writing, firing off speculative stories to magazines, and it was the sale of a short story to *Windsor Magazine* that saved him from penury.

He returned to London in 1925, as his parents—particularly his father—wanted him to become a lawyer, and he was sent to study law at Cambridge University. In the mid-1920s, Cambridge was full of Bright Young Things—aristocrats and bohemians somewhat typified in the

Evelyn Waugh novel *Vile Bodies*—and again the mixed-race Bowyer-Yin found that he didn't fit in. He was an outsider who preferred to make his own way in the world and wasn't one of the privileged upper class. It didn't help that he found his studies boring and decided it was more fun contemplating ways to circumvent the law. This inspired him to write a novel, and when publishers Ward Lock & Co. offered him a three-book deal on the strength of it, he abandoned his studies to pursue a writing career.

When his father learnt of this, he was not impressed, as he considered writers to be "rogues and vagabonds." Charteris would later recall that "I wanted to be a writer, he wanted me to become a lawyer. I was stubborn, he said I would end up in the gutter. So I left home. Later on, when I had a little success, we were reconciled by letter, but I never saw him again."[3]

X Esquire, his first novel, appeared in April 1927. The lead character, X Esquire, is a mysterious hero, hunting down and killing the businessmen trying to wipe out Britain by distributing quantities of free poisoned cigarettes. His second novel, *The White Rider*, was published the following spring, and in one memorable scene shows the hero chasing after his damsel in distress, only for him to overtake the villains, leap into their car . . . and promptly faint.

These two plot highlights may go some way to explaining Charteris's comment on *Meet—the Tiger!*, published in September 1928, that "it was only the third book I'd written, and the best, I would say, for it was that the first two were even worse."[4]

Twenty-one-year-old authors are naturally self-critical. Despite reasonably good reviews, the Saint didn't set the world on fire, and Charteris moved on to a new hero for his next book. This was *The Bandit*, an adventure story featuring Ramon Francisco De Castilla y Espronceda Manrique, published in the summer of 1929 after its serialisation in the *Empire News*, a now long-forgotten Sunday newspaper. But sales of *The Bandit* were less than impressive, and Charteris began to question his choice of career. It was all very well writing—but if nobody wants to read what you write, what's the point?

"I had to succeed, because before me loomed the only alternative, the dreadful penalty of failure . . . the routine office hours, the five-day week . . . the lethal assimilation into the ranks of honest, hard-working, conformist, God-fearing pillars of the community."[5]

However his fortunes—and the Saint's—were about to change. In late 1928, Leslie had met Monty Haydon, a London-based editor who was looking for writers to pen stories for his new paper, *The Thriller*—"The Paper with a Thousand Thrills." Charteris later recalled that "he said he was starting a new magazine, had read one of my books and would like some stories from me. I couldn't have been more grateful, both from the point of view of vanity and finance!"[6]

The paper launched in early 1929, and Leslie's first work, "The Story of a Dead Man," featuring Jimmy Traill, appeared in issue 4 (published on 2 March 1929). That was followed just over a month later with "The Secret of Beacon Inn," starring Rameses "Pip" Smith. At the same time, Leslie finished writing another non-Saint novel, *Daredevil*, which would be published in late 1929. Storm Arden was the hero; more notably, the book saw the first introduction of a Scotland Yard inspector by the name of Claud Eustace Teal.

The Saint returned in the thirteenth issue of *The Thriller*. The byline proclaimed that the tale was "A Thrilling Complete Story of the Underworld"; the title was "The Five Kings," and it actually featured Four Kings and a Joker. Simon Templar, of course, was the Joker.

Charteris spent the rest of 1929 telling the adventures of the Five Kings in five subsequent *The Thriller* stories. "It was very hard work, for the pay was lousy, but Monty Haydon was a brilliant and stimulating editor, full of ideas. While he didn't actually help shape the Saint as a character, he did suggest story lines. He would take me out to lunch and say, 'What are you going to write about next?' I'd often say I was damned if I knew. And Monty would say, 'Well, I was reading something the other day . . .' He had a fund of ideas and we would talk them over, and then I would go away and write a story. He was a great creative editor."[7]

Charteris would have one more attempt at writing about a hero other than Simon Templar, in three novelettes published in *The Thriller* in early 1930, but he swiftly returned to the Saint. This was partly due to his self-confessed laziness—he wanted to write more stories for *The Thriller* and other magazines, and creating a new hero for every story was hard work—but mainly due to feedback from Monty Haydon. It seemed people wanted to read more adventures of the Saint . . .

Charteris would contribute over forty stories to *The Thriller* throughout the 1930s. Shortly after their debut, he persuaded publisher Hodder & Stoughton that if he collected some of these stories and rewrote them a little, they could publish them as a Saint book. *Enter the Saint* was first published in August 1930, and the reaction was good enough for the publishers to bring out another collection. And another . . .

Of the twenty Saint books published in the 1930s, almost all have their origins in those magazine stories.

Why was the Saint so popular throughout the decade? Aside from the charm and ability of Charteris's storytelling, the stories, particularly those published in the first half of the '30s, are full of energy and joie de vivre. With economic depression rampant throughout the period, the public at large seemed to want some escapism.

And Simon Templar's appeal was wide-ranging: he wasn't an upper-class hero like so many of the period. With no obvious background and no attachment to the Old School Tie, no friends in high places who could provide a get-out-of-jail-free card, the Saint was uniquely classless. Not unlike his creator.

Throughout Leslie's formative years, his heritage had been an issue. In his early days in Singapore, during his time at school, at Cambridge University or even just in everyday life, he couldn't avoid the fact that for many people his mixed parentage was a problem. He would later tell a story of how he was chased up the road by a stick-waving typical English gent who took offence to his daughter being escorted around town by a foreigner.

Like the Saint, he was an outsider. And although he had spent a significant portion of his formative years in England, he couldn't settle.

As a young boy he had read of an America "peopled largely by Indians, and characters in fringed buckskin jackets who fought nobly against them. I spent a great deal of time day-dreaming about a visit to this prodigious and exciting country."[8]

It was time to realise this wish. Charteris and his first wife, Pauline, whom he'd met in London when they were both teenagers and married in 1931, set sail for the States in late 1932; the Saint had already made his debut in America courtesy of the publisher Doubleday. Charteris and his wife found a New York still experiencing the tail end of Prohibition, and times were tough at first. Despite sales to *The American Magazine* and others, it wasn't until a chance meeting with writer turned Hollywood executive Bartlett McCormack in their favourite speakeasy that Charteris's career stepped up a gear.

Soon Charteris was in Hollywood, working on what would become the 1933 movie *Midnight Club*. However, Hollywood's treatment of writers wasn't to Charteris's taste, and he began to yearn for home. Within a few months, he returned to the UK and began writing more Saint stories for Monty Haydon and Bill McElroy.

He also rewrote a story he'd sketched out whilst in the States, a version of which had been published in *The American Magazine* in September 1934. This new novel, *The Saint in New York*, published in 1935, was a significant advance for the Saint and Leslie Charteris. Gone were the high jinks and the badinage. The youthful exuberance evident in the Saint's early adventures had evolved into something a little darker, a little more hard-boiled. It was the next stage in development for the author and his creation, and readers loved it. It became a bestseller on both sides of the Atlantic.

Having spent his formative years in places as far apart as Singapore and England, with substantial travel in between, it should be no surprise that Leslie had a serious case of wanderlust. With a bestseller under his belt, he now had the means to see more of the world.

Nineteen thirty-six found him in Tenerife, researching another Saint adventure alongside translating the biography of Juan Belmonte, a well-known Spanish matador. Estranged for several months, Leslie and Pauline divorced in 1937. The following year, Leslie married an American, Barbara Meyer, who'd accompanied him to Tenerife. In early 1938, Charteris and his new bride set off in a trailer of his own design and spent eighteen months travelling round America and Canada.

The Saint in New York had reminded Hollywood of Charteris's talents, and film rights to the novel were sold prior to publication in 1935. Although the proposed 1935 film production was rejected by the Hays Office for its violent content, RKO's eventual 1938 production persuaded Charteris to try his luck once more in Hollywood.

New opportunities had opened up, and throughout the 1940s the Saint appeared not only in books and movies but in a newspaper strip, a comic-book series, and on radio.

Anyone wishing to adapt the character in any medium found a stern taskmaster in Charteris. He was never completely satisfied, nor was he shy of showing his displeasure. He did, however, ensure that copyright in any Saint adventure belonged to him, even if scripted by another writer—a contractual obligation that he was to insist on throughout his career.

Charteris was soon spread thin, overseeing movies, comics, newspapers, and radio versions of his creation, and this, along with his self-proclaimed laziness, meant that Saint books were becoming fewer and further between. However, he still enjoyed his creation: in 1941 he indulged himself in a spot of fun by playing the Saint—complete with monocle and moustache—in a photo story in *Life* magazine.

In July 1944, he started collaborating under a pseudonym on Sherlock Holmes radio scripts, subsequently writing more adventures for Holmes than Conan Doyle. Not all his ventures were successful—a screenplay he was hired to write for Deanna Durbin, "Lady on a Train," took him a year and ultimately bore little resemblance to the finished film. In the mid-1940s, Charteris successfully sued RKO Pictures for unfair competition after they launched a new series of films starring George Sanders as a debonair crime fighter known as the Falcon. But he kept faith with his original character, and the Saint novels continued to adapt to the times. The transatlantic Saint evolved into something of a private operator, working for the mysterious Hamilton and becoming, not unlike his creator, a world traveller, finding that adventure would seek him out.

"I have never been able to see why a fictional character should not grow up, mature, and develop, the same as anyone else. The same, if you like, as his biographer. The only adequate reason is that—so far as I know—no other fictional character in modern times has survived a sufficient number of years for these changes to be clearly observable. I must confess that a lot of my own selfish pleasure in the Saint has been in watching him grow up."[9]

Charteris maintained his love of travel and was soon to be found sailing round the West Indies with his good friend Gregory Peck. His forays abroad gave him even more material, and he began to write true-crime articles, as well as an occasional column in *Gourmet* magazine.

By the early '50s, Charteris himself was feeling strained. He'd divorced his second wife in 1943 and got together with a New York radio and nightclub singer called Betty Bryant Borst, whom he married in late 1943. That relationship had fallen apart acrimoniously towards the end of the decade, and he roamed the globe restlessly, rarely in one place for longer than a couple of months. He continued to maintain a firm grip on the exploitation of the Saint in various media but was writing little himself. The Saint had become an industry, and Charteris couldn't keep up. He began thinking seriously about an early retirement.

Then in 1951 he met a young actress called Audrey Long when they became next-door neighbours in Hollywood. Within a year they had married, a union that was to last the rest of Leslie's life.

He attacked life with a new vitality. They travelled—Nassau was a favoured escape spot—and he wrote. He struck an agreement with *The New York Herald Tribune* for a Saint comic strip, which would appear daily and be written by Charteris himself. The strip ran for thirteen years, with Charteris sending in his handwritten story lines from wherever he happened to be, relying on mail services around the world to continue the Saint's adventures. New Saint books began to appear, and Charteris reached a height of productivity not seen since his days as a struggling author trying to establish himself. As Leslie and Audrey travelled, so did the Saint, visiting locations just after his creator had been there.

By 1953 the Saint had already enjoyed twenty-five years of success, and *The Saint Detective Magazine* was launched. Charteris had become adept at exploiting his creation to the full, mixing new stories with repackaged older stories, sometimes rewritten, sometimes mixed up in "new" anthologies, sometimes adapted from radio scripts previously written by other writers.

Charteris had been approached several times over the years for television rights in the Saint and had expended much time and effort during the 1950s trying to get the Saint on TV, even going so far as to write sample scripts himself, but it wasn't to be. He finally agreed a deal in autumn 1961 with English film producers Robert S. Baker and Monty Berman. The first episode of *The Saint* television series, starring Roger Moore, went into production in June 1962. The series was an immediate success, though Charteris himself had his reservations. It reached second place in the ratings, but he commented that "in that distinction it was topped by wrestling, which only suggested to me that the competition may not have been so hot; but producers are generally cast in a less modest mould." He resented the implication that the TV series had finally made a success of the Saint after twenty-five years of literary obscurity.

As long as the series lasted, Charteris was not shy about voicing his criticisms both in public and in a constant stream of memos to the producers. "Regular followers of the Saint saga . . . must have noticed that I am almost incapable of simply writing a story and shutting up."[10] Nor was he shy about exploiting this new market by agreeing to a series of tie-in novelisations ghosted by other writers, which he would then rewrite before publication.

Charteris mellowed as the series developed and found elements to praise too. He developed a close friendship with producer Robert S. Baker, which would last until Charteris's death.

In the early '60s, on one of their frequent trips to England, Leslie and Audrey bought a house in Surrey, which became their permanent base. He explored the possibility of a Saint musical and began writing some of it himself.

Charteris no longer needed to work. Now in his sixties, he supervised the Saint from a distance whilst continuing to travel and indulge himself. He and Audrey made seasonal excursions to Ireland and the south of France, where they had residences. He began to write poetry and devised a new universal sign language, Paleneo, based on notes and symbols he used in his diaries. Once Paleneo was released, he decided enough was enough and announced, again, his retirement. This time he meant it.

The Saint continued regardless—there was a long-running Swedish comic strip, and new novels with other writers doing the bulk of the work were complemented in the 1970s with Bob Baker's revival of the TV series, *Return of the Saint*.

Ill-health began to take its toll. By the early 1980s, although he continued a healthy correspondence with the outside world, Charteris felt unable to keep up with the collaborative Saint books and pulled the plug on them.

To entertain himself, Leslie took to "trying to beat the bookies in predicting the relative speed of horses," a hobby which resulted in several of his local betting shops refusing to take "predictions" from him, as he was too successful for their liking.

He still received requests to publish his work abroad but had become completely cynical about further attempts to revive the Saint. A new Saint magazine only lasted three issues, and two TV productions—*The Saint in Manhattan*, with Tom Selleck look-alike Andrew Clarke, and *The Saint*, with Simon Dutton—left him bitterly disappointed. "I fully expect this series to lay eggs everywhere . . . the only satisfaction I have is in looking at my bank balance."[11]

In the early 1990s, Hollywood producers Robert Evans and William J. Macdonald approached him and made a deal for the Saint to return to cinema screens. Charteris still took great care of the Saint's reputation and wrote an outline entitled *The Return of the Saint* in which an older Saint would meet the son he didn't know he had.

Much of his time in his last few years was taken up with the movie. Several scripts were submitted to him—each moving further and further away from his original concept—but the screenwriter from 1940s Hollywood was thoroughly disheartened by the Hollywood of the '90s: "There is still no plot, no real story, no characterisations, no personal interaction, nothing but endless frantic violence . . ." Besides, with producer Bill Macdonald hitting the headlines for the most un-Saintly reasons, he was to add, "How can Bill Macdonald concentrate on my Saint movie when he has Sharon Stone in his bed?"

The Crime Writers' Association of Great Britain presented Leslie with a Lifetime Achievement award in 1992 in a special ceremony at the House of Lords. Never one for associations and awards, and although visibly unwell, Leslie accepted the award with grace and humour ("I am now only waiting to be carbon-dated," he joked). He suffered a slight stroke in his final weeks, which did not prevent him from dining out locally with family and friends, before he finally passed away at the age of 85 on 15 April 1993.

His death severed one of the final links with the classic thriller genre of the 1930s and 1940s, but he left behind a legacy of nearly one hundred books, countless short stories, and TV, film, radio, and comic-strip adaptations of his work which will endure for generations to come.

> *I was always sure that there was a solid place in escape literature for a rambunctious adventurer such as I dreamed up in my youth, who really believed in the old-fashioned romantic ideals and was prepared to lay everything on the line to bring them to life. A joyous exuberance that could not find its fulfilment in pinball machines and pot. I had what may now seem a mad desire to spread the belief that there were worse, and wickeder, nut cases than Don Quixote.*
>
> *Even now, half a century later, when I should be old enough to know better, I still cling to that belief. That there will always be a public for the old-style hero, who had a*

clear idea of justice, and a more than technical approach to love, and the ability to have some fun with his crusades.[12]

---

1 *A Letter from the Saint*, 30 August 1946

2 "The Last Word," *The First Saint Omnibus*, Doubleday Crime Club, 1939

3 *The Straits Times*, 29 June 1958, page 9

4 Introduction by Charteris to the September 1980 paperback reprint of *Meet—the Tiger!* (Charter), the last ever print edition.

5 *The Saint: A Complete History*, by Burl Barer (McFarland, 1993)

6 PR material from the 1970s series *Return of the Saint*

7 From "Return of the Saint: Comprehensive Information" issued to help publicise the 1970s TV show

8 *A Letter from the Saint*, 26 July 1946

9 Introduction to "The Million Pound Day," in *The First Saint Omnibus*

10 *A Letter from the Saint*, 12 April 1946

11 Letter from LC to sometime Saint collaborator Peter Bloxsom, 2 August 1989

12 Introduction by Charteris to the September 1980 paperback reprint of *Meet—the Tiger!* (Charter).

WATCH FOR THE SIGN
OF THE SAINT!

THE SAINT CLUB

And so, my friends, dear bookworms, most noble fellow drinkers, frustrated burglars, affronted policemen, upright citizens with furled umbrellas and secret buccaneering dreams that seems to be very nearly all for now. It has been nice having you with us, and we hope you will come again, not once, but many times.

Only because of our great love for you, we would like to take this parting opportunity of mentioning one small matter which we have very much at heart . . .

—*Leslie Charteris,* The First Saint Omnibus *(1939)*

Leslie Charteris founded The Saint Club in 1936 with the aim of providing a constructive fanbase for Saint devotees. Before the War, it donated profits to a London hospital where, for several years, a Saint ward was maintained. With the nationalisation of hospitals, profits were, for many years, donated to the Arbour Youth Centre in Stepney, London.

In the twenty-first century, we've carried on this tradition but have also donated to the Red Cross and a number of different children's charities.

The club acts as a focal point for anyone interested in the adventures of Leslie Charteris and the work of Simon Templar, and offers merchandise that includes DVDs of the old TV series and various Saint-related publications, through to its own exclusive range of notepaper, pin badges, and polo shirts. All profits are donated to charity. The club also maintains two popular websites and supports many more Saint-related sites.

After Leslie Charteris's death, the club recruited three new vice-presidents—Roger Moore, Ian Ogilvy, and Simon Dutton have all pledged their support, whilst Audrey and Patricia Charteris have been retained as Saints-in-Chief. But some things do not change, for the back of the membership card still mischievously proclaims that . . .

> *The bearer of this card is probably a person of hideous*
> *antecedents and low moral character, and upon*
> *apprehension for any cause should be immediately released*
> *in order to save other prisoners from contamination.*

To join . . .

Membership costs £3.50 (or US$7) per year, or £30 (US$60) for life. Find us online at www.lesliecharteris.com for full details.